DEDICATION

This book is dedicated to the lovers still looking for their one and only. Just because there are many sharks in the sea, doesn't mean you should stop fishing.

ACKNOWLEDGMENTS

Special thanks to Monica Guetre, all my beta readers and dedicated fans. Thank you for pushing me beyond my capabilities.

CHAPTER ONE

"You have mail!"

The robotic voice sliced through my random thoughts as I poured my first cup of coffee. Glancing at my laptop precariously perched on the kitchen counter, I spotted the quick flicker of the screen as new messages streamed down. The morning spew of spam was no surprise. Daily, the first login was the largest. As an author and a popular Internet blogger, my email was constantly downloading something. Thirty minutes at the start of each day was wasted sorting through the mess. For the moment, I ignored them. Cobwebs still floating around in my head, I was not ready to work. I loved self-employment.

Turning away, I went back to adding cream to my oversized mug filled with Java. Taking a cautious sip, I sighed with contentment. *Perfection!* Satisfied, I grabbed the steaming cup in one hand, the laptop in the other and headed to the kitchen table. I got comfortable and turned my attention back to the email to examine the new messages with mild interest. Besides the usual crop of spam, most were press releases from various sources, including research for a current story I was working on. I sipped my coffee while mentally prioritising the list.

The soft click of claws on hardwood flooring signalled that Belle had decided to appear. She rarely stayed in bed once I was up and moving around. Trotting down the hall from the bedroom, she slid to a not-so sudden stop when she spotted me in the kitchen. I'd recently replaced the carpet and she was still not used to the slippery floor. I stifled a giggle at her puzzled expression.

When I bought the little rustic A-frame, it needed some work, but I was up for the task. Formerly used as a hunting cottage, I cleaned it out and turned it into a cosy little hideaway. My private paradise sat nestled in the centre of a pine clearing. The tiny cottage consisted of a working kitchen, a cosy dining area, and a four-season porch. My favourite feature was the massive Fieldstone fireplace which served as a functioning wall between the master suite and the living room. Sprawling on the king-sized bed or couch to enjoy a crackling fire was heavenly. The entire suite was romantic, yet functional.

I also loved the corner Jacuzzi complete with a crystal glass waterfall placed in the nook of the master suite. Surrounded by candles and live tropical plants, it was my oasis. Replacing the aged and disintegrating trophies from past hunters, every vacant wall is lined with solid oak bookcases. Shelves overflowed with a collection of hardcover books, some dating back to the 1800's. The cottage was built as a lover's hideaway, but I turned it into a home for me and my dog. For her, I added a chain-link fence in the backyard both to keep her in and wild critters out. Beyond the fence was my own secluded swimming hole, left over from the gravel operation that once mined the site. Having my own private beach was why I bought the place. The cottage was a bonus.

"Got to go outside for a pee?"

In response, Belle's wagging tail sped up before she trotted eagerly to the door. Who says dogs don't understand English? Setting my laptop aside, I obliged her morning ritual. She nearly toppled over with excitement as I reached down, giving her grinning face a quick scratch before accepting the role of door-keeper. A swift glance at the gate, assured me it was secure. I'd learned the hard way to always double check. If it was left open, it usually meant I'd be making a frantic dash around the neighbourhood trying to play "catch the crazy Pomeranian", Belle's favourite game. Based on her indignant grunt, Belle was not as enthusiastic about the closed gate. All thoughts of her great escape shot. I chuckled at the sulky look she tossed at me before trudging off into the back yard.

Knowing Belle would be occupied for a while; I re-entered the house and turned my attention back to emails. Seventy-two new messages! *Great, I'm going be here for a while.* I start weeding through the missives. Glance. Click. Delete. I soon had a rhythm going until forced to pause about two-thirds of the way through. The words *"For your information"* jumped out at me. I did not recognise the sender. *Great, more spam.* Click – wait! I paused, my finger hovering midair over the delete key. The first few lines of the email had caught my attention.

"You do not know me, but you and I have a common "friend"," read the first line. As a former member of social networking chatrooms, I was no stranger to the odd "outing" email. It was common to warn the community about scammers and troublemakers. One could never be too careful and in the world of internet dating it was especially important. It was our way of watching out for each other. I would read them and take them under advisement, but never passed them on. Looking forward to killing time with some gossip I gave in to my curiosity and continued to read.

"A few weeks ago, I was at a party when I met Stephan," the note continued. Stephan? I blinked in momentary surprise.

Now the message had my undivided attention. This was not just another "outing" email. Stephan and I had been dating for almost two years. At first life was wonderful. He was everything I was looking for in a man - handsome, charming and sweet. Things were going so well that when he proposed, I eagerly said yes, but due to our hectic schedules setting a wedding date still eluded us. Instead, we discussed cohabitating but the closest we'd gone was to exchange house keys for our individual homes. I broached the subject of moving in and getting married a few times, but he was full of apologies. Regardless, neither of us looked too eager to surrender our freedom, and I was okay with that. I was in no rush anyway. Nor did I want to scare him off, so I never pushed it. Maybe this email would shed light on some of those excuses. I was shocked and a little bit scared.

"It was an event hosted by a group of people through the hookup site called AdultPlayBuddy," AdultPlayBuddy? I never had heard of it before. Making a mental note to Google it later, I continued to scan.

"We were both at a swingers party," Party? What party? It is funny how a few simple words could send up several red flags at once. I was having trouble getting past each sentence without fifty questions popping up. We still had separate apartments, but since the

engagement, we spent nearly every day and night together. I would have recalled him mentioning a party. I knew we hadn't attended this one together; I would remember that too. I did not like where this conversation was going. I start to feel nauseous. Swallowing hard, I forced myself to continue.

'I know that you've been together for a few years, but I wanted to warn you. You might want to reconsider this relationship. I have been following your blog and realise how much you care for this guy and you need to know he does not deserve it. You are naive to think he is being faithful to you. He was not. I hate to break this to you, but he has been cheating on you – and not with just one person. I know you won't believe me so I have attached proof. The attached photos were taken at a party Stephan attended a few weeks ago with "friends". I am really sorry to be the bearer of bad news, but I consider you a friend and do not want to see you hurt. You deserve to know the truth and you may want to investigate this further. If you have any questions, feel free to contact me."

It was signed *"A concerned friend."*

My heart ached as my brain registered the words clearly spelt out in black-and-white. It felt like someone had sucker punched me in the chest. Near panic, I pushed the laptop aside. This had to be a prank or a case of mistaken identity. Everything about the note confused me. There had to be some mistake. I had just decided to ignore it when I spotted the attachments.

The files were unnamed, but it was obvious by the file extension the attachments were photographs. *I should delete this message NOW*, my inner voice screamed. I did not want to see any more, the implication was bad enough. If Stephan was hiding something, then I needed to know. As his future wife it was my RIGHT to know, especially if he was cheating! First and foremost, I needed to protect myself; sexually transmitted diseases were an epidemic after all. Second, if my fiancé was living a lie, I had to know and the sooner, the better. Lord knows I did not want to become one of those women married to a man incapable of fidelity. Now was the time to find out, not after walking down the aisle.

Despite my anxiety, I scrolled to the bottom of the page and let out a horrified gasp. The first image had popped up before I was ready. There was no disputing what I was seeing. My jaw dropped and my stomach hit the floor. Instantly I regretted my curiosity - scanning the incriminating evidence my guts rolled. Retching, I turned away quickly; barely getting my face over a nearby mop-pail. My first cup of coffee reappeared violently and I kept retching until the dry heaves took over. Sweating, I wiped my mouth with a nearby napkin. It took a few minutes before I could focus on the naked bodies plastered across my screen.

There was Stephan, sitting on what appeared to be a cheap hotel room bed. Even worse - he was bare-assed naked. An equally nude female lay sprawled across the bed on her back; brunette hair strewn onto his lap. His hands were busy caressing her breasts while a second woman knelt on the floor with her face buried between his partner's thighs. The deeply dimpled grin on his face said it all. He wanted to be there. There was no doubt in my mind at all. It was obvious he was enjoying every moment in his ringside seat, eager to lend a helping hand if needed.

Hurt and shocked, I gasped for air and fought for control as I nearly hyperventilated. Soon I could not swallow the uncontrollable well of tears. *This has to be a cruel joke.* A surge of anger replaced my hurt. There was no disputing what I saw; images do not lie. I did not even have to ask when they were taken. The date stamp in the bottom right corner reads January 27. *This is not a joke.* I was losing it and quickly. Desperate for an explanation, I grabbed my day planner, nearly tearing it apart until I found what I was looking for. *Damn it!* I cursed silently.

CHAPTER TWO

According to my organiser, Stephan and I had dinner plans that particular night. My original note of 'dinner date' was crossed out. An added note was jotted in the margin. *No dinner! Back hurt - change of plans.* Thinking back, I recalled calling him before walking out the door, intent on letting him know I was heading over.

"Hey Babe," he said when he finally picked up the phone. He never called me by name; it was always "Babe".

"How are you?" I asked. He sounded exhausted. For a brief moment I felt guilty about our plans. At the same time, an evening out was a rare adventure these days due to our busy schedules. I was looking forward to spending time with him.

"I could be better; I slipped on the ice at work today and wrenched my back," came Stephan's strained reply. His voice conveyed the pain so I did not doubt him.

"Are you okay?" with instant concern. After suffering whiplash years ago because of an automobile accident, I personally experienced the intensity of back pain. Back injuries are never an easy fix.

"Yeah, I should be in a few days after some sleep. I stopped at the chiropractor on the way home from work and had a treatment. I have another appointment tomorrow morning. I should be okay after taking it easy for a few days." He sounded confident, which helped ease my concern. Besides, he hated being coddled so I refrained from babying him. But that did not mean I wasn't interested.

"I am sorry to hear that! Glad you got it checked out though, you don't want to take any chances," I offered sympathetically. "I just wanted to let you know that I was on my way. Or have plans changed?" I hesitated, knowing I was giving him an opening. Selfishly, I hoped he wouldn't take me up on the offer.

"I believe that under the circumstances, I will stay in tonight and rest my muscles," Stephan took my bait. "I am going to run a bath, then hit the sack early."

I stifled my disappointment; I had excitedly waited for our date all week. But his physical well-being comes first, no doubt about that.

"Not a problem, want me to come in and take care of you?" I asked, secretly hoping he wanted company. Besides, I could make myself useful, I'd been told many times I gave a decent massage. I waited eagerly hoping for a yes.

"I should be fine. I'm going to take an anti-inflammatory and a hot bath. It will definitely be an early night. Besides, it's pretty cold and the streets are icy, you might want to stay home anyway. I'd hate to have to get you out of the ditch," he laughed. The joke made me giggle. We were having a bad year for snow; I'd already gotten stuck in my driveway twice in the past month.

Resigned to sleeping alone, we chatted for a while longer before ending with assurances. I was perfectly fine with spending a quiet evening snuggling on the couch, watching movies with Belle.

"Do you want to come over tomorrow night instead? I should feel better by then," he asked hopefully. I brightened at the invite. Any doubt and disappointment about our cancelled date was gone in a flash; replaced by anticipation.

"Sure, I look forward to it. You take care of yourself and get some rest. Love you."

He hung up before I got a response.

The next night when I popped up at his apartment, Stephan looked better than he sounded on the phone the night before.

"I actually feel pretty good today," he responded to my inquiry about his back. "As a matter of fact, after I got out of the bath, I felt so good that I went out for a few beers at the pub down the street."

"Oh really? That's so great! Glad you are feeling better." I said, covering my surprise. "Still up for a houseguest?"

"Sure, see you in a bit," he responded. "I can't wait to see you!"

Curled up in his arms later that night, I sighed in contentment while he told me about his night out. It certainly sounded innocent enough at the time. Drinks and a few games of pool with his work crew. While I did feel resentment for getting ditched for his cronies, I also knew that this was an important piece of his life. Going out with them was not a big deal. If I expected him to understand my needing to hang out with my friends, then I needed to extend the same consideration.

I never thought about questioning him further. I trusted him implicitly.

Until this very moment, I had no reason to distrust him.

Tossing my day planner aside with disgust, I turned my attention back to the email.

There were a few more pictures attached. Like a rubbernecker driving past a car crash, I looked. In each picture Stephan wore a shit-eating grin while watching another woman have sex with the female he was touching. It didn't take a rocket scientist to figure things out. The photographs left no doubt. Including the photographer, there had to be at least four people at this "party". To make matters worse, I knew every single person in the photograph; two of the women even claimed to be friends.

The sickening feeling of betrayal coursed through my veins. This is uncharted territory for me. I'd been in a few relationships, but as far as I knew, no one had ever cheated on me. I wasn't quite sure what to think. The longer I gaped at the pictures, the more my emotions changed. My hurt turned to outrage. There had to be some rational explanation. The investigative journalist in me kicked in and in a split second, my decision was to know what was going on. I would dig until I couldn't dig any more. If Stephan was up to something, I was going to find out what and for how long. Before I did anything rash I would line up the facts; then make an educated decision.

Opening a second browser, I entered *AdultPlayBuddy* (APB) into the search engine. My mind blurred once I found what I was looking for. Clicking on the highlighted link a new page opened; "Sex, Dating, and Personal Encounters" the website's header promised. Glancing at the various sample profile pictures, the purpose of the site was obvious. Adult encounters, a dating site specifically for sex. Red flags were flying everywhere.

As I aimlessly clicked on various links on the page, my imagination went wild but I was not deterred. With each click of the mouse, I felt like someone hoofed me in the gut. Instead of normal face shots popular on dating sites, this site featured profiles complete with genitalia shots; male, female and couples. Nothing is left to the imagination of the viewer. I felt like a voyeur, but the more I looked, the more determined I was to find out how Stephan was connected to this particular situation. My quest to know the truth overruled my senses. I tried clicking on a few profiles, but nothing came up. To view the actual profiles, I would have to become a member. *Why would a guy in a relationship be a paying member of a 'dating' site?* My mind was on emotional overload. I had to figure this out and there was only one way I would discover the truth. I had to sign up as a member.

Spotting a free trial membership option, with a click, I joined. I harboured no scheme other than a need to conduct an extensive investigation on my fiancé. Despite the photographic evidence, I still thought he was innocent of such deception. As I filled out the registration form for the 'dating' site, I promised myself that my integrity would remain intact. I would cancel my membership as soon as I was done my search. Despite that decision I hesitated. I was fully aware that joining an adult site could open a can of worms I may not be able to contain. Ignoring my inner voice, I created a screen name and logged into the chat system for the very first time.

As a limited member, I could retrieve basic information, but not see full profiles. This needed full membership, but I could access the member search engine to perform random searches. Now the challenge was to see his profile, if he had one. Referring to the damning emails, I looked for clues for what chat-name he could be using but they were absent. I briefly pondered emailing the sender directly to ask for a chat-name point blank. I was not ready for that particular confrontation. Not knowing the email's origin, any inquiries could also send the whistleblower scurrying to warn Stephan. While unlikely, I was not going to take a chance.

Expecting to find the worst, I took a deep breath and steeled my nerves. When ready, I typed in a few random user searches, but nothing familiar jumped out at me. I skimmed over a few pages containing various user names and pictures without avail. The results were vague and incomplete. There was only one way I would be able to do this; I would have to pretend to look for a hookup. Coming back to my newly created profile, I reluctantly filled in the blanks. I quickly typed in my information based on age and location; then clicked *SEND*.

Moments later, a few dozen profiles filled my screen. Scanning the list, most of the men who matched my settings lived within a thirty-mile radius of Winnipeg. Each user was listed in descending order based on the last time they logged into the chat system. Profiles with pictures appeared at the top of the list. Skimming over the first page, none of the names or photos rang a bell. The same went for page number two. It looked like my luck would run out on the third page, until a photo attached to a profile halfway down the list caught my attention immediately.

The snapshot was unmistakable. Even without a proper face shot there was no doubt in my mind. It was Stephan! My vision blurred as I recognized the undeniable image of his naked torso. He was naked except for a royal blue towel wrapped around his waist. I knew it was him because he'd sent me that particular photo privately. Last summer, he'd returned from the beach, sporting horrific sunburns after falling asleep in the scorching sun. His magnificently moulded chest was scarlet, but the distinct ripples of his ABS were still clear and sexy. At the time, seeing the picture had warmed my insides; and a few places further south. Recognising it now, anger and hurt heated me up, not pleasure. Recognising the familiar coat-of-arms tattooed on the right side of his chest was the final blow.

Trembling, I took a deep breath and clicked on the incriminating profile. The page opened and I read the header; *looking for a good time, not a long time*. Marital status listed him as single and looking for 'casual encounters'. His sexual preference stated 'women and couples'. My stomach started to heave again. Glancing at his contact list, there were over three hundred names, mostly female. Obviously he was not a casual visitor.

There were even comments on his profile where "recommendations" could be listed. *Kudos on your performance* said one note. *Seriously? Who all was he screwing behind my back?* There were also links to his public responses in the forums. It was obvious he had been a member long before we started dating.

On one hand, I was not surprised. After all, our relationship began on a dating site very similar to *AdultPlayBuddy*.

CHAPTER THREE

I still remember how my best friend Debbie strong-armed me back into the dating scene. Since the day we met at a wedding show over a decade ago, we were inseparable. I was covering the event as a reporter for *Exposed* magazine. She had a booth set up advertising services as a marriage commissioner. I was working on a feature article for the magazine on unusual relationship origins. Assuming that she would have many interesting stories to share, we soon kicked up a conversation. The discussion eventually leads to the topic of online relationships and how it fit into the dating scene. She was a wealth of information on the issue and helped me finish the article which became the best wedding piece published to date in the magazine's five year history.

While working the story, I found out that Debbie met the love of her life on *TheFishPond*. She signed up after reading about the group in a Miss Broken-hearts column in the local newspaper. For her, it was a non-threatening way to meet someone after fleeing an abusive marriage. Not long after joining, she met Ron, a long distance truck driver. He'd gone online after discovering it was difficult to find anyone of substance while on the road. What began as a casual email exchange between complete strangers became a hot love affair and within six months, Ron was dragging her to the altar.

Our relationship changed from professional to friendship when she asked if I'd photograph her upcoming nuptials. Honoured, I accepted. My role as photographer changed to friend when the frantic bride nearly succumbed to a fit of hysterics after finding the best man and maid-of-honour half naked in the laundry room. When I found the fiery redhead, she was berating the pair loud enough the entire neighbourhood could hear. I stepped in when it became evident that the best man would be accessorizing his suit with a black eye. Admittedly, there was something hysterical about seeing the petite spitfire in flowing white taffeta threatening to throttle a man nearly twice her size. Thankfully, Debbie found humour in the situation - after gratefully guzzling the second glass of white wine thrust in her direction.

After that, we became steadfast friends. When she performed ceremonies she held no bias. She catered to couples looking for a unique experience. If they were happy and in love, no request was too outlandish. She even conducted a wedding on a nudist resort! Thanks to Internet dating, couples all over the country were getting hitched, which usually involved travelling. Working freelance allowed me the freedom to play wedding photographer for some of her ceremonies. We travelled to Nova Scotia, Alberta, Minnesota and even as far as Texas.

Debbie was still a member of the site, even though she was happily married. Her new role was as a "success story" which she eagerly shared with anyone who'd listen. It was also good for business. Her services were in high demand. When she was not marrying people, she was playing matchmaker. Considering herself a regular online Cupid, I became her next target.

"Are you dating yet?" Debbie demanded one afternoon over coffee. She was not one to beat around the bush. "You know that you need an active sex life to remain healthy right?"

I just laughed. She was constantly nagging me about what I was eating, who I was seeing and letting me know that worked too much. She was also a secret dating diva and loved to tease me about my self-imposed celibacy. With Debbie, playing the field while dating was just as fun as playing summer slow-pitch - it was never serious, just a game.

"You're going to get cobwebs in your panties," she continued.

"Cobwebs?" I howled with laughter. "That's a little dramatic!"

"Don't laugh; I've heard it can happen," she replied. She was serious! I rolled my eyes in amusement.

"How am I supposed to get a date? I live in a small town and most of the men are married. The rest go to church and couldn't be bothered with someone like me. I am too liberal for the men in this town." I argued, taking a generous swig of my coffee. The coffee liqueur Debbie snuck into my cup when I wasn't looking loosened and warmed me.

Not that there was anything wrong with me. I was once married, for almost half a decade, but it did not last. Melvin and I got married straight out of high school. Our conservative community dictated that the correct way of life was to finish school, get married, have sex, birth children and, be a stay-at-home wife and mother for the remainder of your life. What were frowned on were deviations to that order. To make it work, you needed a husband capable of an income for two; someone willing to support his family while the good wife stayed home to keep a perfect home. Don't get me wrong, I knew women who were perfectly happy with that type of life. They seemed to thrive in old fashioned domestic bliss. However, it was not the life for me.

Melvin worked hard and was out of town a lot. I loved him for it, but I felt deserted and alone. I always wanted more out of life. Eventually, due to distance, we drifted apart. After five years of being a part-time wife and a bored housewife, I let him know that I was going to get a job. That conversation ended with his ultimatum. Either I stayed home and fulfilled my wifely duties or he would move on. HE needed to know I was at home waiting. HE needed me to be consistent. HE needed me to take care of him. What I wanted and needed did not matter. I bravely told him, I was going back to school and starting a writing career. His response was to go out of town. I was served divorce papers two weeks later.

I was crushed. I'd always been taught to stand up for myself but never at the cost of somebody else's happiness. Melvin promised that he would never hinder my happiness. He had made me believe I could be both a wife and a creative member of society. He lied; it was nothing but an empty promise. When it came down to it, I had to make a choice. It was my happiness or his. Staying just to please him would have finally killed me.

As a newly available divorcee, I became an immediate threat to every woman in my friendship circle. Former female acquaintances avoided me. I was no longer invited for coffee, dinner parties or crafting circles. They even avoided me on the street! I felt completely isolated. So I threw myself into work and studying to make up for the loneliness. During college, I discovered a passion for writing investigative pieces. I got a thrill out of research, and looking for the proverbial needle in the haystack. Finding the final piece of a puzzle was almost as good as sex.

Ten years later, I had built myself quite a reputation as an investigative journalist for *Exposed*. Since its conception, the monthly magazine prided itself in telling the truth, and no subject was taboo. I scored the job after responding to an advertisement in the local newspaper. The call out was for writers capable of producing full featured research pieces, complete with pictures. I bravely presented a controversial piece demanding that consumers consider pet adoption from rescues instead of buying from breeders. It was a graphic expose based on several recent puppy mill raids; a rare look into the life of a puppy mill dog. Impassioned by what I found during my research, I swore to never buy a pet from a store. Then I found Belle languishing abandoned on the side of the road and my words became more than an opinion. I did not think twice about it. I saw the frightened pooch, and turned her into the sweetest lap dog ever.

I got a dog - and the job.

Where I was once languishing and lonely, I was now too busy to worry about fitting in with the locals. I'd even published several underground novels in my genre of choice, erotic fiction. It was my secret moneymaker; even Debbie was clueless. The money in good erotica was almost as good as pornography, but without the stigma. I could delve into my darkest fantasies without spreading my legs. Based on my bank account, I was good at it.

One fact remained; I was thirty-four years old and completely out of the dating loop. Other than a few casual coffee dates with perspective clients, I had not been on a date since Melvin walked out of my life. I was more than ready; I simply did not think anyone would be interested.

"I know you are busy, but there are ways. Have you ever considered of online dating?" Debbie asked me one evening. When it comes to online dating, she was the self proclaimed expert. Her favourite boast was how she'd personally married seven couples who she'd also introduced to each other.

While many people would scoff at getting a mate through a dating website, to me it actually started to make sense. Our grandparents and great-grandparents would meet through newspaper ads or pen-pal letters, get married and stay married for decades. Now relationships could evolve from Internet dating. I'd also witnessed the happiness of others, so the idea of falling in love with someone you met on the Internet was less ridiculous than it seemed fifteen years ago.

"I already spend too much time online." I admitted. This much is definitely true. With all the hours I spent researching topics for my blog or for freelance articles, some days I was online from dawn to dusk. One tip lead to another and before long an entire day evaporated. Debbie's question made sense. I really wanted to break this pattern. I need a break from technology. Maybe getting out more, communicating with real people instead of looking for another reason to stay disconnected while online.

"No. Seriously! You can make a profile and just check for messages once a day. If you like what you see then you can respond and see where it goes. If you don't enjoy the experience or find what you're looking for, delete it and move on. I still have a profile on *TheFishPond* and it is lots of fun," said Debbie.

I watched her get up to refill our cups. The liqueur was working its magic. I had a slight buzz going. Soon Debbie would be able to convince me of anything I thought, and I was right.

By the end of our third cup of heavily spiked coffee, we were bent over my laptop. I watched mutely as she typed in the web address and *TheFishPond* homepage popped up. She quickly scrolled through some of the local users. From that I could see, it looked harmless.

"See? Everyone seems fairly normal and looking for romance," she said as she pointed out a few male profiles. There were plenty of face-shots and each profile burst with first date ideas and expectations. Dinner, dancing, a walk on the beach. It all seemed normal.

"Besides, what a great story idea. You can do an expose on internet dating. If you don't meet Mr. Right, then you can at least help others understand what dating sites are all about. The good and the bad. Come on Emmy, you know that you want to. Consider it research," she teased. "I will help you fill out your profile." As I watched, she clicked on the link stating "create a new profile".

"Pick a username," she pushed. Her eager fingers twitched impatiently above the keyboard.

"How about Emma?" I suggested hopefully. I was not adept at picking fake names. I lumped creating a false name along with creating a false personality. How can one expect an authentic relationship when it starts out with so much misleading information? While it made sense and provided anonymity, in my mind it was also misleading. For me, I just had to keep things simple. The easier the name, the easier it would be to remember.

"Never use your real name! You want some anonymity and illusion. How about WriterChick? It's perfect for you; you are a woman and a writer. If you do end up writing about this, then you also have a legit handle that doesn't look silly in print. Plus, it's easy to remember," she said with some authority. She was already typing it in, then one click later, it was accepted.

"Now you need a password." Knowing all my passwords, she didn't wait. I watched her enter my most common combination. "There, now you are totally set up."

Glancing at the screen, I found myself staring at a brand new profile, minus specific details and a photograph. I opened my mouth, prepared to offer a suggestion, but Debbie was already filling it in. Within seconds the words *Sexy writer seeks adventurous counterpart* were blasted across the header.

"Not bad," I begrudged. Grabbing my cup, I finished it in one gulp. I found myself slowing down into a submissive puddle of mush as the alcohol loosened my inhibitions. I was definitely more pliable and Debbie knew it. Grabbing our empty cups, I went to the wet bar looking for refills.

Debbie's fingers worked feverishly on the keyboard while I refilled our cups, this time more liquor than coffee. I needed all the boldness I could muster, even if it manifested itself in the form of liquid courage. I was terrified to see what she'd reveal in my profile, but I could always change it later.

"Ready?" The keyboard stopped clacking, signalling that Debbie had finally finished typing. Handing over her cup, I sat down and began to read.

"I am a free-spirited, independent woman, interested in finding a gentleman interested in exploring the world and making memories (or a partner in crime). I enjoy taking my dog on long walks, picnicking on the beach and various outdoor

activities including camping and fishing ~ I can even bait my own hook! A perfect date consists of wine and cheese shared on a blanket under the stars or getting muddy quading in the swamps. I am looking for a loyal, loving companion who is interested in the same."

"You like it?" She asked hopefully before taking a sip of her coffee, which sent her into a sputtering fit. "Boy, is there any coffee in here?"

"Not much and - not too bad on the description," I admitted.

"I didn't think so," she laughed. "Are you ready?"

"Am I ready for what?" I demanded. I felt like I was being thrown to the wolves.

When it came to people, I was a tad dense. When I was growing up, I learned quickly to be quiet and stay in the background. My parents were always gone, so being lonely I tried to make friends. However, I was deathly shy, which was made worse by a nasty stutter. But instead of cowering in a corner, I became the class clown. When I got excited, I would giggle too loud, sometimes I was downright obnoxious. Instead of drawing people towards me, it drove them away. Meeting new people frightened me.

"Once I click submit, your profile goes live. Then you are going to get tons of email. Are you ready?" She repeated. Her sisterly concern was adorable and one of the many reasons why I loved her so much. We'd been friends for fifteen years but we were more like sisters. She always had my best interests in mind, especially when I didn't know what they were.

"It works that fast?" I replied with a note of scepticism. Until now, the only Internet ads I'd ever placed was to list giveaway ads for household items and to sell my car. It always took a few days to get a good response. I didn't expect anything different.

"Trust me, when there is someone new in the pond, guys respond pretty fast. Competition is fierce and they each want to be the first to catch the newbie," Debbie continued.

I nervously chuckled to myself. *Competition?* A visual of men doing a sixty-yard dash, then vaulting hurdles across a finish line popped into my head. Instead of a ribbon, I stood waiting to find out who'd be the first to collapse at my feet. This image nearly sent me off the couch in a fit of drunken giggles. Debbie's glare made me giggle harder. She was the old pro at online dating and by making fun of it, I was insulting her. Swallowing my mirth, I forced myself to seriousness before her feelings got hurt any further.

"So I am a newbie?" The liqueur was kicking in and I sniggered like a teenager again. *Newbie, what a strange word.* I rolled with laughter.

"Grow up! This is serious business here!" she chided. "If you aren't paying attention you're going to end up in bed with some creeper. I don't want to have to wipe your disappointed tears when it could have been prevented by paying attention to me in the first place."

Again, her sisterly bossiness made me chortle.

"Yes, mom!" I guffawed.

"Wait! I forgot something," she cried out.

She was already sorting through several files on my laptop. "Do you have any face shots?" She demanded. Browsing through my photo file, she clicked on various images trying to find the right one. "Aha! Found one!"

I glanced over to find her uploading a picture taken last summer. The photo was shot by a newspaper reporter on the red carpet Media Awards event where I was a guest. I looked like a professional author, but at the same time, sultry. Just as I would imagine a romance writer should look. Satisfied with her choice, she added one of Belle and I playing catch on the beach.

"There, that should get some interest," Debbie looked pleased with herself. "Today, we sit back and wait. Want to check up on the forums?"

"What are the forums?" I demanded. Boy, was I ever naive!

"There are chat forums where local invitations are posted to group coffee meets, bowling, baseball and even dancing nights," she explained while clicking on the page. As the page loaded, I could see lists of topics up for discussion. She clicked one called "Take a walk on the WildSide". "Oh look, there is a group meeting on Friday at WildSide Club. Want to come with me? I'll be your wingman, or in this case – wing woman."

"This coming Friday?" I hesitated, swallowing my uprising panic. This was fast. Friday was only five days away. Mentally going through my calendar, I failed to find a plausible excuse. With Debbie, I'd have to be on my deathbed to get out of plans she made.

"No excuses. You have no plans, Ron's out of town so we are going!" she said. Her frantic typing redirected my attention just in time to see her posting an RSVP on the page. "There, now they will be expecting us; you can't bail on me now."

I issued a non-committal grunt. Debbie's enthusiasm was contagious, but it was also overwhelming. Normally I needed a day or two to adjust. In Debbie's case, spontaneity ruled her life. I wished impulsiveness was in my nature, but it wasn't. To be blunt, the thought of coming out and meeting a group of complete strangers was frightening. However, if I was going to do this, having a pro at dating like my best friend would be an immense relief. Besides, at this point arguing was futile. I shrugged my shoulders helplessly.

"Don't worry so much; you will be okay," said Debbie, trying to offer reassurance. "Also, just because you are going to see someone doesn't mean you have to plan a wedding. This is for fun, to gain friends and to try new things. You need to live a little!"

Glancing at the clock, we both realized that it was close to midnight.

"Oh shit! I have to get out of here, my babysitter is going to want to get home," she said while jumping up from the chair. Like a whirlwind, she flew around the room gathering her purse and jacket. Typical Debbie, her stuff was scattered all over. "I've got to run. Today is Monday. That gives you four days to get a few friends and then Friday, we are going out and having fun. No arguing."

Grabbing her keys, she made for the door, then stopped in her beeline for the exit. She'd suddenly noticed that I was just waiting quietly off the side. It was a habit of self-preservation. When she got to move around in a hurry, one stayed out of her way, or got trampled. I tried to stay out of her way.

"You okay? You went quiet." she asked before running back to me for a quick hug. "You will be fine; stop looking so terrified. Now go check your incoming messages." Planting a quick kiss on each of my cheeks, she flew out the door before I could protest.

After watching her back out of my driveway from my kitchen window, I wandered back to my laptop. The tiny envelope icon was already flashing. There were five messages in my Inbox. *Ugh, already?* Ignoring them, I slammed the laptop lid closed and shuffled back to the front room.

Belle was already curled up on her favourite blanket waiting to snuggle. Plopping down carelessly on the couch, I pulled her into my lap. She moaned in protest as I leaned over to grab the remote. I brushed her off and switched on the Late Show with David Letterman. She sighed in satisfaction once I fell back down beside her and pulled her close. By the first commercial break, we were both contentedly snoring.

CHAPTER FOUR

The next morning, I woke up to Belle's wet tongue caressing my cheek. Half asleep, my hand went up to wipe away the doggy-pom slobber. Belle's way of asking to go for a morning patrol was always messy. She jumped down expectantly as I tossed the blanket aside and dragged myself up.

"Who needs an alarm clock when you have a dog," I laughed at Belle dancing around at my feet. She was looking pretty dire. As soon as the door opened, she was gone in a cream-coloured flash. Guess she really needed to piddle, I chuckled.

A persistent, dull pounding in my head reminded me that I drank almost an entire bottle of chocolate liqueur the night before. As I shook out a couple of Tylenol and grabbed a bottle of water, the rest of the night came back to me. I shuddered involuntarily. Why had I allowed Debbie to talk me joining a dating site? Have I taken leave of my senses? Well, maybe she is right. I really didn't not want to become the crazy dog lady. I wanted love, I wanted companionship and yes, I wanted a happily ever after, but would anyone want me? I guess, thanks to Debbie, I was about to find out.

Hearing Belle's yip at the doorway, I promptly let her in. Following her to the kitchen, I refilled her dished with food and fresh water. Once Belle was taken care of, I wandered over the laptop. I reached for it with some hesitation. For a second, I was afraid to touch it. Suck it up, I chided myself. Having no clue what I'd find, I opened the lid and wiggled the mouse.

When my computer finally came alive, I blinked. My personal ad Inbox was still open on my desktop. The night before there were five messages waiting; now there were over a dozen messages awaiting my scrutiny. I was momentarily taken aback. This was not what I'd expected. I'd jokingly told Debbie that maybe I would get a note or two. I definitely didn't expect more than a handful. Once again, she was right and I was wrong.

Clicking on the first message, I started reading. As a writer, I expected to be wooed with words. I barely got through deciphering the first sentence before I wanted to delete it. My pet peeve glared back at me in black and white. I could handle two-fingered typists, but I could not deal with bad writers. As a writer, I was easily seduced by crisply written, mistake free emails. With spelling and grammar checks available on every chat service, email and writing programs there was no reason for typos, other than laziness. The message was also full of distracting mistakes, which made it difficult to understand. Click. Delete.

The next three messages also hit the trash folder. Other than to tell me how hot I was and how much they'd like to "do me", the notes offered little else for content. A few notes contained indecent proposals such as asking outright for a hookup or even offering cash for a date. They were promptly deleted. I was starting to get a little annoyed. This was definitely not what I imagined. *Does anyone take this seriously?* What a colossal waste of time. I would have to give Debbie hell for setting me up like this.

I was starting to lose interest, but giving up with not an option. I wanted to finish reading through the messages. Debbie was right; this was good research. There were a few messages that caught my attention and they looked legit enough, and then I went and checked their profiles.

One respondent was a truck driver; he seemed interesting and handsome, but I did not want another long distance relationship, so I put it aside.

Some of the men seemed sane, others seemed full of bitterness and it showed in their profiles. These I deleted, I wanted a man, but I did not want the baggage. The last thing I wanted to do was listen to a man whine about his ex wife screwed him over or that he was sick of sending child support. I sent back a few hellos to the more polite messages, but for the most part, I didn't take any of them seriously. *Maybe I just was not into this type of thing,* I thought.

Once I'd gone through my Inbox, I paid another visit to the general message forums. This was where the banter took place. I quickly found Debbie's post from the previous night. She had not been joking. She'd publicly declared that she was coming on Friday along with me. She even attached a link to my profile as an introduction to the group. From the looks of it, several bachelors were keen on seeing me. Double-checking the names in my Inbox confirmed their readiness.

"She's never going to let me bail now," I grumbled in Belle's direction. Hearing my voice, Belle cocked her head in my direction. When I didn't continue or invite her over, she gave out a disappointed sigh and resumed her nap.

By the time Friday rolled around, I had to admit I was pumped. Over the past few days, I spent some time going over the forum threads to familiarize myself with the regular posters. Very quickly, it became obvious which people were there for fun, who the couples were and who was just sleeping around. While the majority of the people on the site were there for legitimate dates, there were also just as many looking for a quick roll in the hay. I needed to be prepared for the worse.

Debbie came on my doorstep at 8 o'clock, looking like she was going to a beauty contest. After spending an hour preening, I thought I looked pretty good too. My long brunette hair lay in luxurious waves down my spine. The evening promised to be unseasonably warm so I had pulled on a mid thigh, skirt and added a standard black tank top along with a plain jacket. A pair of white and black stilettos complete with four inch heels added a much-needed pop to my outfit. Doing a little spin of admiration before the mirror, I felt confident in my appearance. Debbie, who looked hot in a hunter green silk mini-dress and thigh-high black leather boots, disagreed.

"You need to change. You look like you're going for a job interview. You are NOT going to a meeting," Debbie stated emphatically as she pushed her way into my living room and surveyed my outfit. Her look of fashion horror nearly shattered my confidence. "Come on, let's hit your closet," she said.

"What's wrong with what I am wearing?" I asked, while admiring my reflection. I thought my business suit looked smart.

Plus, I adored the shoes. They added several inches to my five-foot six-inch frame, causing my legs look incredible.

"We are going DANCING not to a Chamber of Commerce banquet," she said with exasperation and undeterred in her mission. She was already carelessly tossing the contents of my closet into the bed. "Here, try this." She was clutching a transparent ebony chiffon blouse. "Take off your jacket and put this on."

"I would never wear these shoes to a Chamber dinner," I muttered as I obeyed, shrugging into the delicate blouse. Looking at my reflection in the mirror, I had to admit the diaphanous chiffon was a deliciously feminine choice.

"Impressive! Now you need some bling," she said while already rummaging through my meagre jewellery collection. Finding what she was looking for, I was handed a bracelet with big gems and a pair of matching earrings. I slipped them on without arguing. She grinned and stepped back to see the entire ensemble. I had to admit, her version of my look rocked. "You look perfect. If you do not make an impression then these guys are dead, blind or playing for the other team."

"Thanks, I think!" I laughed. Her enthusiasm was contagious and I found myself starting to get excited again.

"Come on, we want to make an entrance, but we don't want to be too late. Most people couple off by ten so if you want a chance, we have to roll," she said.

She was already on her way to the door. How did I end up with such a whirlwind for a best friend? I was going to need an energy drink just to keep up with her.

"Hope I can keep up with you tonight," I uttered once we were on the road.

"It's not me that you have to keep up with dear. Wait until these guys get a look at you, you are going to be the life of the party," she said with a laugh.

"If you say so," I retorted, still not convinced.

"You will see and then you will owe me," Debbie replied.

"Owe you what?" I asked, instantly suspicious. Owing Debbie could cost me more than I was ready to pay. Her idea of payment could include Parasailing or bungee jumping.

"Don't worry, I will make it painless," she chortled and knowing damn well her teasing was not helping the situation or my nerves. I chose to brush her off and cranked up the radio to Hot 103.1 and dance music filled the cockpit. The thirty-minute drive flew by as we got into the spirit and cranked up the volume. We sang harmonies all off-tune to every song and my nervousness was soon forgotten - until we arrived at our destination.

Pulling into the back alley behind the club, I spotted a handful of people gathered around the doorway smoking. Obviously they recognized Debbie's canary yellow Shelby Mustang because a few arms went up to wave hello. She honked the horn and waved back before continuing into the parking lot to find a space. Finding an empty spot near the door, she moved in and parked.

"You ready?" she asked, taking her keys out of the ignition.

"As ready as I will ever be," I said. I was terrified, and that would not change.

"Suck it up buttercup, this is your night," she said and gave my hand a quick squeeze before we jumped out of the car. Locking the doors behind us, Debbie headed towards the back door of the Club. In her excitement, she forgot that I was following and I ran to keep up. She finally slowed just before we reached the front entrance of the building.

"DEBBIE!!" a chorus of voices cheered as we moved around the bend. Two couples were finishing their cigarettes when we reached the door. Debbie quickly ran over; giving each one a huge hug and kiss. Introductions were tossed in my direction, but I nervously shrugged them off. I would remember them later when given an opportunity to chat one-on-one, until then, it was all a blur.

"This is my friend Emma; she just joined our group earlier this week," she advised the group. The door to the Club opened and another group of revellers spilled out to join us. "This is Emma, she is single and VERY available," she informed the newcomers. I giggled. This was getting a little too awkward for me. I felt like a sideshow from all the attention I was getting.

"I love your blouse," said one woman, with friendly green eyes. Debbie had introduced her as Judy. "You are very beautiful!"

"Thank you," I responded politely. "I love your clothes," I said. She looked delicious wearing a slinky black dress with capped sleeves. Scrutinizing the women gathered outside, I was grateful Debbie made me change. I would have stood out like a sore thumb in my work clothes. At least now, I looked just as sexy and sleek as all the other single females.

"How do you keep your hair so long and shiny?" another woman asked. Her welcoming smile put me at ease quickly. "By the way, my name is Sheryl."

"Hey Sheryl, I am an Aussie girl," referring to my favourite hair product. "It's a pleasure to meet you."

"Personally, I think your legs and ass are your best features," delivered a male voice from behind me. Spinning around, I came face-to-face with the biggest pair of green eyes ever. Even under the glow of the streetlight, I could see they were a deep jade ringed with golden-brown. *I'd bet they even changed colours with his emotions.* I blushed and gave myself a mental shake.

"Excuse me?" I demanded. His bold observation astonished me. Caught off guard I pretended not to hear him. Instead of responding, I pointedly surveyed him like a farmer checking out a prize bull at auction. The first thing that caught my eye was the flashy silver buckle at his waist that accented his slender hips. Skinny tight denim clung to his beefy thighs, accented legs that obviously worked out. His denim shirt fit snugly around bulging arms. Everything about this man radiated physical power. He was fit and unyielding.

"Your legs, in that skirt, go forever. I'd love to know what you have underneath," he continued with a smirk, obviously enjoying my discomfort. *Did he really just ask me if I was wearing underwear?* Boy, it has been way too long since I'd gone clubbing. Such intimate questions used to be taboo, except in private.

"Do you always talk to strangers like this?" I laughed awkwardly. I couldn't believe the audacity of his remarks. I glanced around looking for help from Debbie but she was on the other side of the group yakking to her friends. I was completely on my own.

"Nope, just the ones who I think would look breathtakingly beautiful in the daylight, under moonlight; but especially sensual under the glow of candlelight," was his tranquil response. "I bet you are positively splendid, lying bare-assed naked beneath the stars."

"Oh really now," I sputtered, unsure of how to react. I had faced self-assured men before, but this one took the cake. His confidence nearly knocked me off balance. *Was he for real?*

"Back off Dom, you're going to scare her off," Debbie retorted as she rejoined me. I tossed her a grateful smile. She gave my elbow a reassuring squeeze and winked mischievously in return.

"Emmy, this is Dom. Dominic, this is my best friend Emmy and if you hurt her, you answer to me," her voice steeled with a warning. She moved closer to me while glowering at the obnoxious male.

"Hey, it's okay. I was just introducing myself. You know I'm harmless," he said. He must be familiar with her temper because he took a few steps back and threw up his arms.

"Harmless my ass; you are not going to charm this one into submission," Debbie's arm went around my waist protectively. "This one is too sweet to be messed with by the likes of you. Play nice," she admonished.

Dominic laughed in amusement, then shrugged, but he must have taken Debbie seriously. He shot me a tremendous smile and got up to depart. He held my hand gently in his enormous grasp.

"It was a pleasure to make your acquaintance Miss Emma. I hope to get another chance to charm your pants off," he chuckled, before leaning over to kiss the back of my hand. I mentally rolled my eyes. Flashing a cheeky wink in Debbie's direction, he spun away and headed back inside the club. My eyes watched his backside as it disappeared into the building. There was nothing wrong with that view, I admitted before snorting in self disgust.

"You okay?" Debbie asked, suddenly very worried.

"I am okay, but what was that about?" I asked, trying to shake the mental image of Dom's behind out of my mind. I got the impression I was missing something.

"That was Dominic. He is the room charmer. He thinks he is Mr. Wonderful, and boy is he ever. Most of the women would kill for a date with him. Handsome, charming, rich, he is a great catch; but he also has a shady reputation. I have yet to see him with the same woman twice. I'd advise you to avoid him at all costs; at least for now," she suggested. Taking a last drag of her smoke, Debbie flicked it into the sidewalk ashtray like a pro. She sounded harsh, but I knew better. Her genuine affection towards Dom was evident.

"He's a member of the group?" I inquired curiously. What was a man like him doing on a dating site? He was delicious and obviously too good to be true. There had to be something seriously wrong with him. I was not prepared to accept it, but I was somewhat intrigued.

Dominic had definitely made an impression - I am sure it was just what he meant.

"Yep, and now you are going to play some more," she said. "By the end of the night, you will forget about meeting Dominic."

Before I could protest, she grabbed my hand and dragged me into the club.

I soon found out that when the *TheFishPond* group got together, they partied hard. Inside the dance club, the room was packed with men and women, all dressed to impress. WildSide was privately owned by one of the group's regular members. He leased the recently vacant club for the exclusive use of the group. It was open Friday and Saturday nights only. Presently, the hexagon shaped dance floor was packed, as both sexes attempted to perform a choreographed line dance. The floor was surrounded by jovial spectators, who only stopped chatting long enough to tease dancers who performed with two left feet. Nearly every table surrounding the base and outer walls was running over. It was literally standing room only. There had to be close to one hundred and fifty people, yet everyone knew each other in one way or another.

I still felt like an outsider. To make matters worse, I hated crowds. If I had gone to the party alone, I would have discretely bailed. According to our plan for the night, Debbie was my ride home and unfortunately I was at the mercy of her agenda. I pushed my way towards the crowded bar and ordered a glass of white wine. By the time I got served, Debbie had wandered off again. Finding myself alone once again, I sauntered off to the side, leaned against a pillar and watched the room.

"Why is a lovely lady like you hiding in the corner like this?" A male voice said close to my ear. Turning, I noticed the attractive male standing beside me, holding what appeared to be a coke.

"Pardon me?" I asked, glancing in his direction before looking back to survey the room. I was still trying to spot Debbie but she was as elusive as a butterfly in the crowd.

"Are you hiding from someone?" he asked again. This time, I caught a hint of an accent, but with the pounding bass and rumble of voices, it was hard to tell. I loved accents, and he sounded western European.

"Not really, just catching my breath," I lamely offered. He didn't need to know that I was secretly plotting an escape. Turning to face him, I conducted a quick visual inspection. By my estimate, he was about forty years old and took care of himself. His biceps bulged beneath his well-fitted white tee shirt and I could make out every ripple of his chest. His skin-tight Levi's clung to well-formed thighs. He was definitely drool-worthy. I caught myself ogling.

"Like what you see?" he grinned, bringing the drink to his kissable lips. I watched as the glistening glass caressed his sensual mouth while he took a sip. "Hello?" was all that I could muster.

Realizing I was staring, I blushed. "Sorry," I lamely stuttered in embarrassment. *What is wrong with me?* I was reacting to every handsome male who entered my orbit. Maybe Debbie was right, I'd been celibate way too long.

"My name is Stephan and you my dear, are utterly enchanting," he said. This time there was no mistaking his accent; he was definitely British.

"I am Emma." I responded. I tipped my glass bottle in his direction. "It's nice to meet you!"

"Nice to meet you too Emma," he replied. "Would you like to dance with me?"

Looking down at my glass, I didn't realise that it was almost empty. I devoured the remainder in one swallow.

"I will grab you one after we dance," he volunteered. Before I could react, he set his drink down and led me to the dance floor. As we merged into the swaying crowd, he gracefully pulled me into his arms while I assumed a chaste distance for the ensuing slow dance.

"You know, I may be English, but we are not dancing before the Queen; you can move closer to me you know," he suggested. I laughed and allowed him to pull me closer.

"You're from England?" I asked.

"Yes, I came here about five years ago," he volunteered.

"Do you have a wife?" I asked, secretly hoping he said no.

"Would I be on a dating site if I did?" He replied. Good question and unfortunately one I didn't know how to respond. The premise is that everyone is single, but you just never know. I didn't know who visited dating sites. After all, I was still a newbie.

"Have you been on *TheFishPond* long?" I asked. I was curious as to know how long the dating process took most people.

"I joined about six months ago. I've been on a few dates but I haven't met the one I want to run away with... yet," he said. His eyes never left my face as he placed extra emphasis on the word "yet". "And you?"

"I just joined four days ago," I admitted sheepishly. At this point, I was not sure being a newbie was beneficial or not.

"And why would you do that?" He asked. It was difficult for me to not giggle at his comical face.

"My girlfriend was tired of me living vicariously through her. She was getting tired of sharing the details of her sex life without me having anything important to dish to her." I admitted.

"So you let her suck you in huh?" His amused laughter warmed me, instead of rubbing me the wrong way. At least he wasn't mocking me.

"Yep, pretty much!" I admitted.

"Well, I am glad that she did," he admitted, drawing me closer and wrapping his arms around me. Strangely, I felt safe. His gentle touch and teasing nature made it easy for me to lighten up. I was soon laughing freely at his silly antics as he attempted to charm me. The dance ended way too soon. I actually saddened when we pulled apart.

"Come outside with me?" he asked as we came back to where he'd set down his glass. He downed the remainder in one gulp.

"Sure," I replied. I needed a smoke to calm me down. I hated to admit it; I was having fun, but it was all very unsettling. There was something about the way he talked and made me laugh. His charm made it easy. His hand settled on my waist with familiarity as he pointed me towards the door.

"You know, I have a confession to make," he said, offering to light my cigarette. I took a deep drag, savouring the soothing nicotine as smoke flooded my lungs.

"Isn't it too soon for confessions," I teased.

"Not really! I was not going to come tonight; I've been on the site for months, but this is my first meeting too," he admitted. I tried to pay attention, but leaning casually against the brick wall of the club, he looked more like a bouncer than a guest. *Damn, he was cute.*

"What brought you out tonight?" I enquired.

"You!" he said. He watched me for a reaction.

"Me?" I demanded. That statement was ludicrous in my opinion. No one made a trip anywhere, just for me.

"Yes. You!" He said with a wicked twinkle in his eyes as he teased me. "Deb's on my Facebook so I've seen you before. I've also checked out your magazine and online blog. You are a good writer."

He researched me? I was suddenly uncomfortable. I wasn't sure how it made me feel about this stranger admitting familiarity to both me and my work. While I was used to meeting fans in unexpected places, blatant adoration bothered me. I wrote because I enjoyed it, not because I wanted to be recognized or stalked. I also tended to over-share personal things on my blog; things only people who knew me would understand how they really affected me. To a stranger, it was like peeking into a secret diary. Sometimes it was almost embarrassing.

"Please, don't pull away," he said, pushing away from the wall. I took an involuntary step backward. He quitted my retreat with a loose grasp of my wrist. "Don't run away either."

Taken aback by his gentle but firm grip, I staggered backwards, suddenly caught off-balance in my stilettos. Before I could fall, Stephan reached out and caught me. Instead of letting me go, he pulled me straight into his arms. I gasped with excitement and surprise. Plastered against his chest was like being pressed against a sun-baked brick wall. He was strong, steady and warm.

"Do you mind?" I managed to stutter, well aware of how small I suddenly felt in his grasp. I felt slightly intimidated yet at the same time extremely turned-on. *Oh gawd, I am losing my mind.*

"Do you?" he asked. His eyebrows lifted questioningly. Before I could retort, his face lowered and he pressed his lips against mine. The warmth of his lips as they caressed mine in the gentlest of kisses was mind-blowing. I briefly saw stars. He tasted like tobacco and rye whiskey. *I think there was more than coke in the glass.* All coherent thought scattered as his tongue gently coerced my lips apart. Much to my surprise and shame, I responded, and soon I eagerly kissed him back.

Wrapped within his warm embrace, his mouth worked its magic on my senses. I moaned as his eager tongue pillaged my mouth. I was lost in sensation as flames of desire flared. It has been a long time since I'd made out like this. It was absolutely heavenly. I was oblivious that he'd spun me around and pushed my body backwards against the wall until I felt a brick burning in my lower spine.

"Get a room," someone called playfully as the club's door suddenly flew open. Music flooded the sidewalk, along with a bunch of bodies. No longer alone, we reluctantly pulled apart as the well-inebriated group poured onto the street. Coming to my senses, I pushed him away, trying to put enough distance between us to catch my breath. I adjusted my blouse, which had ridden up during our feverish kiss. Panting, my fingers involuntarily caressed my lips. They were swollen from his wanton advances.

His eyes smouldered with desire as I caught him watching me. I could not recall how long since I'd seen that expression, but I recognised it immediately. He wanted me; there was no doubt about it. The realization frightened yet excited me. My flash of panic must have been visible, because Stephan suddenly backed off and glanced down at his watch.

"I have to go. I start work early in the morning. Can I call you?" He asked hopefully. I should have been flattered, but instead I felt like a doe, panicky and about to flee.

"You want my number?" I couldn't believe I was about to give him my phone number, but admittedly, I wanted to see him again. There was something dangerous, but alluring about him. He made me feel desirable and then there was the accent; his accent warmed me in ways nothing else could.

"Nope, but I will find it; I have ways of getting information when I need it," he chuckled. "Can I have one more for the road?"

Before I could ponder his request, my body was enveloped within his arms once more. As our lips reconnected with torrid urgency, I nearly blacked out. When he finally pulled reluctantly away, I was gasping for breath. Unable to think straight, I staggered with both disappointment and relief. His kiss nearly brought me to my knees.

"Just a little something for you to remember me by," he grinned down at me; before tracing his fingertip lightly across my moist mouth. "Lord knows, I won't forget you."

Before I could respond, he turned on his heels and headed down the street. Stunned, I watched his retreat and absent-mindedly pulled another cigarette out of my pack.

"EMMA!" Debbie yelled as she left the club shortly after. "There you are; I've been looking all over for you. What's wrong?"

She stopped jabbering instantly when she recognized the look on my face. "Are you all right? Do you want to go?"

"No, I am fine. Can we go back in?" I asked with excitement. Debbie looked genuinely surprised. I just laughed and hugged her. Suddenly I felt much more alive and rejuvenated. Kissing Stephan had awakened something inside me; something I'd long forgotten. Fun. People. LIFE. This all awaited. Maybe it was the kiss; maybe it was the wine, but suddenly, I was not ready to leave.

I also needed to find something to do to help me forget about meeting Stephan. Maybe some dancing would give me other things to think about other than dwelling on the tingling left behind by his kiss. As much as I enjoyed it, he knocked me off balance. I definitely needed to forget that he'd made me feel more alive in ten- minutes than I'd felt in a really long time.

"I thought you would never ask. Let's go party!" Debbie hollered loud enough for the entire street to hear. A rambunctious cheer erupted from the crowd assembled on the sidewalk. I laughed too. This was definitely better than spending the night at home again with Belle.

When we finished our cigarettes, I eagerly followed Debbie back into the club. *Let the fun and games begin.*

CHAPTER FIVE

I never arrived home that night. Debbie and I literally danced the night away. Once word got out that I was new to the group, everyone wanted to see me. It was overwhelming at times and I was grateful the drinks flowed freely. Initially I planned to go home back out to the country, but at the end of the night, we called a cab and went to Debbie's home. Eight hours later, I woke up sprawled out on the couch wearing nothing but a tee shirt and panties. That was not surprising.

Alcohol tended to loosen my inhibitions, which usually lead to me losing my clothes. I was never one of those young ladies who got blindly drunk and slept around. However, I was one of the young women who would run naked down the street, or strip naked and play in a public fountain.

Once, when accompanying Debbie to a wedding in Texas, I had a few too many drinks at the rehearsal dinner. During the after-party, I got bored and decided to go for a swim. Riding the elevator thirty stories down to lobby, I jumped in the hotel pool wearing nothing but a tee shirt. I'd even forgot my underwear back in the room. The funniest part was the looks hotel guests gave me when they joined me for the short elevator ride. No one knew quite what to say. Debbie loved this crazy side in me, and encouraged my inebriated alter ego to come out and play. From what I could recall, Emmy did not make an appearance last night. *Thank goodness for that.*

My head throbbed while my mouth felt like it was full of cotton balls. It's been years since I felt this rough in the morning. I despised hangovers, which is another reason I chose not to imbibe. After Stephan left the club last night, I was more than a little unsettled. Once inside, it did not take me long to get back into the swing of things. We danced the night away until our feet couldn't handle another step. A few drinks later and we were ready to dance some more.

I groaned, reluctantly pulling myself off the couch and headed to the kitchen. While rummaging through Debbie's fridge for a bottle of water, I picked up my tablet beeping in my purse. Someone was trying to message me. Brushing it off, I opened the bottle and eagerly quenched my thirst. With each refreshing gulp, I felt the pain in my brain ease and I tossed back a few Aspirin to speed up the recovery process.

Tucking the bottle of pills back into my purse, I grabbed my tablet and pushed the power button. Pulling down the notification window, I opened the email. I blinked in mild shock. There were even more messages than before. I sifted through them, looking for something useful. Several of the notes mentioned seeing me the night before, and some enclosed gushing compliments. I had definitely been noticed.

Halfway down the list was a message marked urgent. It was from Stephan.

"It was a pleasure to meet you last night. Thank you for not slapping me, but I must admit, I really loved the way you tasted. Hope I get another test just to make sure. Message me and we will go for coffee. Stephan."

"Hey girl," I slammed my tablet shut guiltily at the sound of Debbie's voice. I cringed. "Oh. My. God. I have such a bad headache. But man, was it ever worth it." She was already rummaging in the fridge. "Did you grab my last bottle of water?"

"Nope, look in the door." I suggested.

"Got it! Do you have any Aspirin?" She asked. I offered the bottle I'd already pulled from my purse. I giggled as she struggled with the childproof cap. "Yea, I know, outsmarted by a bottle."

She plopped down on the couch beside me; then popped the pills into her mouth.

"So, did you have fun last night?" she asked as I scooted over to make room. She tugged out a portion of my blanket and tucked it round her shoulders. I snapped it back, taking just enough to cover my bare legs.

"Yes, I really did. Thank you for dragging me out," I said. I wasn't lying; I really did have a great time.

"Not like it took much," she teased. That much is probably true. Once I'd made up my mind that I was going out, nothing could stop me.

"You know what I mean," I concurred. Ultimately, I had not put up much of a fight. This must mean that I was finally ready to get away from work and have a life again. Finally! It only took me five years to realize that.

"So, have you heard from Stephan yet?" She asked as she flashed me a quick look; almost daring me to make up a story. My agonizing headache made it too difficult to fabricate anything plausible, so I settled on telling the truth.

"As a matter of fact, he sent me an email this morning." I replied nonchalantly.

"Oh?" Her eyebrows went up in curiosity as she leaned forward with eager anticipation. "What did he say?" Debbie asked.

"He thanked me for not slapping him," I chuckled.

"No way – he didn't! That is funny!," she laughingly replied. She offered me a cigarette before lighting the one already hanging out of her mouth. "Are you going to see him again?"

"No!" I responded, way too quickly. Her eyebrows went up mockingly as she snorted.

"Why not?" she begged. "His online personality seems really sweet. Besides, I've known him since he joined *TheFishPond* and he has always been a gentleman. We've talked privately since the week he joined. As the self appointed welcoming committee I make it my business to know all new members, and show them the ropes. Normally he avoids gatherings so last night was the first time he joined us for a meet-and-greet."

"So he told me."

"Do you know why he came out last night?" Debbie asked, leaning over me to flick her smoke into the ashtray.

"I am assuming it was because there was a meet-and-greet? He wanted to date me? He was looking to get laid?" I scoffed. It was not hard to figure out why people attended these things based on the sum of discrete making out I witnessed. The sexual innuendos left on the forum after these meetings made it even more definite. These meetings were designed to turn singles into couples, even for just a night.

"Actually, I think it was more than that. He was asking questions about you a few days ago," Debbie nonchalantly volunteered.

"Oh really? What was he asking about?" I was momentarily confused. This was the first time she'd mentioned knowing him before last night.

"Yep, he caught my post about you in the party thread, so he inboxed me. We've been chatting for a while so he trusts my opinion on who is datable and who is just playing games. Believe me, there are a few less than savoury people on TFP. You can't be too careful," Debbie continued. She had finished her cigarette and was already looking for another. "I told him that we've been friends for years and you are one of the good ones."

"The good ones, huh? In other words you told him I was boring," I said with some dejection. Just my luck, I'd been sold out by my best friend.

"I can't believe you'd think I would do that! No, it was nothing like that. I told him the truth that you were single and have been for a few years. I also said you were a good person; and if that's what he wanted the he should introduce himself. I even offered to help but he assured me he could handle that on his own," Debbie added.

"Oh, he handled it alright. He definitely introduced himself," I scoffed. Remembering just how he'd introduced himself, I blushed scarlet. It was the first time I ended up plastered against a brick wall with a tongue stuck down my throat. Not only did it surprise me, but I had to admit that I also enjoyed it.

"He got to you! I knew he would!" It was a statement, not a question. Debbie started laughing.

"How could you be so sure?" I demanded as I stood up to grab another bottle of water. However, once in the kitchen, I decided to make a pot of coffee instead. Besides, rummaging through the cupboards looking for filters and coffee grounds kept me out of Debbie's line of vision long enough to regain some semblance of dignity.

"First, I know you're a sucker for accents. Secondly, he's European and they are different from the guys here. They appreciate quality, not quantity." Debbie said. She'd obviously given this some thought. "Do you really think I would have thrown you to the wolves without having a backup plan?"

"No, but you could have warned me," I stated. Satisfied the fresh coffee filter was in place and the coffee was added, I switched on the machine. While I cleaned up, Debbie continued her explanation.

"Warned you? If I'd warned you, you would have found some stupid reason to stay home. I was not about to let that happen. You work too much and tend to forget about life and fun. Go out there and live a little. You're almost forty and if you don't get laid soon you're destined to become a dried up spinster. You need a reminder of the wonders of having someone special in your life, other than Belle. At this rate, you're going to become the crazy dog lady," argued Debbie.

She had a point and I knew better than to argue.

"So you are telling me I should give him a chance?" I demanded. I rejoined her on the couch, grabbing the blanket back in the process. A brief game of tug-a-war ensued until Debbie finally conceded and gave me back enough to recover my legs.

"Yes, I do! I think he's a decent guy and you could do a lot worse. Besides, I'd like to see you deny that you were unmoved by his kiss," she continued. I squirmed uncomfortably. I would be lying if I told her I hated it and didn't want a repeat performance. But I didn't want to seem like some love struck teenager who'd just been swept off her feet. I was a mature woman. I was smarter than this. "At least think about it?" said Debbie. She leaned closer to make sure I was listening.

"I will think about it!" I concurred. I had already decided I was going to respond to his message, I just hadn't prepared my speech yet. I wasn't ready to give Debbie the satisfaction of knowing I was taking her advice - not yet anyway.

"Good. And when you meet, I want all the gory details," replied Debbie with satisfaction.

"I don't kiss and tell!" I chuckled.

"Oh, you will, even if I have to beat it out of you," she hooted, while grabbing one of the throw pillows off the loveseat. Before I could duck, she swung. My head snapped back when the pillow connected. I grabbed another and soon pillows were flying. Fortunately, our hangovers ended the game quickly. After landing a well-placed pillow upside Debbie's head, we both fell over groaning. Neither of us had the energy or inclination to keep going.

"Well, since we have to wait for the coffee, I might as well hit the shower," Debbie said, before tossing aside the blanket and getting up. I watched her stroll down the hallway before reaching for my tablet. I waited until the shower started running before reopening my Inbox. I reread Stephan's message before replying.

"Hi Stephan, It was a pleasure to meet you too. Sorry you had to leave, but I am glad that you had a great time before you left. We will have to do that again soon. Thank you for making me feel welcome, Emma."

Clicking send, I reread the note before filing it away. It sounded pathetic, but I didn't want him to think I was reflecting, reminiscing or yearning for a repeat performance. Nor did I want him to know how delicious I thought he looked. I was a crappy poker player, but I did know that a smart woman never lets a man know she was interested after one encounter. That normally sent them running in the opposite direction. Nope, I would wait until the proper time – IF the right time ever came. But at this point, I didn't even expect a reply.

Getting up, I went back to the kitchen and looked into the coffee. It was done. Debbie was the queen of quick showers, so I filled two cups, added cream and carried them into the living room.

My tablet buzzed just as I was sitting down. Placing the cups carefully on the table, I picked up the still beeping contraption and clicked my Inbox.

"Good afternoon! How is your head?" read his message.

A little sore and definitely foggy. How is yours? I quickly typed back a reply.

"Ha-ha, I am not surprised. I hear you shut the place down."

Yep, Debbie and I made a night of it. I am still at her place. I sat back and waited for his reaction. I didn't have to wait too long.

"I'd like to see you again," read his next message.

Boy he sure went straight to the point. No small talk for this man.

"Oh really?" I replied coyly, not wanting to appear overly eager. If he wanted to see me again, he would have to beg for it.

"Yes, REALLY. What are you doing later this evening? I'd like to get to know you better," he asked.

I have a meeting at 7 o'clock, but I should be free when I am done. I suggested.

"That works for me! I am a night owl by nature. How about coffee on Regent Avenue? There is a nice little cafe that is open twenty-four hours a day. We could take our time getting to know each other," was his immediate reply. It was obvious he was proficient with a keyboard. His reactions were coming in too fast for a two-finger typist.

It sounds great. I'll see you then. My heart caught in my throat as I pressed send. Was I being too impetuous? I needed to give my head a shake. Have I lost my mind completely? I couldn't believe I just agreed to have coffee with a stranger. I thought, if Debbie approved, then it should be acceptable. If it wasn't then I knew who to blame.

"Are you okay?" Debbie asked when she rejoined me in the living room.

"Yeah, I am okay, why do you ask?" I feigned innocence as I reached for my coffee cup. "I poured you a coffee."

"Never mind deflecting! What's wrong? You look like you lost your best friend and I know that didn't happen because I am standing right here," said Debbie. Trust her to get right to the point.

"I e-mailed Stephan back," I reluctantly admitted. She may be a pain in the buttocks, but she never judged my decisions.

"And?" Debbie questioned.

"And, he wants to meet for coffee this evening after I finish my meetings," I responded.

"You have a first date!" Debbie giggled with glee. She was still rubbing her hands together in excitement. I found the gesture irritating.

"Do you have to be so excited? It is just coffee." I retorted. "It's not a date!"

"Well, you have to start somewhere. What are you going to wear?" she asked, pulling the towel off her head. I watched as she finger-combed the damp strands clinging to her skull.

"It is JUST coffee," I said emphatically.

"Well, in TFP coffee is never JUST coffee," she winked mischievously. Her hair was starting to curl as she proceeded to fiddle with it.

"Excuse me?" I was shocked. *Did I miss something here?* "Are you telling me there are hidden innuendos or are you just messing with me?"

"Would I do that?" was her mischievous response. I made a face, which had her roaring in laughter within moments. "You don't have to look so shocked. We are all adults. This is not high school or college. It is a part of the adult dating game. There IS a big difference. People have needs and they find a place to meet those demands. Online dating facilitates that process."

"So you are telling me that I agreed to have coffee with a guy and he is going to expect more than coffee?" I said. Really? This was not expected at all. I was not going to bed with someone simply because he took me out for coffee. Thank goodness, I still had time to cancel.

"I am just warning you to not be surprised if something else happens," said Debbie with a satisfied smirk on her face. She seemed to be enjoying my discomfort and sudden confusion. If she was a stranger, I would have been insulted. But I knew enough to know that she was teasing. "Quit being such a prude! This is not the 1950's where marriage comes first. You can have sex on a date now – it IS okay."

I rolled my eyes. This conversation was becoming ludicrous.

"If you weren't my best friend, I would smack you and walk out of here never to be seen again," I threatened lamely.

"Promises, promises. You know I love you and want the best for you. Most of all, I want you to be happy. You only live once. Let's have a little fun today! Your single, he's single. Trust me, no one will get hurt. HAVE FUN," Debbie encouraged.

She made it sound so easy, but I knew differently. It was difficult to release my inhibitions. When I'd succumbed to my urges in the past, someone always got hurt and usually it was me. Broken hearts suck! It was easier to put myself up on a shelf, never to descend again.

"Come on Emmy, stop being so difficult. Do you want to see him again?" Her voice softened and the teasing stopped. She reached out and laid a hand on my trembling knee.

"I guess so," I hesitated. I wasn't really sure what I wanted, other than Debbie to get off my back. Okay, maybe I did a little. I wanted to go out with a good guy; I wanted to live happily ever after.

"Then what is stopping you?" she urged. Her words brought me back from my wish-filled thinking.

"Nothing," I begrudgingly admitted, to both of us. Shrugging, I conceded defeat. Debbie was absolutely right. It was time to have a little fun. "Fine, I will meet him tonight, but that's it. It's just coffee."

"That's a start anyway," she grinned, knowing she'd won this battle. It remained to be seen who would win the war.

"You're a pain in the ass," I teased. I was joking, but at the same time I wasn't. Debbie was a pain in my ass, but only because I permitted it. Glancing at my watch, I shoved off the couch and began gathering my things. "I better get cracking. I still have to go back to the house and let Belle out before I start my meetings."

"I expect a full update when you get home later!" Debbie demanded, before grabbing my pants off the floor and tossing them in my direction. I slipped them on, trying not to fall over as I tugged while hopping around the living room on one foot. "Promise to call me when you get home? Better still, text me and then swing by. I will still be awake waiting for Ron to call when he parks for the night."

"I promise. I will let you know what happens," I confessed. It may not be right away, but she would get a full report. After looking around the room one last time to make sure I didn't forget anything, I headed towards the door with Debbie trailing.

"I can't wait to hear what happens," she said before handing me a quick hug. "I expect every juicy detail!"

"We shall see about that," I half promised, returning her hug. Pulling away, I turned tail and ran out the door before she could speak another word. Looking up as I pulled out of the driveway, I noticed she was still standing in the doorway. Tossing a quick wave in her direction, I turned away and headed down the street.

I had just made it down the street when my cell phone started beeping. At the next red light, I pulled over and glanced at the message. It was from Debbie.

"Loosen up and have fun! You totally deserve it! Stephan seems like a total sweetheart. Love you!"

Instead of answering, I tossed my cell phone back into my purse.

Begging for information was unnecessary. As my best friend, Debbie already knew she'd be the first to know anything. She just wanted to ensure I knew cancelling my date was not an option. With her expecting a full report, I knew better than to cry off. Stephan may be easy to get rid of, Debbie not so much. She wouldn't let me live it down, nor forgive me. I was totally committed.

On the other hand, maybe I should be committed.

CHAPTER SIX

The sun had already set by the time I finished work for the day. Despite being tired, I headed towards our designated meeting spot. I'd made a promise and I planned on keeping it. As I pulled into the darkened parking lot, I realized I forgot to ask Stephan what type of vehicle he was driving. Nor had I offered up mine. Thank goodness, I knew what he looked like or I would actually have been screwed.

There were only three other vehicles in the car park when I arrived. Two were parked near the employee entrance while a third, a massive black one-ton Duelly sat closer to the doorway. I pulled into the vacant spot next to it and turned off the ignition, leaned my head back against the headrest and closed my eyes. Breathing in deep breathes I struggled to calm my nerves. Driving into the city, I was pretty excited. Now that I had arrived, I was terrified. A million possibilities raced through my mind. What if he turned out to be a crazy person pretending to be a gentleman? What if he was a rapist, hiding on the Internet trying to find an easy victim? What if I was his next victim? Why had I agreed to this? Every worst-case scenario played out in my head.

A light tapping on the driver's side window had my head whipping up in fright. Startled, my heart pounded until I recognized the face peering in through the tinted glass. Stephan! I sighed with relief and rolled down my window.

"Are you getting out or are you going to hide in here all night?" He laughed.

"I was getting a quick nap." I improvised. The last thing I needed him to know was how nervous I really was. My heart rate was beginning to come back to normal.

"You were just trying to decide if you should leave or not," he said, before stepping aside and pulling the door open for me. I grabbed my keys from the ignition, rolled up my window and climbed out.

"How did you know?" I laughed. Locking the door behind me, and slamming it shut.

"Just a wild guess; besides, it's happened to me before," he admitted as we reached the coffee shop door.

I stepped aside as he pulled it open. Instead of barging in first, he patiently waited for me before following. I couldn't help think what a sweet gesture that was. Men did not seem to open doors anymore, so it was a very pleasant change. Once inside we soon realized looks were deceiving. While the parking lot appeared nearly abandoned there was a large group monopolizing one side of the late night coffee shop. I was immediately relieved and started laughing to myself. With others in the place, I felt less threatened. Even if Stephan turned out to be a creep, he wouldn't dare misbehave in a public place.

"What can I get you?" His wallet was already out.

"Cafe Mocha would be perfect," I replied.

"You look pretty perfect," he said.

I blushed at the compliment. Prior to our meeting, I dashed home after work and changed out of my business suit into a pair of jeans and a red halter-top. I guess the effort paid off. It had been a while since someone had complimented me and instantly warmth spread through me.

While we waited for the barista to fill our order, I surveyed the busy coffee shop. There was a vacant table in a quiet corner. With coffees in hand, we headed over and got our seats.

"So how was your day?" I asked.

"It was hectic, and yours?" He replied.

"It was pretty good, but it was nice knowing that I would receive a break later," I volunteered.

"Oh, so you were thinking about me all day?" He laughed at my startled expression. That was not what I intended, but hey, I would play along.

"Yeah, I was wondering what kind of man would agree to meet a woman at a cafe in the middle of the night," I jokingly confessed. "Or at least question his intentions."

"It's only 9 o'clock; far from being the middle of the night," he teased back. "Is it so hard to admit that you were excited about meeting me?"

As a matter of fact, it was! But I was not going to admit it. Instead, I tried to change the subject.

"So, tell me what do you do?" I asked before taking a sip of my coffee. Stephan was so comfortable to be around. The conversation is light and effortless.

"I own my own construction business. We are currently constructing a hotel downtown." Stephan leaned forward and rested his elbows on the table. The mug looked delicate within his burly callused hands. "Pardon my rudeness, but why is such an intriguing woman like you still single?"

"Excuse me?" His question caught me off guard. Men normally beat around the bush when they flirted. Stephan obviously went straight to the point. It was refreshing, yet unexpected. I wasn't sure what to answer truthfully without him jumping to the wrong conclusions. Did I want to admit to swearing off men and relationships? I didn't want him thinking I was still bitter over a long past breakup. After all, I rarely even thought of my previous marriage anymore.

"Why are you still single?" Stephan repeated. "You are obviously smart, attractive and funny as hell, so why don't you have a boyfriend?"

"I don't have time." I replied with partial truthfulness. The truth was I couldn't be bothered. Yes, I was lonely sometimes, but not enough to settle for just anyone. While I've met many available men along my travels, the fact remained that I did not want to be tied down. If I had to choose between a relationship and never achieving my goals; or being single with the ability to satisfy all my dreams, I picked remaining single. The romantic in me believed that when the right man came along, I would be able to make the right choice and it wouldn't be a sacrifice. I had yet to meet that type of man.

"You can make time, if you really wanted to," he suggested. I nodded in agreement.

"So why did you move to Canada?" Not ready to delve too deep into my failed relationships, I tried to change the subject. "What did you do in England?"

"I had a small tavern in Cambridge for about a decade. I always wanted to immigrate to Canada. Yea, I know what you're thinking - tavern owner to construction worker. That's a big career change.," Stephan explained. "I was working as a general contractor when my dad died not long after my thirtieth birthday. He left me the pub. Typical party animal, I thought it would be great, hosting parties all the time; anything was better than slinging a hammer for the rest of my life. The lifestyle turned out very different. When I'd raised enough money, I sold the place, moved here and started my own construction company. Logistically it made more sense to start my own company than to find a job. I am actually supposed to be sworn in as a Canadian in a few weeks!"

"That is pretty cool! Did you have to attend extra classes?" I was really curious. Stephan was the first person I'd ever met who'd actually immigrated to Canada and was trying to become a citizen. Who knows, maybe an expose on immigration was in my future, I couldn't help thinking.

"Yes, I had to attend a few. One of them was an English class, which I obviously did not need," he chortled. "It wasn't that hard. We learned a great deal about Canadian history, but for me it was almost a formality."

"Knowing the language makes it easy," I agreed with a grin.

"Sure does. I'm glad that I did the courses over the winter. Work is getting hectic, so I don't have time for classes now. Now I just have to wait for the swearing in ceremony and I am legally a Canuck," he chortled.

"Why did you come to Canada?" I couldn't imagine relocating to a new country unless I had a valid reason. "Do you have family here?"

"Things are really expensive in England so it was time to move. The money I made selling the tavern tripled when I set foot on Canadian soil. You can't scoff at returns like that. No, I don't have family here but I have been making friends. My parents passed away years ago and I am an only child. I was married once and we have a son. He lives with my ex in London, but he is planning to move here after graduation. I've already started the paperwork," he paused. At the mention of his son, a hint of sadness crossed his eyes.

"There are more opportunities here so it was easy for me to leave. There was nothing tying me down. Moreover, I was ready for a new adventure. One gets tired of listening to every drunk who wanders in blaming the world for their troubles. All they have to do is look at themselves and half of the problem would be solved. I have no patience for ignorant people anymore," Stephan continued. "Be right back, I need a refill. How is your coffee, or should I say Cafe Mocha?"

"I still have a half cup, so I am fine. Thank you," I replied. My eyes watched as he sauntered back to the counter and placed the order. I surveyed how the formfitting boot cut Wranglers cradled his muscular behind. Bulging biceps strained his fitted checkered shirt. He was a prime specimen. Despite his forty-five years, there was not an ounce of flab on his torso. I was very impressed.

"Like what you see?" Stephan chortled when he came back to the table. Oblivious that I was staring, I turned away guiltily. My face was burning with embarrassment.

"I am sorry," I started to stutter, but his chuckle stopped me.

"Don't you dare apologize for enjoying the view. You should never apologize for enjoying life's little pleasures."

"Are you one of life's little pleasures?" I sniggered awkwardly. *Really? Did I really just ask him if he was pleasurable? Well, so much for subtlety.*

"I can be, but let's be clear on one thing; I am far from little!" he guffawed outright at this remark. I really should have known better. Every man I knew was sensitive when the term 'little' came up.

"Typical male," I snorted with amusement.

"What's that supposed to mean? You insult my manhood and I am supposed to just sit here and take it." Stephan teased. His eyes twinkled with amusement. "I understand how it is."

"That was not what I meant and you know it," I hastily interjected. This made him laugh even harder.

"Are you done mocking me?" I teased while pretending to be occupied with the task of working with the frothy whipped cream at the bottom of my cup.

"I am far from mocking you. I just think you are adorable and I would love to get inside your head. I find you fascinating and adorable. My manhood or lack thereof can be discussed at a later date," he suggested with a near future in mind.

"Assuming that we go on another date," I interjected, half joking. While I was having a wonderful time hanging out with Stephan, I did not want him to assume we were an item. That's happened before and didn't turn out well. I had agreed to meet for coffee and the next thing I knew, my phone was ringing at all hours of the day or night. I'd even been forced to change my phone number in the past due to persistent wannabe suitors.

"Why wouldn't we?" He stopped laughing. "Aren't you having a good time? I know I am. You are an engaging and intriguing conversationalist. You are also sexy as hell."

"That is beside the point," I whispered, leaning forward and resting my elbows on the table. When I agreed to meet for coffee, I assumed that was all it would be. However, based on the ease of conversation, I sensed he would ask for another. I tried hard not to panic. I tried to refocus, to think of this date as research, but that did not work.

"So when are you going to tell me about you? Other than the fact that you write, enjoy walks on the beach and picnics, and extremely sexy. I know very little about you." Stephan tried asking, definitely trying to change the subject. "What do you write about?"

"Life; things I like to do, places I've been to or want to go; dreams, fantasies, whatever I fancy at the moment," I answered truthfully. I had no issue discussing the magazine, and I could write whatever I wanted. The same went for my books, but I was not going to admit that I wrote erotica for a living. "Sometimes I write just to keep sane."

"Oh? Why is that?" He leaned forward with genuine interest.

"Because sometimes my thoughts scare me; if I put out in the world how depraved my mind gets sometimes, I am sure I would have no friends." I giggled. "Sometimes, I just like to rant."

"What do you rant about?" Stephan asked as he downed his second cup of coffee.

"How are you going to sleep with all that caffeine in your system," I teasingly asked when he set down the empty mug.

"This is nothing; I still have four cups to go before I reach my daily dose." With that remark, he pushed away from the table and returned for another refill. "Are you still okay over there?"

"Yep, I am good," glancing down at my cup, I noticed it was nearly done, but I knew I wouldn't sleep if I had another. "I have to go soon anyway."

"Why are you rushing off?" He asked once he'd settled back down. Glancing at my watch, we'd managed to kill off over two hours. Time flies when you are having fun and verbally sparring.

"I don't call going home after a two hour coffee break rushing off," I volunteered.

"Oh, so I am just a coffee break," he mocked before emitting an exaggerated sigh of disappointment. "I should have known. Use me for my coffee and then abandon me to my own devices."

He looked forlorn, filled with disappointment. But, I couldn't help but laugh. He was being downright ridiculous and his theatrics were absolutely hysterical.

"Then she laughs at me; I am crushed," he pouted. Clutching his heart, Stephan pantomimed getting stabbed in the chest. The twinkle in his eyes and a hint of a smile tugging the corner of his mouth told me otherwise. I giggled. "Are you trying to break my heart?"

"Do you have a heart?" I teased. "Stop being such a baby."

"Now she calls me a baby! Well, so much for asking for a second date." Pushing his empty cup aside, and get ready to leave.

"This was a date? I thought it was just coffee." I responded quickly.

"It was a coffee date. I just didn't use the word date, because I heard it scares you." Even with his coffee mug mere centimetres' from his face, I could still make out the smirk tugging at his lips.

"You heard dates scare me?" Obviously Debbie failed to mention that part of the conversation. I would have to ask her about it later.

"No, I heard that you love dates, but the word 'date' scares you," he corrected himself.

I couldn't argue; that much was true. I had no trouble meeting people one-on-one, but add the word date and I turned into a bumbling mess. It opened the door too many expectations and those expectations usually left me frozen with doubt and terror. My expression must have given me away, he reached across the table and took my hand. "It's all right, I am just teasing. Nonetheless, I would like to see you again." He sounded so bright that it was difficult to say no.

"What do you have in mind?" I inquired.

"I don't have my schedule here, but can we get together on Friday?" he advised.

"That shouldn't be a problem," I confessed. After the past few hours seemed to fly by, I couldn't find a reason to argue. We had a great conversation, he was handsome, smart and obviously a gentleman. There was no reason that I could tell, why I should run away. Besides, Debbie did tell me to have fun and Stephan was definitely entertaining!

"Of course it won't be a problem; but do you want to see me again?" he implored. He's watching me expectantly, expressive eyebrows raised. "I definitely want to get to know you better."

"Can I get back to you?" I said, needing to check my schedule before I fully committed.

"I guess that's better than you coming out saying 'no' right off the top," he sighed. I was really surprised. He actually looked and sounded disappointed; or maybe it was just me. He scooted his chair away from the table. "Are you ready to go?"

"Yeah, we better leave before we get kicked out, " I agreed after glancing at my watch. It was already long past midnight. Getting kicked out was highly unlikely since the coffee shop stayed open all night, but I was not going to argue. The time had gone by so fast.

Putting our empty cups back on the counter, we left the restaurant in unison. His hand automatically went to my waist as he escorted me to our vehicle's. I did not mind. It's been a while since I'd felt that simple comfort. He waited patiently while I unlocked the driver-side door before moving closer.

"I had a great time tonight," his voice was hoarse. I glanced up and he was watching me under the streetlight.

"I did too," I admitted. He took a step closer and involuntarily I stepped back. My retreat was halted by the driver's side of my car. The way he was staring at my mouth, I knew he was going to kiss me. I tried not to flinch when his hand reached out to brush my hair away from my face. His fingers lightly traced my cheek. Supposing he had changed his mind, or I'd misread his signals I waited for him to retreat; but he didn't. Instead, he pulled me closer.

My eyes closed instinctively as our lips connected. Tentatively at first, his warm mouth caressed mine. The sensual passion of his lips made me shiver in the cool night breeze. He pulled me closer, wrapping his arms around my shoulders. Instead of drawing back, I let him deepen the kiss. I melted within his embrace while his mouth pillaged mine. Tasting, teasing our tongues danced. Each caress of his probing tongue fuelled my passion. Finally, goose bumps erupted, spreading over my exposed flesh. Every inch of me tingled. Breathless, I staggered for a second when he finally pulled away.

"Are we still on for Friday?" He watched me intently until I answered. My brain has ceased to function properly. Befuddled, I tried to shake it off. The last thing I needed was for him to clue into how he affected me. Without thought I responded with a breathy "yes".

"I knew you would eventually see things my way," he grinned triumphantly. He stepped aside and opened my car door. His teasing snapped me back to reality. I realized too late that I'd agreed to a date. Thinking he'd change his mind, I'd deliberately refrained from giving him a definitive answer when he'd asked earlier.

"You tricked me!" I retorted, feigning to be incensed.

"Yep, and it worked!" He laughed as I climbed into my car. "See you on Friday; I will message you with further details."

Before I could think of a fitting retort, he closed the door and waved. Then turning, he headed to the truck parked next to mine. I should have known the pretentious beast was his. Hopefully the oversized gas-guzzler was not overcompensation for smaller things.

Smarten up; stop thinking about this man naked, I chided myself. Shaking my head in self disgust, I backed out of the parking space and headed towards home. My cell phone was beeping by the time I pulled into the driveway. I shifted into park before pulling the phone out of my purse to read the blinking message.

"Thank you for agreeing to meet with me. You are an amazing kisser; your mouth tasted like heaven! I can't wait to see what Friday brings. Sweet dreams. Stephan."

Smiling in fond remembrance, my fingers subconsciously traced my kiss swollen lips. Yep, you're a great kisser too, I mused, keeping that opinion to myself. Instead of responding to his message, I tucked the phone back into my purse. Thank goodness Friday was still three days away. Maybe by then I would stop acting like a love struck teenager.

"So, how did it go?" Debbie demanded before stuffing another donut hole into her mouth. I had barely woken up the next morning when she came barging into my house and bedroom. Grumbling with annoyance, I rolled onto my back and acknowledged the excited ginger. I should never have given her a key to my house, I mentally cursed.

"It went well," I lamely offered before pulling the blanket up to my nose to cover my secretive smirk. That didn't stop her. She bounced onto my bed like a teenager and plopped down beside me.

"Come on, you know better, what happened?" she insisted. Gawd, she really was like a teenager when it came to romance. By her reaction, you'd think I was a sixteen year old never been kissed virgin out on my first date.

"Do you really have to be so irritating? I just woke up!" I exclaimed. I pulled a pillow over my head and tried to ignore her. It didn't work.

"It's already almost noon, you can wake up any time now. Besides, I brought you fresh coffee," Debbie handed me a tall takeout cup from our favourite coffee place. I pulled myself upright and popped open the lid while she propped a few pillows behind my back. "Now dish!" She ordered once I'd calmed down.

"There is nothing to tell," I answered, taking a big swig of the lukewarm Java, and then saluted her with the paper cup. The caffeine hit the spot quickly and I was grateful for the pick-me-up. "Thanks for the coffee."

"Nice try at trying to change the subject. Did he kiss you yet? Are you seeing him again?" Her questions came out in rapid fire like bullets from a machine gun. I really should have known better. Debbie never accepted defeat in her quest for details.

"Yes, he kissed me," I reluctantly admitted. Debbie's excited squeal sent Belle's head whipping up from where she was curled up at the foot of my bed. I reached down and rubbed the poor dog's ears. She offered an indignant grunt, stretched and then sank back down.

"How was it?" Debbie pressed, leaning over expectantly.

"He's English and he's adorable," I admitted. "We have a date on Friday. By the way, why did you tell him dates scare me?"

"Because it's the truth; I wanted to warn him that you might find a reason to bail." Debbie had the decency to look guilty for all of two seconds.

"Well, I didn't bail." I retorted. It was one thing to tease me about ditching a date, but I was insulted she believed that I actually would be rude and stand someone up. Agreeing to meet someone for coffee was equivalent to making a promise in my eyes; and a promise was a promise.

"Stop being so sensitive, you know I am teasing. You would do the exact same thing to me, if our roles were reversed," she volunteered, before embracing me. She knew better than to apologize. Besides, it was not her fault that I was being thin-skinned. "Now get your ass out of bed; we have shopping to do."

I groaned inwardly. I hated clothes shopping. I was probably the only woman in the world who despised shopping with a passion. I had neither patience nor interest in this mundane task.

"Come on you grumpy Gus; you need to get something sexy for your date." She put extra emphases on the word *date*. Incensed, I grabbed a pillow and smacked her upside the head.

"What the hell!" she sputtered before toppling over. Grabbing the other pillow, she returned my blow, nearly knocking me off the bed. Belle got up, shot us a look of disgust, then bolted out of firing range. She sat on the floor looking confused for a few minutes before heading to safer ground in the living room.

"All joking aside, I am really proud of you. I know it was not easy for you to put yourself out there like that, but you did. You have come a long way and now, you may have found someone wonderful to take along for the ride," Debbie offered once we had run out of steam. "Besides, you could do a lot worse. From what I hear, Stephan is a great catch."

"I guess I will have to wait and see," I replied, making sure I sounded non-committal. I refused to count my chickens before they hatched. I also knew better than to argue with her.

CHAPTER SEVEN

It was a busy week, and Friday came around much faster than expected. The majority of the week was spent researching my next article. Debbie was right; online dating was a great story. It was evidently more common than I first imagined. Once I started talking to people it became clear that in today's busy world, more people were turning to online dating sites than ever before. The more I talked about it, the more I discovered that other people I knew in real life had either found their match online, or were currently online and looking. Everyone had a tale to tell; some were good and others not.

For our second date, Stephan and I agreed to meet at the same coffee shop before heading to a house party. One of the regular Fish Pond members was hosting an annual barbecue complete with live music and fireworks. Normally I avoided events like this because of the transportation involved. I refused to drive after drinking and I was never comfortable enough to stay the night. Ultimately, it was easier to fabricate an excuse to be absent, than to appear unexciting by not drinking. More than willing to end my social drought, I was eagerly looking forward to this evening making new friends.

When I arrived at the appointed destination, Stephan was already parked and waiting. Pulling into a parking space next to his truck, I grabbed my bag, locked the car and jumped into his truck.

"You look very lovely tonight," Stephan whistled softly in appreciation after I climbed into the cab. That night, I chose to wear a pair of faded jeans and a white T-shirt. A worn jean jacket and black mid-calf high boots finished my look.

"Thanks, I wanted to be comfortable. It's an outdoor party and it may get chilly later, so I came prepared," I replied. Giving him the once over, he was dressed in jeans and a black fitted T-shirt. It was hard not to notice how it clung to his chiselled chest. He also smelt delicious, but I kept that to myself. "You look good too."

As we walked from our parking spot, I could hear the pounding of rock-and-roll streaming down the street. From the street the venue looked festive and inviting. Between strategically placed bamboo torches and multi-coloured patio lanterns strung along the fence, the front and back yards were softly ablaze with a romantic glow.

The party was in full swing by the time we arrived. A mix of boisterous laughter and chatter from the backyard funneled down the driveway. A handful of revellers sat in a lawn chair semicircle on the front lawn, surrounding a portable fire pit while the latter group appeared to be sequestered in the back yard. We followed the sound of laughter. In the backyard a pool table was put together on the rear deck and a game of doubles had been already underway. More guests were gathered around the backyard fire pit singing exuberantly out of tune. They were just finishing an enthusiastic version of Credence Clearwater Revival's Proud Mary when we wanted around the corner.

"EMMA!" I turned in time to see Debbie flying in my direction. "I didn't know you were coming to this party for your date!"

"It was Stephan's idea," I replied excitedly, returning her enthusiastic embrace. Any apprehension I harboured about the night was gone as soon as I spotted her. It didn't matter now what happened with Stephan. Having my best friend close by meant I was going to have a great time.

"Wow Stephan, two gatherings in two weeks! You've been a Fish Pond member for how long?" Debbie teased, before giving him a warm hug. Turning her attention back to me, she grabbed my hand and pulled me away. "Glad to see you buddy! Let me introduce you to some people."

I tossed a helpless look in Stephan's direction and shrugged. I felt guilty ditching him upon our arrival. However, there was a bunch of people at the party I wanted to meet and talk to. Maybe some would want to participate in my story. It would have been rude of me to refuse.

"Go, have fun!" He chuckled when I hesitated, then he waved me off. "I see some people I know. I will be fine."

Before I could respond, Debbie dragged me off. Soon she began introducing me to various people by their chat names. Most of the handles sounded familiar. I had either followed their comments on the group's forums, or checked their profiles. I was thankful for that tidbit of recognition because if I'd relied on their photographs alone, I would have made a fool of myself. As I made the connection between names and the real people, it became obvious dishonesty was common, at least when it came to photographs. A few of the women had posted pictures of themselves either ten years old or before gaining significant weight. This really bothered me. I didn't understand the point of the deception. What's the point of saying you are 35 years old and 105 pounds when you'd eventually met up and the person would see that you were neither. Yet it was obvious that is exactly what some people did. It made me question the rest of information in their profile. It also explained why people were taken aback when they met me face-to-face. My photograph was fairly current; I was exactly how I presented myself.

Over the next hour or so Debbie lead me from group to group, making sure that everyone knew who I was, that I was new and that we were friends. I came highly recommended, she'd laughing tell everyone. At one point someone handed me an ice-cold beer, which I gratefully accepted. I was getting parched.

As we made our rounds, I skimmed the various groups looking for my date. I finally found Stephan standing by the backyard campfire chatting with a group of women. *Great, he's making friends.* He looked up as I was watching. He smiled and waved. I lifted my hand up in response before continuing to follow Debbie like a sheep. While I enjoyed meeting people, it was also overwhelming. Too many names, too many faces, too many first impressions to mentally store away.

Content that she'd finally introduced me to everyone who mattered, Debbie wandered off looking for another drink. Left to my devices, I was instantly thankful for the peace and tranquility. I needed a moment to catch my bearings and relax. Taking advantage of her distraction, I leaned on the fence, and watched the various groups interact. Everyone seemed to know each other very well and I was briefly jealous of their relationships. Other than Debbie, I did not have a group of friends I could just hang out with. I hated to admit it, but she may be right, joining the online dating community may be a good thing for me. At least at present, I wouldn't feel like such a hermit.

"We meet again," a familiar voice intruded, rudely interrupting my thoughts. I jumped in surprise before acknowledging the source. Dominic stood leaning against the corner of the gazebo a few feet away, watching me intently. He was wearing skin tight jeans and a leather jacket despite the humid July night. "Still, as hot as ever I might add."

"Thanks Dom, how are you?" I stifled any compliments that roared into my head. I would be lying if I didn't find him extremely sexy. I was notoriously attracted to the bad boy look. But that usually meant a bad boy was attached, and those I preferred to avoid.

"I was about to leave when you arrived," he stated with a smirk, before taking a swig of the beer clutched in his grasp. "I've since changed my mind. Suddenly the night promises to get better."

"How do you figure that?" I asked, taking the bait. His casual sexiness was hard to ignore even though it was somewhat annoying.

"You are here!" He grinned cockily before lifting his bottle and tossed a salute in my direction. "Until you walked in, this night sucked."

"I came with someone," I quickly pointed out, not wanting him to think I was alone and available. To prove my point, I searched the crowd for Stephan. I found him quickly. He was still carrying on with the women by the fire, seemingly oblivious to my activities or my companion. From my vantage, he was showing off a couple of his tattoos; some of which I did not know he possessed. The women were eating it up and he was obviously enjoying the attention.

"I saw that! You're too good for him," he said before downing the rest of his bottle with one swallow. "I'm going to get another beer, want one?"

"Sure. Thank you," I said. When he turned back, I retrieved the bottle from his outstretched hand. His blasé comment annoyed me. Who was he to think he could offer me an opinion on the matter. "Why do you think he's too good for me?"

"Guys know these things. He's pretending to be interested, but he's using you," he repeated, shrugging nonchalantly. I bristled with indignation.

"For what though? I have nothing to offer," I was really confused. As far as I was concerned, I had nothing worth using. "How could you suggest that?"

"Trust me, I know; he is not who he says he is," Dominic snapped with slight annoyance. "Besides, how dare you say you have nothing to offer? You are smart, fun, graceful and beautiful. You have a twinkle in your eyes that is impossible to avoid. I'd be careful with him."

I was shocked, first by the warning, then by the compliment. *He thought I was smart and beautiful?* Even Stephan had failed to acknowledge me in that manner. It was still early in the romance though, we only had one date. Wait, Dominic and I had just met too, and here he was, trying to convince me that I was worth being used by somebody. Disconcerted, I swallowed the remaining half bottle of beer in two gulps.

"Whoa! You must really be thirsty! Want another one?" He was already taking out another bottle from the cooler next to him. I must have guzzled the first one too fast; I could already feel a slight buzz as the alcohol flowed through my body. Undaunted, I cracked open the second bottle and took a deep swallow.

"Better?" He'd moved closer and was now standing right beside me. To anyone watching from a distance, they might consider our pose intimate. The quickly guzzled beer was definitely giving me a buzz. Afraid I would wobble if I stepped away from the fence, I refused to move away. Dominic took it as acquiescence.

"You know, you are the most beautiful woman here tonight; you were the other night too," he confided. I blushed uncomfortably, in sudden need of rescue. Glancing back towards the fire, Stephan was still engaged, oblivious to my company. So much for getting his attention and help.

"Emma!" Hearing my name, I jumped. Looking up, I spotted Debbie heading quickly in my direction; her fierce look never leaving Dominic's face. I smiled in relief.

"Hey Debbie, how's it going?" He asked before giving her a hug. Her expression softened. She may be annoyed with him for spending time with me, but she obviously harboured a fondness towards the big guy.

"I am great Dom; you better be behaving. We've had this talk before, remember? Emma's off limits to you!" she admonished. He fidgeted guiltily under her disapproving glare.

"I know better than to disobey a direct order from you, Miss Debbie. Nevertheless, she was standing here all alone and what kind of man would I be to leave a beautiful woman leaning against a fence all by her lonesome." His engaging explanation charmed a grin out of Debbie. Her stance softened slightly.

"Well, in that case, how very sweet of you." Debbie hugged him back. "Where's the bike?"

"Parked on the street," Dominic pointed into the darkness with his beer. "Don't worry, I won't drink and drive. My Harley is hard enough to handle sober."

"You're a smart man. Now, if you don't mind, the fireworks are starting in a few minutes and I want to make sure Emma gets a good seat," Debbie reached out to take my arm.

"That's okay. I was about to leave soon anyway." He looked disappointed that I was being hauled away. "Remember what I said Emma."

Debbie looked at me with questions in her eyes. I waved her away. *I'll explain later,* I mouthed. She just nodded.

"I will take that into consideration. Thank you for the warning," I muttered in Dom's direction. With that, I allowed Debbie to lead me away.

"Wait – EM," Hearing Dominic call my name, I stopped and turned towards him.

"If you're planning on entering the wet T-shirt contest I may consider sticking around a while longer," he grinned, pointing towards the front lawn. Sure enough, our host was setting up the garden hose and prizes. His dimples deepened as he grinned mischievously. "It's a standing tradition at these parties. Our host is an ex biker so when we get together, there is always a wet-t contest. He insists and since it's his birthday, he gets what he wants."

"Thanks, but no thanks. I think I am a little too old for that," I retorted before turning on my heel to join Debbie. She had already staked out the perfect spot to watch the fireworks and was waving me over.

When the first Cherry Bomb went off a few minutes later, everyone ran to the front yard to watch the colourful display. Our host had spared no expense. As I stood leaning casually against the picnic table enjoying the show, I felt a hand slip around my waist. Stephan had returned to my side.

"Are you having a good time?" he asked, giving me a warm squeeze. I moved closer until my back was pressed against his chest. His arms came up, forcing me closer.

"Yes, I am, and you?" I asked. I already knew the answer based on the earlier display by the fire.

"As a matter of fact, I am. It's been a great night. Are you almost ready to call it a night?" He asked.

"We can go after the fireworks if you want," I suggested.

"Sounds like a plan; we can continue this party back at my place," he winked suggestively.

"Oh? What do you have in mind?" Feeling playful, I started giggling. *Must be the beer*, I thought.

"How about going back to my apartment and we can see what I have in mind," he grinned. "You can come for another beer before you head home, or better still, you don't have to go home."

"Yeah, your couch may prove to be handy tonight. I've been drinking so it might be the smartest idea," I admitted. While I hated to sleep one someone else's couch, other than Debbie's, I was not going to take a chance and drive. One night of stubbornness was not worth a lifetime of regret.

The fireworks show came to an end and people started drifting back to their previous activities. Debbie wandered over to where I was still standing, wrapped in Stephan's arms.

"What's the plan?" Debbie's words were slightly slurred. It would be a while before she would want to leave the gathering. This would make our escape easier.

"I think we are going to head back to Stephan's place," I deliberately ignored Debbie's blink of surprise.

"Are you sure?" The look of concern in her eyes was legit. She wasn't going to let me leave with Stephan until she was positive it was what I wanted. It was her way of playing overprotective sister. I appreciated her concern. It was unusual for me to leave with a near-stranger. She visibly relaxed when I winked.

"I will be okay. We are going back to his place for another drink. And yes, I promise I won't get behind the wheel so save the lecture," I informed Debbie before she could protest.

"Well, if you're ok then I am okay; have fun and play safe." Debbie quietly slurred into my ear as we hugged. "Don't forget to call me tomorrow. I expect all the juicy details."

"I will," I promised, hugging her back. "Have fun too, and don't do anything I wouldn't do."

"You know I will do everything that you wouldn't do; one of us has to enjoy life and it might as well be me," she laughed before pulling me into another drunken embrace. "You're going to confess everything to me tomorrow," she whispered before pulling away.

"We shall see," was my non-committed response. We both knew better than that. Whoever was conscious first would be calling the other for a full report come morning. The real question was who would be the first to call.

"You ready?" Stephan's hand was back on my waistline.

"Yep, let's get out of here," I said with nonchalance.

As we walked back to the truck, the unmistakable growl of a revving Harley engine came up from behind. We paid no attention. Stephan was unlocking the truck door as the motorcycle finally pulled up alongside us.

"Have a good night, sexy," came Dominic's helmet muffled voice. Tossing a quick nod in Stephan's direction, he roared off before I could react.

"What was that about?" Stephan asked once we'd climbed into the truck cab and snapped on our seat belts.

"Nothing," I lied. I was grateful Stephan didn't question me further. Instead, he shifted the truck into gear and headed back to the apartment. During the fifteen minute ride to our destination, I reflected on Dominic's words. His persistence alarmed me. What did he know that I didn't?

Or maybe, he was just playing games with me.

CHAPTER EIGHT

Twenty minutes later, Stephan guided the truck expertly into a parking spot along a quiet residential street. On one side, cookie cutter bungalows lined the street while in sharp contrast, several three-story apartments building filled the other. Unsure of which direction we were heading, I waited until he got out of the truck.

"Nice neighbourhood," I offered when the passenger door popped open. I took his extended hand, and let him help me descend. Without running boards, even with my height I would need a stepladder to get and out of this beast. I chuckled at the visual that popped into my head.

"Are you coming in?" He asked hopefully.

"Well, obviously I can't drive home, my car is still at the coffee shop and I assumed we're at your house?" My words sounded slightly slurred and I giggled ridiculously.

"Pretty much, I figured we could throw back a few more drinks and talk. It is also less crowded in my apartment," he continued. I caught him watching me intently. "Besides, I don't think it would be a good idea for you to be driving right now."

"Lead away," I agreed and started navigating my way in the general direction of the doorway. Two steps later, I stumbled as my heel snagged a crevice on the street. I would have fallen to the asphalt if Stephan hadn't reached out and caught me.

"Follow me!" Stephan took my hand and led me towards the entrance. After punching in his security code, we climbed three flights of stairs and headed down a darkened hallway. There was no elevator in the building.

"Someone forget to pay the power bill?" I joked, attempting to hide the fact I was panting from the climb. Leaning against the wall, I watched him fumble with the keys in the semi-darkness. The clink of the deadbolt signalled that he'd finally found the right one key.

"Welcome to my house," he said, swinging open the door with a flourish before moving away, inviting me to enter first. I walked into a small vestibule and kicked off my shoes while he closed the door behind me.

"Do you want a drink?" he asked while hanging up his jacket in the wardrobe beside the doorway. I weighed my choices. I could have another drink and be forced to spend the night, or refuse so that I could drive home in a few hours. I didn't answer him right away. Instead, I followed him into the kitchen and looked around. He got busy taking out a pair of clean glasses out of the dishwasher.

"Sure, whatever you have would be great." I finally answered. It wasn't often that I found myself in someone else's home in the middle of the night. You only live once, I scolded myself. I busied myself by browsing through his bookcase while he rummaged for fresh ice in the freezer. Stephan obviously loved to read. The walnut shelving lining the room was bursting with a vast collection of novels, including books by Stephan King and Anne Rice. There were also a number of conspiracy theory books.

"I see you found my collection?" Stephan said, coming up from behind me. I nodded, taking the drink he offered. "Here you go; I hope you don't mind jack and coke."

"No, that's fine. Thank you." I took a sip and savoured the warmth of the drink as it slid down my throat and hit my stomach. Whiskey was not my preference, but if that was all he had, it would be rude to decline. "Just what the doctor ordered," I replied.

"Do you mind if I check my email messages? There was a glitch on the job site today and I promised the guys to double check something when I got in. I am not sure how long it will take. Relax and make yourself at home," Stephan invited. Without waiting for a reply, he went to the computer desk and went to work.

I took the opportunity to look around. The apartment was a basic single-bedroom bachelor suite. It consisted of a small bedroom, bathroom, kitchen, dining room and sitting room. I was surprised at how tidy it was; an unusual trait to find in a single man. Glancing at the computer, I could see Stephan deeply engrossed in email. I went into the bathroom to freshen up. Even the bathroom was cleaner than I expected. No facial hair stuck to the sink, toothpaste on the mirror or stale amber ring in the toilet. I was duly impressed.

When I exited the bathroom fifteen minutes later, Stephan was still plugging away on the computer. He was typing frantically and didn't look up when I returned. Not wanting to interrupt, I picked up my drink, headed over to the couch and plopped down. A stray blanket lay strewn on the couch, so I pulled it over my legs. Spotting the remote, I switched the TV on. It went straight to a news station.

"Mind if I change the channel?" I asked.

"Go ahead, I should just be a few more minutes," he replied without looking up.

I spent the next few minutes surfing stations before finally settling on a movie already in progress. Wiggling into a comfortable position, I pulled the blanket up to my chin and curled up. Soon I found myself nodding off. I'd barely closed my eyes when I felt the couch shift. Alarmed, my eyes popped open. Stephan had joined me, sitting on the opposite end of the couch. He glanced over when I stirred.

"Have a good nap?" he chortled. I brushed my hair out of my eyes and tried to get my bearings.

"How long was I out?" I pulled myself upright, searching the room for a clock.

"Not long. About an hour," he responded. Lifting up my legs, he moved closer then laid them gently across his knees. "You know, you can always lie down in the adjacent room."

"In your bed?" I sounded appalled. Half asleep, my questions made me sound like an idiot.

"Don't worry! I will keep my hands to myself," he promised, chuckling at my obvious confusion. I found that hard to believe, considering his hands were lightly rubbing my legs under the blanket.

"I've heard that before," I retorted. Meanwhile, I was fully aware of his hands on my legs, not minding how I felt with the heat of his hands.

"Seriously, I promise to stay on my side of the bed. You won't sleep comfortably on this couch." he insisted. Stephan did have a point, but I still hesitated. "Tell you what, you take the bed and I'll stay here. Just give me a minute to get the room ready."

He returned a few minutes later.

"All right, you can crawl in now," he said, offering me his hand. I took it and stood, allowing him to lead me down the short hallway. The comforter was neatly turned back and the sheets appeared newly changed. He's obviously turned down the bed before joining me on the couch. "There you go, all fresh, just for you."

"Thank you Stephan, you are very sweet. This should be just fine," I replied.

"Do you need anything else? I can still get you a bottle of water, you know, for morning," he volunteered. His words trailed off, lost while he watched me fumble with the buckle of my jeans. Ignoring him, I shrugged them off and abandoned them on the floor. He blinked, taken aback as I hastily stripped, oblivious to his presence. "You sure you don't need help?"

"Thanks, but I should be okay," I answered, before crawling onto the bed and pulled the comforter up to my nose. The sheets felt cool and crisp against my bare legs. I was dying to throw off the rest of my clothes. At home, sleeping naked is not a problem. It only became an issue when spending the night at other people's houses.

"Do you have a T-shirt I can borrow?" I inquired hopefully. His eyes darkened with disappointment.

"Hang on," he replied, already rummaging through a pile of folded shirts on top of a bureau situated against one wall. Finding what he was looking for, he tossed a shirt on the bed. Then he went to the window and shut the blinds. "There, you should be able to sleep in now a little too."

"Thank you Stephan!" I grabbed the T-shirt and brought it within easy reach.

"No problem; see you in the morning. Sweet dreams!" Turning off the light, he left the room, but not before looking back to make sure I was comfortable. As soon as he was gone, I slipped off the rest of clothes, put on the shirt and crawled back under the comforter. Thanks to the few drinks I'd consumed earlier, it didn't take long for me to drop off to sleep.

The smell of bacon and coffee filtering into the bedroom the next morning enticed me out from under the covers reluctantly.

Opening my eyes, it took a few minutes to realize I was neither at home and Belle was not curled up at my feet. I sat bolt upright – Belle – I'd forgotten about her. The poor pup must be frantic already. I did not normally stay away all night, so I was sure she would be having issues. I stood up and quickly finger-combed my hair before leaving the room.

Stephan was in the kitchen preparing breakfast when I finally joined him.

"Good morning sunshine," he looked up and smiled. Setting down two empty coffee cups on the counter, he came to where I was standing in the doorway watching. His arms wrapped around me and I allowed him to pull me close in a warm hug. "How did you sleep?"

"Actually, I slept very well. You have a comfortable bed," I hugged him back. My nose caught the scent of freshly showered skin and a woodsy type aftershave. He looked good and smelt delicious. Pulling away abruptly, I turned and went to the bathroom to freshen up. After splashing some water on my face and brushing my hair, I rejoined Stephan in the kitchen.

"Can I use your phone? I need to call my neighbour and ask her to check on Belle. I've never left her alone this long before and I am sure she's exploded all over the house already, if you know what I mean," I quickly explained.

"Of course, poor dog. Sure, be my guest. The cordless phone is on the wall around the corner," he said before turning to open the oven to check on the bacon while I went in search for the phone. Finding it, I dialled my neighbour. Thankfully, she was more than happy to check on Belle. Since we moved in five years ago, Chris had shown an avid interest in the pint sized pooch and Belle loved her right back. I hung up assured that she would be well taken care of. Chris even offered to take her for a walk. I made a mental note to pick up her up a gift-card on the way home to express my gratitude.

"Is everything okay at home?" Stephan inquired when I returned.

"Yep crisis averted. Chris is going to check on Belle and take her for a stroll in a little while. Thanks for letting me borrow your phone. I feel so much better now. This mine?" I pointed to a steaming coffee waiting on the table. Stephan smiled slightly and nodded.

"I take it this means you don't have to run off right away?" He looked like he didn't want me to leave. Admittedly, I was feeling comfortable too, so I wasn't in any hurry to leave either.

"Nope, I am good for a few more hours." I replied, then tried to change the subject. "What's for breakfast?"

"Well, I made bacon and home-made hash-browns. Want green onions in yours?" Stephan asked. I nodded, nibbling on a slice of toast that I'd grabbed off a nearby plate. Suddenly I realized was famished. "How do you like your eggs?"

"Over easy works." I replied, taking a seat at the counter. From my vantage point, I could watch him buzz around the room without getting in the way.

"Awesome. Sounds just like me. That keeps it simple; I'm an over-easy pro." He returned to the stove and stirred the butter into the waiting hot pan. "Care to set the table?"

The kitchen was a tight fit so I tried to stay out of his cooking space while I rummaged through his cupboards searching for plates and cutlery. Once the table was set, I stepped back with satisfaction. I'd even found a candle for the centrepiece.

"Very nice," Stephan said, while cracking a trio of eggs into the hot skillet. "You ready to eat? This won't take long." He was right. In a matter of minutes, there were two overflowing plates on the table. He'd even cut fresh fruit, I marvelled as he set down a plate of cantaloupe and melon in the middle. "Dig in."

Obeying, I took a place at the table. Suddenly famished, we both dug in with gusto. It had been years since a man made me breakfast so this was a real treat. "Oh my goodness, this is so good. What did you add to the eggs?"

"A little Tabasco sauce," he volunteered. "It's a little trick my mother taught me."

"These are the best eggs I've ever had!" I wasn't lying.

"So what are your plans for the day?" Stephan asked before plugging his mouth with toast.

"Well, I have to go after breakfast. I can't leave Belle alone much longer. She is going to be crazy when I finally get home." I could already picture it. She would jump all over the furniture, barking for attention until I finally settled down. It was her routine every time I returned. The intensity of her greeting depended on how long she was alone. Since I'd been gone for the night, I expected Belle to take a good half hour before finally settling down enough for an actual cuddle.

"You sure love that dog huh?" he chuckled.

"Yeah, she's my family," I admitted, before shovelling in a mouthful of hash browns. It was hard to tell if he was amused or annoyed. I was an animal lover and for his sake, it better be amused.

"Well, I hope to get a chance to meet this family of yours. She sounds like quite the character. I love dogs, but I can't have one here," he admitted.

Obviously Stephan planned to see me again; and meet my dog. This was good. I smiled to myself. "I am sure that you will get a chance sooner or later," I offered, not wanting to appear too eager.

"Well, hopefully it will be sooner than later," expressed Stephan.

Our breakfast plates clear, Stephan got up and started to clear the table. "As soon as I clean up, I can give you a ride back to your car."

"Thanks that would be awesome." I pushed my chair back and took my plate to the sink then went back to clear the table.

"I will clean this up later, why don't you gather your things together?" He started stuffing dishes into the dishwasher as he spoke. I went into the living room to collect my things. Then returning to his bedroom, I put on my clothes from the night before. Giving the apartment one more walk through to make sure nothing was forgotten, I turned back to the kitchen and placed my overnight bag by the door.

"Ready whenever you are," I said.

Stephan slipped on his boots, and grabbed his keys and said, "Let's roll babe."

Fifteen minutes later, we were pulling up to the parking lot where my vehicle still waited from the night before. I was relieved to find it still in one piece.

"Next time you come over, you park at my place," Stephan stated definitively. "If I hadn't called the coffee shop last night, they would have had it towed."

"You called the coffee shop?" I was surprised by his thoughtfulness.

"Of course, I am a regular, so it was easy to ask them to leave it where it was. Next time, just leave it at the apartment." He repeated.

Next time? I smiled to myself. It was obvious he planned on calling me again. Instead of responding, I gathered up my bags.

"Thank you for the wonderful night and the amazing breakfast. I had a great time." I rummaged in my purse, looking for my car keys. Finding them, I reached for the handle, ready to get out of the truck. His hand on mine stopped my exit.

"No, thank you! I had a great time too." His hand felt warm, or maybe it was just me. "Can I email you later?"

"I would like that. We'll to do this again." I promised, fully meaning it. I had a great time, and I definitely wanted to see him again.

"Do you mind?" he asked. I was confused, but before I could react, he was leaning over, looking intently at my lips. Instinctively, I leaned forward and our lips touched. A million garbled thoughts popped into my head, then darted away. I found myself melting into his arms. I was lost and breathless when we finally pulled apart.

"Whoa," we both sputtered once we'd pulled apart. Realizing we'd both said the same thing at the same time, we burst into laughter.

"Yeah, whoa," Stephan guffawed. "You better get out of here before I decide to take you back to my apartment." Sighing, I was almost disappointed that he didn't try. At the same time, I was extremely grateful he was being a gentleman. It would be too easy for me to give in to my carnal cravings. Cravings I'd long forgotten about.

"I better hit the road, talk to you later?" My hand was already opening the door. I had to get out of the truck and fast before I embarrassed myself. Climbing out, I turned back to thank him before fleeing to my vehicle. He was watching me with an intense look on his face.

"Check your Inbox later," he promised, before giving me another kiss. "Have a great day sexy."

"You too Stephan, thank you again," I replied, then closed the cab door and turned to my car. He waited until I unlocked the door and climbed inside before starting his truck. When I got out of the parking lot, he was right behind me. For a brief moment, I thought he'd changed his mind and was following me home. My pulse sped up in anticipation.

At the next light, he changed lanes and turned back towards his apartment. I exhaled deeply, not realizing I was holding my breath. My disappointment was immediate and shocking. Ugh, one night at a nightclub, a party and then a sleepover; and I was more than ready to have him follow me home? *Was I losing my freaking mind?*

Later that day when I finally found a few minutes to check my email, I found a message from Stephan.

Hey, EM - thank you for the great time at the party. I can't wait to see you again; what are you doing this Friday? I'd like to make you supper. Let me know your thoughts. Stephan.

Not wanted to appear too eager, I waited a few hours before I answered.

Thanks for sharing your bed; Friday sounds great. It's a date, EM.

CHAPTER NINE

The ringing of my phone in the middle of the night two days later forced me to change plans. The alarm clock sitting on the night stand flashed 4:00am.

"Hello?" I mumbled, half asleep into the receiver.

"Emma? I am sorry to wake you up," it was my editor Jason Rutledge. Hearing his voice, I knew something was wrong. We received story leads in the office constantly, but he never woke me up in the middle of the night. I was instantly alert.

"It's okay, Jason, what's up?" I asked, rubbing the sleep from my eyes.

"You know I wouldn't wake you unless it was an emergency, but we just had a huge story break. You need to head out of town for a few days to investigate as soon as possible," he responded.

"Where am I going?" I asked. "Am I leaving right away?"

"Yes, but you have to be prepared, this could be a big one," Jason continued. "Are you awake enough to pay attention?"

"You have my undivided attention. What's going on?" I replied. Pulling a cigarette from a pack laying on the table, I lit it and took a drag.

"You have to head to Baudette. There was a huge explosion just outside of town and someone says it came from the local senator's house. I've been trying to contact the local police department but have not been able to confirm anything other than emergency crews are still on scene," Jason explained. "It just happened about an hour ago."

"Who called you?" I asked curiously. Finding a notepad and pen, I quickly jotted down what Jason had already told me.

"A woman. She asked for you personally," he replied. "She wouldn't tell me who she was, other than you would know once you met face to face. She sounded frightened."

"That is an odd request," I admitted. "Did she say where she knew me from?"

"No, other than she was very confident that you would want the story. She was very insistent that she'd only talk to you," he replied. Even Jason sounded confused. "Get home and throw a few things together. I've already made arrangements for you to travel. Your plane leaves in two hours."

"She didn't give you any clues about what happened?" I inquired.

"Not really, but I got the feeling there is more to the story," he replied. "You better get moving or you will miss your flight. There will be a rental and hotel room waiting when you land. There is something strange going on. Keep your cell phone charged and close. Be safe!"

Jason passed on a few more travel details before finally disconnecting. I quickly showered then gathered up my clothing. Halfway out the door, I realized I'd forgotten to make arrangements for Belle. I scribbled a quick note with instructions to slip under my neighbour's door. Giving the cottage another swift look to ensure I'd not left anything behind, I headed for the airport.

When I landed at the Baudette Airport, a cab was already waiting to take me to the only hotel in town. True to his word, Jason had booked and prepaid for my room. The concierge handed me a note after I signed the guest book.

"This was left for you," he said before handing me a white envelope. Clutching it tightly, I headed to the room. Safe inside, I tossed my bags onto the bed and tore open the message.

'Hi Emma, thank you for coming. I will come to your room as soon as I can. I will explain later, H.'

I looked at the clock sitting on the hotel night stand; it was almost noon. I'd already been travelling for several hours so I needed to freshen up. Unsure of how long it would be until my surprise guest arrived, I jumped into the shower. I was blow drying my hair when there was a knock on the door. Looking through the peep hole,

I recognized the petite blonde standing on the other side of the door immediately - Hannah Remington. I gasped in shocked surprise.

Where had she been?

Hannah and I went back to college days. We started out as assigned roommates then evolved into best friends. She came from an affluent family and I was a former foster child. I never knew my parents, and spent my younger years being moved from foster home to foster home. It was a miracle I even made it to school. When I turned eighteen, I was offered an apartment and a welfare check. Instead, I applied for student aid. I worked hard to maintain my grades, I was determined to rise above the system. Unfortunately, being a foster child left me with trust issues. Some called me anti-social, others thought of me as a snob. I was neither. For the most part, I was shy and insecure. I just managed to hide it well.

To Hannah, that was a lifestyle she could not imagine. Her father was a lawyer and her mother lived at the country club. Somehow she managed to maintain her fun side despite her uptight parents. Or maybe that is why she was such a wild child. She did more partying than studying. I had to study hard for every pass.

At first we were both studying Creative Communications, we often hung out, or studied together. After a few months of classes, she decided journalism was not her forte. She dropped out and attended nursing school instead. The last I heard, she'd graduated with a Bachelor of Nursing and was a Director of Nursing in the Baudette General Hospital. We had not spoken in over fifteen years.

"Hannah!" I exclaimed, throwing open the door. She looked relieved to see me. Without hesitation she threw herself into my arms.

"Thank God you came!" she blurted, holding me close. I hugged her back awkwardly. "I need your help."

"Hannah, what are you doing here?" I asked. No longer trapped in her arms, I took a good look at her appearance. I had never seen her so tired and sad. Her pale blue eyes were puffy and swollen, it was obvious she'd been crying. They also glowed with fear.

"I knew you would come," she replied, ignoring my question. She glanced around the room desperately. "I knew when I called your magazine, you were the right person to help me. You are very good at your job and I trust you will not betray my confidence."

Taking her hand, I lead her to the settee sitting at the foot of the bed. She collapsed onto it gratefully.

"Would you like some coffee or tea?" I offered.

"Tea would be nice, please," was her reply. Her voice trembled. "How was your trip?"

"It happened fast," came my honest reply. "Can you tell me why I am here?"

"I need your help!" she quietly responded. "Before I tell you what's going on, you have to make a promise. You can't tell anyone what I am about to tell you."

"You know me, secrets die with me!" I replied. Yes, she did know this. One of the reasons why she dropped out of college was an unplanned pregnancy. Struggling with grades, Hannah went to her professor and begged for extra credit. Instead, she ended up pregnant and alone. After the professor denied any wrongdoing, Hannah dropped out of school. For the rest of her pregnancy, she stayed with me and I took care of her. Initially she planned to have an abortion. Then a childless couple we knew stepped forward and offered to adopt the baby. She met with them several times before deciding they'd be the perfect parents for her unborn child.

Even though she had no income, I allowed her to stay in the apartment for the remainder of her pregnancy. When I was not in class, I took her to doctor appointments and made sure she took care of herself. When the time came to give birth, I accompanied her to the delivery room. Like any expectant father, I became her breathing coach and stayed during labour and delivery.

Outside, the new adoptive parents waited impatiently in the hallway. After seven years of infertility, their dreams were about to come true. To expedite the private open adoption, the soon-to-be adoptive father claimed to have fathered the baby. No one ever questioned his claim; even though his real wife waited outside the delivery room at his side. I overheard a few of the nurses muttering under their breath. Whispering about how brave and generous the infertile woman was for accepting her husband's illegitimate child as her own. Yet no one ever questioned the story.

After twelve hours of labour, Hannah finally pushed her tiny daughter into the world. The nurses cut the cord and asked if she wanted to hold her. Hannah refused. Once the tiny girl was cleaned up, a nurse placed her into my arms. When I looked at the new mother, she shook her head and looked away.

"Are you sure you don't want to see her," I asked, cradling the tiny infant close. With a thick tuft of blonde curls and sapphire eyes, she looked just like her mother. Hannah remained steadfast in her refusal.

"I don't want to see her," she sobbed, before turning her entire body to face the wall. I didn't pursue the issue. Instead, I headed into the hall and presented the parents with their tiny daughter. While they celebrated amid tears of joy, I slipped back into the delivery room where Hannah was still facing the wall sobbing her heart out. I halted my approach when she waved me off.

"You should go home and get some sleep; it's been a long day," she whimpered. "Thank you for being here and all your help. I could never have done this without you, but I need to be alone for a while."

"I don't want to leave you alone," I argued gently, full of concern. While I could not even begin to understand how she was feeling, I was smart enough to recognize this was not a normal situation. Hannah would need as much emotional support as she could get. No woman could carry a baby inside them for nine months, then walk away unscathed. I was afraid to leave her alone.

"I will be okay; the nurses want me to rest now and when I am ready, you can come and take me home," Hannah assured me. "Go and get some rest, I am at least here for the night."

Unsure of what to do, I gave my friend the space she needed. I headed home for some much needed sleep. When I returned to the hospital the next morning to pick her up, I found her room empty. A unit clerk at the nursing station informed me Hannah had already been discharged. Her parents had come and picked her up about an hour earlier. Any attempts to contact her were futile. She refused to take my calls, so I eventually gave up.

Now, she had hunted me down and was asking for help once again.

"I need you to swear that for now, what I tell you remains between you and me," Hannah started. Her trembling hands clutched the cup of tea until it threatened to slosh all over the place.

"Are you okay?" I gently questioned. My initial shock from seeing her after all these years had started to dissipate.

"Did you hear about the explosion?" she started.

"Yes, Jason told me that a senator's house blew up," I admitted. "That was all he could tell me."

"It was my house," came her quiet response. My head flew up in shocked surprise. Her gaze met mine and she nodded confirmation. I had not misheard her.

"Your house? What are you talking about?" I tried to stifle my alarm. My mind burst with questions. I bit my tongue. I knew better than to push Hannah to confide in me. Just because she came to me, did not mean anything was changed. This was her story. She would share it when she was ready.

"My husband blew up our house!" she replied. Then she burst into tears. I started to get up to offer some comfort but she waved me off. "I am fine, this is just hard for me. It was such a shock to get the call from the police this morning. You were the first person I could think of to call. But it's been so long, I didn't have a phone number for you. I've seen your stories in *Exposed*, and I knew I could find you if I tried hard enough. I was right."

"Why did you get the call from the police?" I asked. "Were you not there?"

"I moved out about two months ago," came her quiet response. "I've been hiding from him."

"How do you know it was him who blew up the house?" I gently pried.

"The police found him lying on the front lawn, reeking of gas. He is currently in a coma in the local hospital. They are not sure if he will survive," she replied, then started sobbing again. I put my arm around her and held her while she cried. There was nothing else I could do. I hated feeling helpless.

"Why did you call me?" I asked once it appeared she was ready to speak again.

"I know he was trying to kill me, but I need help trying prove it," Hannah explained. "I need your help!"

"I think you need to tell me what's going on and why you think your husband is trying to kill you," I pushed. It was hard to believe anyone would want to murder Hannah.

"No one will believe me when the truth comes out," she started crying again. "He's a well respected senator, and I am no one. I can't believe he did this. How could he hate me so much?"

"Hannah! What is going on?" I demanded.

Ignoring me, Hannah got up and walked to the window. I watched as she looked out over the parking lot, as if checking to see if she was followed.

"Sorry, old habits die hard," she said, turning back to address me. "I've been looking over my shoulder for months. Even though I know he can't hurt me at the moment, I still expect him to jump out from behind closed doors."

"That bad?" I softly asked. It was a dumb question. Hannah was obviously terrified, and I still did not have an explanation. "Talk to me."

Hannah's shoulders slumped and she returned to the settee. Once she sat down I offered her another cup of tea. She declined.

"I've had enough for the moment, but thank you," she politely refused. "I guess I should tell you what is going on. But you have to promise me - this is our secret for now. You cannot tell anyone."

"I swear," I promised. She studied my face for a few more moments, then visibly relaxed. "Now talk to me."

"George and I have known each other for ten years," she started to explain. "We met and fell in love before he was appointed to the Senate. After I had the baby, I went home with my parents and went to nursing school. I am sorry I just left without saying goodbye. I had a lot to deal with."

I nodded in mute understanding, grateful for the belated apology.

"George's father had a heart attack. During his recovery, he was one of my patients. George spent a lot of time at the hospital at his father's side. He was always charming and generous. He never came to visit empty handed. After his father was discharged, George returned to thank the staff. Along with a huge bouquet of flowers was a handwritten invitation to dinner. I accepted," Hannah recalled. "He was charming and thoughtful; I told him all my secrets - even my darkest one - yet he loved me anyway. I fell in love with him immediately. When he finally proposed, we married quickly and settling here in Baudette. Life was perfect."

"So, what happened?" I asked hesitantly when she finally took a break. I knew better than to push, but something about this story was making me tremble with excitement. Jason was right, there was an exclusive here.

"What happened was he caught me emailing Samantha's father," she quietly answered.

"Samantha?" I asked in confusion.

"My daughter," Hannah replied. "They called her Samantha. She's fifteen now."

"You've talked to her?" I demanded. Admittedly, I was surprised. I knew all parties agreed to an open adoption. That meant photos and birthday cards could be exchanged over the years. Actual contact was a different story. Normally that was discouraged.

"A few times, and George found out," Hannah admitted, then stopped cold in the middle of her recitation. Her azure blue eyes darkened with anger briefly, then reverted to fear. "He was infuriated."

"How angry?" I asked hesitantly.

"He was furious!" Hannah admitted. "It would have been different if we had our own children. We've been trying to get pregnant since our wedding day, but despite our efforts it hasn't materialized. Initially, it was not a big deal, but the more we tried and failed, the angrier George got. We went to doctors who said we would get pregnant eventually, but we remained childless. Discovering that I was talking to my only daughter drove him to the edge."

"I came home from work one night, and George was furious. Samantha had called and left a message on the answering machine. She wanted to go shopping for a prom dress. He had no idea I was spending time getting to know my daughter. Emma - she is amazing. Bright, beautiful and smart as a whip. I wasn't trying to hide it from him; we had simply not discussed it until now. I walked through the doorway and he was waiting. He grabbed my hair and dragged me into the bedroom. I cringed as he raged in fury.

"I'd never seen him like this before. In all the year's we'd been together, he'd never shown me such anger. He completely lost all self control. At one point, I stood up and began to protest. I tried to reason with him, but he refused to listen. Instead, he punched me in the mouth. Falling onto the bed, I could taste blood on my lips. I was completely stunned. No man ever put a hand on me before. I tried to fight back, kicking and screaming, but I missed. He overpowered me and kept punching me until he ran out of steam. I must have blacked out because when I came to, he was gone. I did not wait for him to return. I packed my bags and took flight. I've been hiding in the local women's shelter ever since, trying to figure out what to do next."

"Then he found me," she sighed deeply. Tears threatened to spill as she hesitated. "Can I have more tea?"

I got up and poured her another cup. She took it gratefully and I returned to my seat across from her and waited patiently for the rest of the story.

"He found you?" I inquired.

"I had a meeting with my lawyer a week ago," Hannah continued with her story. "I started proceedings to file for divorce. I was not going to stay in a marriage where my husband was beating me. I have a protection order against him, but when I got to the lawyer's office, there was a message waiting for me. George wanted me to come to the house to get the rest of my things. There were a few things I wanted; childhood mementos, photos, things like that. He even set a date and time. Against my lawyers better judgement, I agreed to meet at the appointed time."

"You agreed to meet him?" I was stunned. After everything she'd just told me, you'd think she would steer clear.

"I agreed - but then I changed my mind. Something did not feel right," Hannah paused. "I was right; he blew up the house."

"What do you mean, he blew up the house?" I was appalled and concerned about my friends' safety.

"I was supposed to meet him there yesterday afternoon. I changed my mind and did not go," she started to cry again. "This explosion was intended for me; I am sure of it. He invited me home pretending to be helpful and cooperative. He never intended to allow me to leave with my things!"

The ringing of Hannah's cell phone interrupted her recitation. I watched her rummage through her purse. When she finally pulled out the offending device, she answered the call. Based on the look on her face, I could tell it was not good news. Deciding to give her some privacy, I went into the hotel bathroom and closed the door. I was in a complete state of shock. I really didn't know what to think. I thought I came here for a story. Instead, I reconnected with an old friend and fell smack dab in the middle of what seemed to be an instance of domestic abuse turning into attempted murder. The public was going to have a field day with this story and I was here with the victim. She had tracked me down after all these years. I decided to stick around and find out why.

Through the closed door, I could not discern the conversation happening on the other side. After a few minutes, I emerged. Hannah had hung up the phone and was standing by the window.

"That was the police. I have to go to the station and give my official statement. They want to ask a few questions," Hannah said quietly, turning towards me. "Will you be here when I am done? I want to come back and fill you in. I'm going to need your help and support. Please, will you stay for a few days? I beg you."

"My editor sent me here for as long as I need. It looks like you are stuck with me. Do you want me to go with you to the police station?" I asked.

"No, I have to do this alone. I will call you later," Hannah promised. Giving me a quick hug, she grabbed her purse and headed to the door. She paused, then turned back with a grateful smile. "Thank you for being here. You have no idea how much this means to me."

Then she was gone.

CHAPTER TEN

After Hannah left, I gave Jason a quick call at the office. Unable to get to him, I left a message on his answering machine.

"I arrived safely. Met with Hannah and wow, not sure what's all going on yet, but I have a feeling this is a big one. I'll be in touch," I said, then disconnected the call. I yawned and stretched. The morning travel time was catching up with me, so I decided to lay down to give my eyes a break.

Knock. Knock. My eyes popped open. It took a few moments to remember where I was. Glancing at the clock on the nightstand, I groaned. It was already late afternoon. I must have fallen asleep. *Knock. Knock.* I cursed quietly to myself. Whomever was at the door was persistent.

"Hang on," I called while fumbling with the privacy chain. Hannah pushed into the room, the moment door was unbarred. Her face flushed and eyes swollen from crying, she looked a wreck. Instead of sitting down, she restlessly paced the tiny room.

"I was right. He tried to kill me," she blurted almost hysterically. "The police just confirmed it. They're investigating the possibility that he deliberately left the natural gas on with the intent of blowing up the house with me inside it."

"Hang on Hannah; are you sure? Sit down. Would you like some tea?" I calmly asked, busying myself with the kettle. "Tell me what happened."

"I went to the police station after we spoke. They questioned me for hours. They wanted to know where I was last night and what I was planning for the future. I told them I was living at the woman's shelter and why," she exclaimed, wringing her hands as she sat stiffly on the edge of the bed. "George is still in critical condition in the hospital. According to the officers, it looks like he cracked open a gas line going into the house. He was in the upstairs living room when the furnace pilot light kicked in and ignited the gas pooling in the basement. He was blown clear. Fire crews found him unconscious on the lawn."

"Why would he do that? I don't understand," I was extremely confused. George was understandably pissed off that Hannah was hiding from him. However, there is a huge difference between being angry and wanting someone dead.

"We won't know for sure until he wakes up; if he wakes up," Hannah replied. "George is a lawyer with an agenda. The only reason he's in the Senate is because his father was a huge supporter. I don't think he can stand the pressure. He's getting older and has yet to produce a son. All these years he's blamed me. To find me talking to a daughter, I gave up for adoption, when we haven't had children, pissed him off. It was like having salt rubbed in the wound. George also knows that once he beat me, I would leave him forever. He will fight a divorce tooth and nail. I've always felt like his property, not his wife. He would never let another man have me," Hannah's voice faded away. I gave the tea to her and waited for her to go on. She remained silent, staring into space. Her brow furrowed with worry.

"The police said that after they are done collecting evidence, I can go the property and check things out. They want me to do a walk around and take note of inconsistencies. Items missing, proof he did set things off, that sort of stuff. Only I would know what is missing, other than George. They also warned me media from all over the country are camped everywhere. Will you come with me?" Hannah hesitantly asked. "I am afraid to go alone."

"Did they give you a rough idea when you can go?" I asked gently. I didn't want her to think I did not want to stay. However, if she wanted me to stay longer, I'd have to incur further expenses approved by Jason.

"They said they would let me know as soon as it was safe," she answered. "The earliest it will be is tomorrow."

"That should be ok then, I am here until the day after tomorrow, no matter what," I promised. Her shoulders dropped, she looked visibly relieved.

"Is there more?" I pressed, after giving her a few minutes to gather her thoughts. She remained silent, as if weighing her next words before opening her mouth.

"There is something else you should know; I had to tell the police the main reason why I fled," she finally whispered. "I just found out I was pregnant."

My teacup hit the table with a clatter. She'd just dropped a bombshell. She looked up with a pleading expression in her tear soaked eyes.

"George does not know; nor can he! Can you please help me?" she begged. Before I could answer, she glanced at her watch. "Oh crap, I better get back. They have a curfew at the shelter. If I am not back, it's assumed I went back home and they lock the doors. I will be in touch as soon as I can."

Hannah gave me a quick hug before heading out the door. For the second time in a single day, my old roommate left me with a million questions and no concrete answers. I tried calling Jason again. This time he answered on the third ring.

"Hey EM, you all settled in?" he demanded once he'd picked up the phone.

"Yes, the hotel is small but cosy. Thanks for taking care of that for me," I replied.

"What have you found out?" Jason questioned. "I just finished watching the news, and the house is gone. Nothing left but a foundation. Have you talked to Hannah yet?"

"Yes, she was here twice, but had to leave," I replied, then quickly filled him.

"Holy shit! There was nothing like that on the news," came his stunned reaction. "You know that if he is a wife beater, and attempted to kill her, this is a huge story. You have to find out more."

"I know, but it's not easy. Hannah is petrified. I have to be very careful with this. I could either help or make things worse," I went on. "I still do not know why she wants me here though. She wants my help but hasn't told me why yet."

"Well, it sounds like a potentially dangerous situation. Please be very careful. When do you see her again?" Jason asked.

"She had to go back to the shelter, but I expect to see her in the morning," I replied.

"Have you contacted the police yet?" Jason paused. I told him no. "At least let them know you are in the area."

"Not a problem. I wanted to talk to you first to see if there was a story, or if I was just here as a friend," I replied. "I should know more tomorrow."

"Okay, like I said though, be careful! I realize George was still in the hospital, but you don't know who his supporters are. He's in a position to hire a cleaning crew to cover his backside. He can also hire protection," Jason countered with care. I could tell he did not want to alarm me more than I already was. "When are you heading to the site?"

"I was thinking of going after dinner. Things should have settled down a little by then," I answered back.

"Take your cell!" Jason stressed, before ending the call.

Hanging up, I decided to make use of the rest of the day. Calling the local police department, I was unable to speak to the investigating officer. He was still at the site of the explosion. Impatient, I jumped into the rental car and started looking for the blast site. It was not that hard to find. As soon as I hit the outer limits of Baudette, I could see the flash of red and blue emergency beacons in the distance. I steered the rental car toward the flashing lights.

Nearing the site, news crews and cameras lined the route. Two squad cars blocked access to the grounds, and investigators were everywhere. The driveway was marked with yellow police tape and no one was getting in or out. Crawling along in low gear, I surveyed the rubble. It was pretty much a disaster area! From my vantage point lumber, furniture and appliances were strewn all over the yard. There was nothing left of the house except for remnants of a concrete foundation. The fire commissioner's office van was parked towards the back and firefighters were moving from building to building.

Pulling into the driveway, an officer walked over to the car.

"This is a crime scene; you cannot be here," the officer barked once I opened my window.

"I am sorry. My name is Emma and I am a reporter with *Exposed* magazine," I explained.

"I don't care! You should not be here. Media are over there," he turned and pointed to the flock of reporters gathered along the main road. "Get over there where you belong."

"Excuse me?" I was shocked by the officer's rudeness.

"There is nothing here to see at the moment. You need to leave now," the officer insisted. "If you refuse, you will be arrested!"

I bristled with indignation. I was used to rude police officers on the job, but this one took the cake. He'd apparently run out of patience dealing with the paparazzi. I decided to change tactics. Turning on the charm, I smiled apologetically.

"I am sorry, I called the station and was told the chief was here," I replied sweetly.

"Yeah, he's here but he's not talking to the media. He will be releasing a press release at the end of the day. Go sit on the road and wait with the rest of the vultures," the cop barked. "You won't receive anything until then. Now GO!"

He stepped backwards and pointed back to the highway.

"Thank you. You've been very helpful," I called out before closing the window. Backing onto the road, I ignored the media who rushed the car as I puttered past. I guess they assumed that since I'd spoken to the officer briefly, I'd be privy to information they still wanted. Waving them off, I headed back to town and the waiting hotel room. With Hannah requesting my help, I did not need to sit on the side of a highway waiting like a vulture. I have the inside scoop.

Back in my hotel room, I replied to email and checked my voice messages. There was a message from Debbie chiding me for leaving town without telling her, and a message from Chris informing me that Belle would be at her house until I came back. Checking my emails, I found a note from Stephan.

"Hey Beautiful; hope you are well. I am really looking forward to our dinner date on Friday. Tried calling, but there was no answer. I hope everything is fine. Give me a call when you can. Stephan."

I replied immediately.

"Hey Stephan. Sorry, I did not get your call. It's been an insane day. I got called out of town on a huge story. I hope to be back by the weekend, but I am not sure. I will let you know the outcome either way. After the week I am having, it

will be nice to have a quiet evening of spoiling. Hope you had a great day, EM." I clicked send.

The hotel room phone rang about fifteen minutes later. It was Hannah.

"The police called. They said they will be finished in the morning. I have to go to the house tomorrow, can you come with me?" Hannah asked. "By the way, George is still in a coma. I called the hospital and he took quite a blow to the head. Apparently a tree stopped his flight when the house exploded. They are keeping him sedated until the swelling goes down in his brain. Either way, it looks like he will be in the hospital for a while."

"Is he being charged?" I demanded.

"Yes, the police are laying charges, but they have not compiled a list yet. This will depend on what I find tomorrow too. The police will meet us there, but we can start earlier. I am also hiring a security company to guard the place until we figure out what needs to be done. The police have also contacted the Department of Environment. They have to test the grounds to see if the gas has seeped into the property. If it has, there will be cleanup involved," Hannah explained. Her voice faded off towards the end of her recitation. She sounded exhausted. "This could turn into a total nightmare."

"It will be okay, Hannah," I promised. "What time do you want to go?"

"I will stop by your room after breakfast. Someone wants to use the phone. See you tomorrow," she said, before hanging up.

After showering and preparing for bed, I climbed into the softness of my king sized bed and switched on the late night news. The explosion was top news on every broadcast. It was not every day that a senator's house blew up. At one point, the captain stood before cameras and delivered his official statement.

"I confirm that Senator George Connelly remains in hospital in critical condition after being found unconscious in front of the remains of his house. No one else was found on the scene. Our initial investigation also confirms the explosion was deliberate, but that is all we can say at this time," he told reporters. "Our investigation will continue once Senator Connelly regains consciousness. Until then, we have no further information."

The next morning, Hannah arrived early as planned. We took my vehicle so the media would not recognize her car. It was a small town and through the process of elimination they would eventually identify and find her, if they thought it was worth hunting her down. So far, media reports speculated that she was overseas travelling Europe with friends. Understandably, Hannah wanted to keep it that way for as long as possible.

"Are you sure about this," I asked, breaking the silence. Since we left the hotel, neither of us spoke. Hannah rode along quietly fidgeting with her purse strap.

"Yes, I have to do this. The police will be meeting us there eventually. I just don't know what I will find," she admitted sadly. I reached over and clasped her cold hand in mine. She squeezed back gratefully and we continued our drive in silence.

Reaching the homestead, the curb side media circus had grown significantly overnight. Everyone stopped milling around and watched as we pulled into the driveway. The same officer who kicked me off the property the night before sauntered towards my car. I pulled up and rolled down my window.

"You again? I told you that you couldn't be here," he barked before leaning over and glaring at my passenger. "And this time you brought a friend?"

"This is Hannah Connelly; she lives here. I believe your boss is expecting us," I responded smugly. He glared at me then looked pointedly at Hannah with disbelief.

"Do you have identification ma'am?" he asked gruffly. Hannah handed over her driver's license. The officer glanced over it quickly before handed it back. "I am really sorry Mrs. Connelly. You have to understand the media has been relentless. We cannot let anyone in to spoil the crime scene."

"It's okay, I understand. You are just doing your job," Hannah replied.

"Let me open the gate for you," the officer responded apologetically before moving away. Once the tape was pulled down, he waved us through. I drove slowly down the driveway while Hannah gasped loudly.

"Oh. My. God. The washing machine is in the garden," she gasped, pointing towards the trees behind where the house once stood. The dryer was about five feet away the foundation. I pulled up in front of the detached three car garage and parked. I got out first, then waited for Hannah to follow. She looked shell-shocked when she finally left the vehicle. Taking my arm, she pulled me close and gave me a silent hug, then we walked towards the rubble together.

The closer we got to the foundation, the more the yard resembled a war zone. Splinters of lumber, tufts of insulation and remnants of the furnishings were strewn around the skeletal remains of the basement foundation. Everything within the basement was covered with a dense layer of ash and rubble. Household and personal items not thrown clear by the blast were destroyed in the ensuing blaze. It looked like a bomb had gone off. Amazingly the detached garage, a huge shop in the back and several other buildings appeared unscathed.

"My beautiful home! Everything is gone," Hannah exclaimed tearfully. "It is even worse than I imagined."

Pulling away suddenly, I watched in silence as she headed towards a charred box lying about ten feet from where the front door used to be. Hannah picked it up and opened the lid. I watched as she rummaged through the contents, then sighed with relief.

"Thank goodness. This is my mother's jewellery box. Other than being a little charred, it managed to survive," she explained. She looked immensely relieved. "I wonder what else we can find?"

Taking her lead, I wandered around looking for personal items. We managed to get a few things; a cluster of photographs, the odd cup or plate, even the family Bible was found charred but otherwise still readable. Finally, we managed to collect about two small cardboard boxes of assorted items. We were just finishing when a police car pulled up and an officer stepped out. It was the police chief from the news broadcast the previous night.

"Hi Hannah, how are you today?" he addressed Hannah with concern.

"I have been better," Hannah replied sadly. He smiled and nodded in agreement. "This is Emma, the reporter I was telling you about. She is helping me here."

"Hey, my name is Police Chief Graham Alexander," he said, turning to me. "You're a reporter for whom?"

"I write for *Exposed* magazine," I responded. He nodded with recognition.

"I've heard of it and you. Just so you know, whatever we talk about here, is off the record. I will not have our investigation ruined because you can't keep your mouth shut," he bristled. I would have been insulted by his bluntness, but I was used to dealing with police. Until they know and trust you, their initial reaction to the media in these situations was always negative.

"I understand; I am here for Hannah," I replied. "Besides, we are a monthly and I still have a few weeks before deadline. By then, I expect most of your investigation will be over by then, so we should be okay."

"Well, you can't run to other media either," he insisted. He unsuccessfully tried to stare me down.

"Like I am going to share my exclusive," I replied with a cheeky grin. Grant it, the story would be old news by deadline. Even so, having the inside scoop would guarantee me exclusivity. I was still the only media with access to the wife. Satisfied, he turned back to Hannah.

"Do you mind if we walk around a little? I want you to do a visual inspection and let me know if you notice anything unusual," he addressed Hannah with gentleness. It was obvious he was a professional, yet empathetic.

"I'll let you do that Hannah, and I will continue wandering around collecting personal items" I volunteered. Grabbing the already full boxes, I headed to the car intent on loading them into the luggage compartment. "I will join you in a few minutes."

Hannah and the chief both nodded and headed across the yard while I continued to scavenge for items my friend would want. When I was done, I spotted the pair standing in the middle of the driveway, staring at a blackened pile of ash on the gravel. Hannah looked distraught and frightened. They both looked up as I neared.

"It looks like he piled my things up right here in the middle of the driveway and set fire to them," she sobbed. On closer inspection, I could make out a few semi-recognizable items. A blackened watch, complete with cracked glass; jewelled cufflinks, along with several charred picture frames. "He even burned all my childhood pictures!"

"These were personal items?" Chief Alexander asked.

"Yes, these were MY items, things I had asked for but he refused to hand over. He refused. Then the day before the fire, he phoned and asked me to meet me here. He told me he'd packed for me and all I needed was to pick up my stuff," Hannah replied, wiping away her tears. "I can't believe he did this! All of this!"

"I hate to say this Hannah, but some people just crack when they split up," the chief kindly suggested. The ringing of his cell phone interrupted. He moved away, then took the call. When he rejoined us a few minutes later after ending his call, we knew something had changed.

"That was my deputy stationed at the hospital," he addressed Hannah carefully. "I have to go; George woke up five minutes ago."

CHAPTER ELEVEN

The next twenty-four hours were spent helping Hannah get her affairs in order. The insurance company joined the police with the investigation. It was soon noticed that George had cancelled the house insurance after she moved out, then for some reason he reinstated it a few days before the explosion. Innocent or not, this action alone suggested premeditation.

Hannah passed this info on to the police and her divorce lawyer.

Before I went home, police officially laid charges against Senator George Connelly. The string of charges included six counts of arson causing negligence, willful destruction of private property, several weapons charges and animal cruelty. The animal cruelty charges were laid after police discovered Hannah's boxer tied up in a back building, shot full of arrows. Poor Duke suffered greatly at the hands of his attacker before his throat was mercifully slashed. Hannah was heartbroken when she found out the news. She admitted to struggling with the decision of leaving her adored four-legged companion, but the shelter did not allow pets. Duke was one of the things she was slated to pick up that black day. George's fingerprints were found on a cross-bow discovered hidden in the garage rafters.

Despite the overwhelming evidence against him, George screamed innocence. Where he once slipped past the scrutiny of the media, his every sin was dug out and laid bare. A deeply hidden history of animal cruelty and physical abuse slowly surfaced. There was even two outstanding protection orders against him from ex-girlfriends.

While Hannah's name was briefly mentioned in the media, no one knew where she was, other than me. True to my word, I remained her confidante and did not disclose the behind-the-scenes story to anyone, other than my editor Jason.

"You know you have to be careful with this," Jason reminded me when I passed on my most recent update. "He sounds like a dangerous man, and you need to steer clear of the situation."

"I can't just abandon my friend," I reasoned. While I appreciated Jason's concern, his mother-hen attitude was sometimes overwhelming.

"I am not asking you to abandon her. I am reminding you to keep perspective. You may be treading on dangerous ground," Jason pressed. "Not only are you personally at risk, there are liability issues too. We don't want a lawsuit on our hands. This is not Joe-Blow down the street - he is a senator!"

Jason was absolutely right. Pissing off someone in government was risky business. They had connections, they had people who would do anything for a promise and they had access to information and funds.

Connelly's alleged actions not only brought down the hand of the law, they also attracted the attention of the government. The federal government stepped in as soon as the police released information that charges were laid. The Prime Minister's office announced that Senator Connelly was on a forced leave of absence. Until the matter was resolved, he was not welcome in Ottawa. If found guilty in a court of law, he would be forced to resign immediately.

Until Connelly's trial, things would remain up in the air. I went home after promising Hannah to be available at a moment's notice. I also promised to be back for the trial. Unfortunately, it would be a while until I heard from her. Until Connelly's sentencing Hannah might as well have been in witness protection.

Chief Alexander was very strict about contact. It was too dangerous, he said. He'd already tried to kill her, and there was nothing stopping him from trying again. That was the only way the trial would not proceed. As much as I wanted to be there for her, we were both advised against it. There was too much of a risk of someone finding her. We couldn't meet, talk on the phone or email. He was kind enough to pass on a message here and there. Otherwise, there was no contact. I had no choice but to wait for until it was safe again. I couldn't imagine how scared she was, carrying her second child while hiding in some undisclosed location. She must be frightened. It killed me that I could not be at her side.

After making Chief Alexander promise to keep her safe, no matter what the cost, I had no choice but to go home.

When I returned from my trip, things picked up between Stephan and I quickly. I'd just walked through the door when my cell phone started ringing.

"Hey EM, how are you?" Stephan asked once I answered. His accent sounded sexy on the phone. After the stressful few days in Baudette, it was nice to hear his voice.

"I am great, how was your trip?" I asked. In the middle of all the excitement with Hannah, I'd received an email telling me that he'd suddenly needed to fly to Toronto.

"It was as expected. The architect messed up the drawings and I had to go and straighten things out with the engineers. Everything is sorted out now, but it was a hectic few weeks," he explained. "Care to come over for a drink? I miss kissing you."

I snorted at his tenacity. Glancing upward at the clock sitting on the mantle, I was relieved to discover it was still early. I had already decided to put aside my research for the night. Besides, it was a stressful few days. It was a good idea to walk away for a few hours. I'd been wracking my brain trying to figure out my next story, but kept coming up short. I had many ideas, but nothing was coming together. I hate writer's block. Debbie would tell me there was no such thing. She believed the problem could be solved with a serious romp in the hay. I strongly disagreed on that one. Frustrated, I almost tossed my notes in the fireplace, just to have a reason to start from scratch.

"Sure. Want me to bring anything?" I asked.

"Just yourself would be nice," came his reply. "I have a surprise for you."

"Oh?" I was suddenly curious.

"Yep, but you will have to wait until you get here," came his reply. He sounded amused by my childish squeal. I loved surprises. "You might want to pack a few things; and plan to spend the night."

"Seriously?" Now I was really paying attention.

"Seriously! Now get moving. I will be waiting for you," he ordered, then hung up before I reply.

An hour later, I pulled up to Stephan's apartment. I punched in the four digit door code, then headed upstairs. On the drive in, I nearly turned home several times. It seemed impetuous rushing to the city at the invitation of a near stranger. Grant it, there had been a lot of communication via text message and phone calls while we were apart. Face to face was a little more intimidating. Or perhaps it was because I knew his intentions were ultimately to get me into bed. It was obvious he was interested. Recalling his kisses still made me blush.

The earnest underlying plea in his voice had triggered an array of emotions ranging from fear, excitement and much to my shame, arousal. I pondered calling Debbie before I left; but I knew she would encourage me to go. What I needed was someone to talk me out of this. Nope, I was a grown woman. I could do this alone.

Arriving at his door, I paused for a moment to catch my breath then knocked. My knock turned into a caress as I heard the lock turn. The door swung open and I nearly collapsed. He could have at least gotten dressed! The little blue towel tied around his waist left little for the imagination. He's obviously just got out of the shower. Catching myself staring, I flushed. Forcing myself to look up, our eyes met briefly, then he reached out, pulling me into his apartment.

"I was waiting for you! I am so glad to see you," he said, pulling me close against his tanned skin. His skin was still moist and smelt of Old Spice. As he held me tightly, the heat emanating from his half naked body soaked into mine. It was comforting after all I had witnessed while helping Hannah.

"You were?" I was surprised that I could speak. It felt safe to be wrapped within his arms. Instead of responding, his fingers caressed my cheek, while his thumb traced my lips, before gently parting them. I gasped in surprise as his thumb invaded my mouth, caressing the inside my lips. The entire time, his blue eyes devoured mine.

My arms snaked up to wrap around his neck. I was having trouble standing on my own volition. Time stood still as I watched his lips draw closer to finally brush my aching mouth. His hot mouth tasted mine lightly at first, before pressing into me harder. I felt myself drift away. Each caress of his gentle lips melted my resolve further, until I feel myself slip. His hands clasp my waist. *Damn the man knew how to kiss.*

"You okay?" he demanded, pulling away slightly. His right hand reached up to brush my hair away from my cheek. His touch made me shiver and melt.

"Yes. I am all right," I managed to mutter. My tongue was having trouble forming words. Stephan chuckled softly against my throat.

"Come on, I have a surprise," he took my hand and lead me into the living room. For the first time I noticed all the lights were off in the apartment. The place was bathed with candlelight. The window sills, the mantle, the coffee table. Candles in profusion were burning everywhere. A single rose lay across the coffee table, between two glasses of wine. I was very impressed. "Care to join me?"

"Do you think you should put some clothes on?" I inquired, starting to feel overdressed.

"Does my outfit bother you?" he laughed softly.

"What outfit? You're wearing a towel and it's distracting." I reluctantly admitted. There was no way that I would admit any vulnerability. The last thing he needed to know was how his nakedness was making it impossible for me to think straight.

"Fine, be right back," his voice faded as he disappeared into the bedroom only to emerge wearing a robe. "Is this better?"

"Much better. Thank you," I replied with a giggle. Sure, he'd only donned a robe, but it was significantly more modest than a mere towel. It's kind of funny now. A naked man should not be intimidating; however, when confronted by one I suddenly wanted to jump in my car and go home. Meanwhile, deep down, I will admit to wanting to grab him by the hand and drag him to the waiting bed. We'd eventually end up there anyway, wouldn't we? Why should I wait? *What would Debbie do?* Debbie - I snickered to myself - would drag the man to bed and ride him like a cowboy going for the gold buckle.

"What's so funny," Stephan asked as we sat down.

"I was just thinking about what Debbie would do if she'd answered the door to find a man standing in nothing but a towel. I told you to get dressed; she would have ripped off the towel," I sheepishly admitted. His eyebrows popped up in surprise. Apparently he was not expecting such a good reaction.

"Hey, I understand. I rented a movie and pizza should be here shortly. Is that okay with you?" He looked genuinely worried that I wouldn't like his idea.

"No, that's awesome. What a perfect way to spend the evening; curled up on the couch, drinking wine, watching movies," I concurred. "You did an outstanding job. This is a nice surprise."

"Topped off with me seducing the clothes off you," he added hopefully.

"It's not that easy," I countered.

"That's good. I don't like easy," his dimples deepened when he grinned. I found myself enjoying making him grin. It meant we were connecting. The chemistry between us was undeniable.

"So what are we watching?" I asked, attempting to shift the subject.

"My favourite movie, *Men in Black*," he responded. Picking up the remote he pressed play. "Thank you for coming. I missed you."

Taking the glass of wine he offered, I smiled.

"You already said that," I giggled.

"That's because I mean it," he put down the glass and faced me. His fingers grazed my chin before lifted my face to meet his gaze. "I really do mean it!"

"You are intense, aren't you," I stammered. His sudden boldness startled me.

"Only when I find something that I like," he stressed.

I was grateful for the soft knock at the door. The pizza delivery had arrived. While Stephan squared up with the delivery boy, I got the time to gather my scattered senses. There was no doubt in my mind that I believed him. When it came to people, I went with my gut. In the past, I had run into some less than savoury characters, and somehow I knew to steer clear. When it came to this particular man, my stomach was aflutter, but not from disgust.

I got up and looked around the room. Unlike most men I knew, he had a number of family pictures on his television stand. I missed checking them out during my last visit. This time, I picked one up and examined it closer. The handsome young man looked exactly like Stephan, yet different - younger. This must be his son.

"That is Michael," Stephan confirmed, having come up behind me. I turned to see him set the pizza on the coffee table, along with napkins and a pair of plates. "Do you need a fork?"

"He looks like you! Who needs a fork for pizza? It's the ultimate finger food," I snorted with laughter, as he turned to take two forks back to the kitchen. "English manners?"

"Yes, but I am not in England anymore; time to get messy," he laughed. I deliberately watched as he carefully pushed his fingers under a slice, then popped a huge portion into his mouth. A trickle of sauce remained on the edge of his lip.

"You know, when you look at me like that, I just want to pull you into my lap and kiss you senseless," he declared. He started to lean over; and I backed up with a mischievous grin.

"I thought we were watching a movie," I laughed, attempting to refocus his attention. It worked perfectly. He pressed *play* and we went back to enjoying our pizza. For the next few hours, the movie became background noise while we learned about each other. Once dinner was done, we curled up on the sofa under a blanket and talked. I particularly enjoyed hearing about England and Stephan loved talking about his native land.

"I had a great life there, but I have no regrets about coming to Canada. If I hadn't, I would never have met you," he said. "I've been thinking about going home, but I am now having second thoughts."

"What do you mean, second thoughts," I demanded.

"Well, I'd decided that once this job was done, if I didn't meet someone special I would consider going back to England. I suppose that's why Michael wants to come here. He thinks that if he does, I will remain in Canada. It gets lonely when everyone you love is so far away," he admitted. Stephan looked lonely and vulnerable and sad. I wrapped my arm around his chest and gave him a hug. He smiled and hugged me closer to his body. "I could get used to this."

"Me too," I yawned.

"Are you getting bored with me?" Stephan leaned sideways to look me in the face.

"Hell no, just worn out. It's been a stressful few days," I admitted. "I should get my things together and go home."

I started to sit up, but he blocked me.

"You do not have to leave," his voice trailed off. "You've been drinking and my bed is big enough for two. I've already shown to be a gentleman. Besides, I have plans for us tomorrow and figured we could make an earlier start if you spend the night."

"Plans?" I demanded. My tiredness was briefly replaced by curiosity.

"We are going for a short road trip," he teased. "I ran out of materials and could not find a driver on short notice. We have to take a run to Crystal City and be back in twenty-four hours. Debbie already said she'd check on Belle."

"Debbie knows about this?" I laughed. That explained the radio silence. Normally we texted each other throughout the day; stupid, meaningless things that we would normally say to each other if we were side by side.

The only message I got today said "*Have fun *wink wink*".

I typed back *"What do you mean?"*

She never even responded.

"What time are we leaving?" I inquired, taking the conversation back to the present.

"It takes about seven hours to drive to Crystal City, and I have to be there by dinner. I'd like to get out of here by 10 o'clock in the morning at the latest. You are going to spend the night," he asked hopefully.

"No, I will stay here," I conceded.

"I will go get the bed ready," he replied with a satisfied smile, and so headed to the bedroom.

"I want the couch," I reasoned, realizing I sounded like a prude. I was terrible at flirting. Now wonder men found me so hard to understand.

"The couch is not comfortable," was his reply. "I promise to behave, like last time. Besides, you will be thankful for the good night's sleep tomorrow after you bounce around in a truck for eight hours straight."

"Fine, just give me a few minutes to freshen up," I conceded, grabbing my overnight bag and headed to the bathroom. When I returned ten minutes later, Stephan was still in the living room, watching the late night news.

"Everything is ready for you in the bedroom. If you wish, go ahead and get comfy. I will join you in a few minutes," he said.

Suddenly exhausted, I nodded and yawned.

"Thanks, see you in a moment," I replied, before adjourning to his bedroom. The bed was already turned back and waiting. He'd even left a glass of wine on the night stand. I stripped down, pulled on a tee shirt and crawled under the covers. Grabbing my tablet, I quickly checked my emails and finished the wine. Thirty minutes later and he'd still not joined me. Finally conceding that he must have changed his mind and was going to stay on the couch, I got comfortable and turned out the light. I was sleeping within a matter of minutes.

Sometime around dawn, I awoke unable to breathe. Any attempts to move were hindered by an unusual weight. Half asleep, I panicked. Forcing my eyes open, I glanced around the room. It took a few minutes to remember where I was. Sometime after I'd fallen asleep, Stephan claimed his side of the bed. He was now the reason I was unable to move. During the night, he had curled up pressed against me; his arm was sprawled across my chest, and a leg strewn across my thighs kept me pinned to the bed.

I should have been upset by his intimate embrace; instead I was oddly comforted. As I lay there and pondered getting up, it hit me. I really do not want to move. It was nice waking up curled in someone's arms. I am sure Belle would hate to be replaced as my snuggle puppy, but honestly, Stephan was much more appealing. Glancing at the clock on the night stand, there was still five hours before we had to wake up. Shutting my eyes, I wiggled back into a comfortable position and slipped back off to dreamland.

CHAPTER TWELVE

Over the next forty-eight hours, I learned road-trips with Stephan could be a lot of fun. The trip was spent listening to loud music while singing out of tune, talking about life, dreams, our families and pasts. It was a relaxing break compared to the hectic previous week.

After a six hour drive, we pulled into Crystal City, where Stephan informed me our return trip would take place the following day.

"I have a hotel room already booked for the night," he informed me once we hit the city limits. "I will drop you off and finish dropping off the truck. When I come back, we will hit the steak house across the street for supper."

"Sounds like a plan," I agreed. We pulled into a *Motel 98*, and checked in. Then he went out to complete his errand. Alone in the suite, I kicked off my shoes, and my clothes were soon a pile on the floor. Needing to shake off the day's long hours in the truck, I climbed into the shower. The hot water eased my tired muscles just enough to take off the edge.

Once showered, I turned the water off, grabbed a waiting towel and headed back to the room. Finding my silk robe in my bag, I slipped it on and started to get ready for supper. I was still blow-drying my hair when Stephan returned.

"Don't you knock?" I laughed. He walked over and pulled me close and I breathed deeply of his wintery fresh smell. It was an intoxicating blend of fresh air, cigarette smoke and diesel. I shivered, suddenly aware of my thin silk wrap. Abruptly I pulled out of his arms, wincing at the quick movement.

"Are you okay?" he asked, as he kicked off his boots.

"Yeah, I am just sore from bouncing around in the truck," I admitted before wandering to sit on the futon placed strategically at the foot of the king-sized bed. He followed suit.

"I can fix that for you," he offered, flexing his fingers flirtatiously in my direction.

"You can? What are you offering?" I flirted back. He looked devilishly handsome as he smirked back at me. His eyes glinted with mischief.

"I've been told I give a mean massage," he responded. He didn't wait for my answer. His hands were already on my waist, facing my back towards him. Before I could protest, his hands found my tender shoulders and began working their magic. My eyelids drooped as his fingers gently rubbed my sore and tired body. Starting at the base of my neck, he worked his way along my spine up and down. I began to weave as I relaxed beneath his skilled hands. He caught me as slowly sagged against his chest.

"God that feels good." I managed to murmur, catching myself and trying to pull upright. As much as I loved the tender manipulations of his fingers, I needed to keep a safe distance between us physically. He pulled away and stood up.

"Be right back," he hurriedly stood and headed to the bathroom. "Let me clean up first."

I leaned back against the pillows and channel surfed while he went about his business. Within minutes I heard the shower turn on. Shutting my eyes, I listened to the water hit the ceramic tiles. It was as calming as a warm spring rain-shower. Realizing that I was in danger of sleeping, I pushed myself up and went to the side table to grab the cup of coffee I'd left behind while doing my hair. I cringed with every movement.

When I turned, Stephan was standing in the doorway, blocking my escape.

"You know, I could really work the soreness out for you," he said. He leaned over and pulled me into his arms. As I watched, his mouth descended towards mine. I gasped in surprise as our lips joined in a moist embrace. I was suddenly aware of the thinness of my robe as he swept me up in his strong arms. I tried to pull away, instead he gently took my wrist and guided me to the bed.

"Permit me," he invited gently. He watched me intently, searching for some sign of dissent. There were none. His hands lowered to widen the opening of my robe. I shivered in quiet anticipation. In moments, my bare flesh was exposed to his hungry gaze. My skin flushed as his eyes devoured my nakedness.

"Come on, lay down," he quietly ordered. Obediently, I climbed onto the bed and lay down on my stomach. I could feel his gaze burning my flesh as I positioned myself on the bed. The mattress shifted as he put a knee on either side of my legs and straddled my bottom. I tensed, expecting to feel his weight, but it never arrived. Instead, his hands were warm when he finally found my skin. I sank into the mattress as he slowly massaged the aching muscles up and down my back.

"Aren't you a little overdressed?" I suggested. The hotel bath towel was rough against my tender flesh.

"Good point," he concurred. He pulled away briefly. I sank into the mattress deeper. Moments later I heard the towel drop to the floor and he straddled me again. This time, I could feel his flaccid member pressed against the crease of my bottom. I tried to ignore the tingling starting between my thighs.

Stephan's attention returned to my sore muscles, bringing my attention back to my cramping back. With each stroke of his determined hands caressing my body, I became more aware of his growing arousal pressed against the softness of my backside. Every nerve of my body tingled in anticipation as he rubbed down my back. I allowed my mind to wander. I tried to imagine what he was thinking, having me completely exposed and at his mercy.

"Are you okay?" he leaned over and whispered against my ear. Goose bumps erupted over my exposed flesh, making me shiver.

"Oh Gawd yes," I muttered. "Your hands feel amazing on my back. This is exactly what I needed."

"I am glad you are enjoying this," he responded. His lips brushed the back of my neck, before he righted himself. A moan of pleasure escaped my throat.

"Your fingers are magical," I groaned.

"You have no idea doll face," he chuckled.

"Oh?" I inquired, intrigued.

"All in due time my dear, all in due time," he replied. Giving my bottom playful smack, he slipped off to lay beside me and pulled me into his arms. "This is very nice. I certainly could get used to this."

"Used to what?" I inquired, turning my face towards him. Without his physicality teasing my senses, my thoughts were slowly coming back to reality. His withdrawal left me curious and confused. This was a first - one minute we are laying naked, close to making love, and then suddenly there was complete withdrawal.

"Lying here, with you in my arms," he smiled teasingly. "You fit me just right."

I agreed! It was nice to be held so sweetly and lovingly. While the chemistry and passion between us was formidable, Stephen was a gentleman. Our relationship evolved into something beyond sex. We were developing a friendship based on mutual understanding and trust. The physical attraction was merely a bonus.

As I got to know Stephan the next few months, I began to see a man harbouring a damaged heart. I found out about his first marriage and how the love of his life betrayed him. They had one son, Michael. Nevertheless, he admitted that owning a tavern took a toll on their relationship. It didn't help that while he was serving customers, she was apparently sleeping with them behind his back. He caught her in the act. I could feel some lingering resentment and annoyance about the circumstances of the breakup throughout our conversations. Finding his wife in bed with another man had brought him to the brink. I found him on his way back. Despite our lack of a real sexual relationship, I was confident he would never cheat. His own pain was too real.

Soon his apartment become my home away from home. He even gave me the key! While I wasn't sure I wanted a relationship, it was fun having a great guy in my life with no strings attached. While that was the basis of our relationship, we spent a lot of time together. He loved impromptu road trips, so many weekends were spent travelling to various job sites. I loved those long, leisurely weekends. They gave us time to be alone and we did a lot of talking. I shared my heart, my fears, and my dreams. With each reveal, I felt myself letting go of my walls, little by little.

In November, he had shoulder surgery to repair a past injury. I took a week off from work and at his request, stayed with him in the event of complications. I drove him to the hospital, waited for him to regain consciousness in the recovery room, then took him home and took care of him during recovery.

It was not a huge sacrifice. Stephan had somehow become my life, away from my home and I looked forward to our time together. We were doing so many 'couple' things that it was hard not to think of us as a couple. I treated him as I would any boyfriend and I had the same expectations. By Christmas and New Years, I was spending every weekend at his place – we had become inseparable.

Admittedly, my first clue that something was 'off' surfaced our first New Years Eve together. We were both invited to WildSide for a Fish Pond party. It was my first official NYE invitation to a private club party and over two-hundred people were expected. Rumour was that due to leasing issues, the Club was closing its doors forever, so I was looking forward to it.

Debbie and I spent the day scouring the mall for the perfect outfits to ring in the New Year. We even booked manicures. I was especially anticipating the event because it would be one of the last ones Stephan and I would spend together for a few weeks. His flight to England to visit his son was booked two days afterwards. I deliberately primped and preened to give us enough time to call a taxi for the party. Stephan, on the other hand, was dragging his feet. Two hours before midnight, I finally asked what was up.

"Are you going to take a shower?" I inquired, standing in front of his desk. Trying to get his attention, I did a little spin. Wearing a short black skirt, black thigh high books and a red chiffon blouse, I looked both classy and sexy. He never looked away from his computer.

"Stephan?" I tried again. This time, he glanced in my direction.

"You look great. I will shower in a minute." he promised, before turning back to the screen. Miffed at his dismissal, I wandered over, expecting to find him working on some project. Instead he was playing an online golf game.

"You're playing a game? I thought we had plans!" I was starting to get annoyed. I'd been talking about this event for a few days, he knew I was excited to see our friends. Besides, it was supposed to be our first official event as a couple.

"It only takes me ten minutes to get ready. Relax," he responded. I did not feel pacified, but I sat down and waited while channel surfing. The televised celebrations all over the globe did nothing to cheer me up; instead it fed my anxiety. Knowing how badly I wanted to attend the party, his blatant dismissal of our plans was starting to piss me off. To make it worse, he was obviously ignoring me.

"Stephan?" I asked again. Instead of answering, he pushed his chair away from the desk, but kept clicking his mouse. I waited with growing impatience.

"Okay, I am going," he finally stated, getting up from the computer. I watched as he retreated to the bedroom to grab a few things and head into the shower. My cell phone started vibrating across the coffee table, and I snatched it up before it hit the floor.

"*Are you coming?*" asked the message from Debbie.

"*We should be there shortly. Stephan's dragging his feet,*" I typed back.

"*You better hurry, there is a big surprise planned at midnight,*" was her response.

"*I will text you when we are on our way,*" I promised.

Stephan finally emerged at about 11 o'clock, showered, dressed and ready to go.

"Have you called a cab yet?" I demanded. Not knowing who to call, I left booking a cab in what I'd assumed were his capable hands.

"Doing that right now, babe," he replied. Grabbing the cordless phone, he punched in the number for the cab company. Based on his end of the conversation, it was obvious we would not be getting a taxi any time soon. When he got off the phone, this was confirmed.

"Well, I have some bad news; we have about a two hour wait," he told me after he hung up. My disappointment welled immediately.

"In other words, we are not going?" I questioned. Mentally, I was cursing like a sailor, but I kept my mouth shut.

"No, we can still go, but we will be late," he retorted. He actually sounded annoyed that I was disappointed.

"Look at the time, if we leave when the cab comes it will be 2 o'clock in the morning. By then everyone will have gone home. We can take my car," I suggested. "It's only a ten minute drive."

"I don't want us driving. The police will be out in full force, and if we get stopped, you could lose your license," he answered back. This much is certainly true. On New Year's Eve there would be check stops set up and I did not want to take the chance.

"Then I suppose I should put on something more comfortable. There is no point in going now if we have to wait that long for a cab.

The point of going out for New Years Eve is to be someplace special or being with someone special at the stroke of midnight, not two hours later," I confessed. With that said, I went into his room and changed out of my clothes, fighting hot tears of disappointment. I would not let him see me cry.

I quickly texted Debbie, telling her plans had changed. She was pretty pissed at me.

"You're going to let him keep you at home? He better have something special planned," came her texted response. *"Well, have fun. Really wish you were here with us. By the way, Stacy got engaged! Isn't that amazing? Garry got down on one knee in the middle of the dance floor and proposed."*

"I guess that was the surprise everyone was buzzing about," I responded, full of disappointment and resentment. That sucked. I can't believe I missed another Fish Pond engagement.

Returning to the living room, I reclaimed my position on the couch. Stephan was back on the computer playing his game. I wound up spending the next few hours sulking and watching international festivities on television while he completely ignored me. Needless to say I was quite hurt. *Why invite me over, if he's going to ignore me? Why was I still sitting here, letting this happen?* A million questions ran through my head, but I did not open my mouth. Nor did I leave.

A few days later, he left for England. The original plan was for him to travel back before Christmas, but surgery delayed the trip. Knowing how much he missed Michael, I was glad he went, even though I missed him like crazy.

During those two weeks, I did a lot of thinking and reflected over the last six months of our relationship. It hit me that while we claimed to have a no strings attached relationship; I was falling for him, despite my attempts to deny that fact. As the day came closer that he would return, I grew more confident in my heart and I couldn't wait to share my exciting news.

However, things were noticeably different when he came back. I collected him from the airport late Friday evening then spent the entire weekend at his place. For the most part, everything was normal, but there was a chill when crawled into bed together at night. The man who at one point could not keep his hands off me, suddenly seemed reluctant to demonstrate any physical affection. Chalking it up as jet lag, I left it alone. We spent two consecutive nights sleeping in the same bed, but we did not make love until the final night.

"What's going on?" I tentatively asked, as we lay in each other's arms sharing a post-romp cigarette.

In a half asleep sex satiated state, he told me he'd been thinking about us during his trip.

"After this job is done, I'm thinking of moving back to England, I don't want to get tied down before I leave," he continued. I was floored. Talk about having a bombshell dropped. My brain scattered as I tried to digest his words. However, if I wanted, he suggested that we remain "friends with benefits'" until he went away. Then he rolled over and fell asleep almost immediately.

I was shattered emotionally. Here I was, planning to lay it on the line and bear my heart to him and it killed me to hear his words. I was tense and anxious and could not sleep. Suddenly claustrophobic, I had to flee. I stealthily grabbed my clothing and slipped out of his apartment in the middle of the night. I had never walked out on a man before, but something was not right. Something had happened since his surgery and he was not being completely honest with me.

When I got home, I sent him an email, explained why I walked out of his apartment in the middle of the night. Maybe he was right. Maybe we should call it off before we get in deeper.

"Dear Stephan: I am sorry for taking off before you woke up. I wasn't doing much sleeping, and I really needed to get out of there. I had a feeling that you would be coming back with a very heavy heart. I also knew, that you were considering staying in England, or returning as soon as you could.

You mentioned that you did not want to make promises that you could not keep; I have never asked for any promises - I don't want promises because they always get broken. However, what I want - is the chance to cherish every moment I have with you - short term or long term - I don't expect a marriage or anything like that - I just want to live! To me, any time we spend together is not wasted time - and who knows - I have never been to England. I could build my cottage in the bush. You know Stephan - you can have it all - the kid, the job, the girl - you just have to want it, then reach out and grab it. I will talk to you soon, hugs Emma"

I received his response via email a few hours later.

"I wanted to write this, because you disappeared so quickly after my last comment that you never gave me a chance to get it straight. You know full well, that when I'm talking, sometimes I get carried away, and the things I say don't

exactly come out sounding the way they were supposed to. I can't find any words that make sense. It's too hard trying to find words with a lump in my throat. I do, however, understand why you don't want to see me. The words, "I'm sorry" just don't seem to cut it, Stephan.

Instead of responding I filed the email away without further thought. At the moment all I could think about was that I needed to get my head on straight. I was starting to fall for Stephan, and if he was leaving, it would be a waste. While I cared about him, following him to another country was not something I was prepared to do. Especially if he didn't want to be with me.

CHAPTER THIRTEEN

Stephan and I entered a brief cooling off period. Part of this was made easy thanks to a phone call from Hannah. Senator Connelly's trial was in a few days, and she wanted me to show up for moral support. I left Stephan a quick note that I'd be out of town for a few days and left.

"Don't know if you'll get this before you leave or not, but just wanted to say Good Luck. I'll be thinking about you, and hoping for the best. Have a great day, and I'll speak to you later, gorgeous." read his message. So much for cooling off.

When I got to Baudette, Hannah was a mess. Understandably so, too. Things had really heated up after I went home. She failed to fill me in until I was sitting across her the day before the trial. She was convinced her ex was stalking her. Due to his political position, he was quickly released on bail pending trial. Hannah was hiding in a safe house. After three months, she was forced to leave the woman's shelter.

Her counsellor helped find her a condo in a gated community. As it was, Hannah worried she's been found. A black pickup truck was often spotted parked a block from the gate. She was convinced it was George.

With the trial pending, Hannah had also pushed for the divorce. I soon learned proceedings hit a brick wall when it came to splitting the property. . By the time, I got back to town she was exhausted, scared and frustrated.

Chief Alexander encouraged me to come for the trial. Hannah wanted me at her side. While she was in town, he kept her under protective custody swooped in like a mother hen. Hannah was happy to see me. The day after I arrived, the trial started. I held her hand while we sat in the audience. It was quickly obvious why she wanted me beside her. She'd lost weight and managed to hide her growing middle, but she wasn't taking any chances. I deliberately kept between her and George's line of vision.

George sat defiantly and smug in the accused box along the left side of the courtroom. Whenever I looked up, I found him staring coldly in our direction. If looks could kill both Hannah and I would be a pile of ash on the floor. I despised him on sight.

There was no jury, only the judge, lawyers and defendant. Throughout the trial, George maintained his innocence. He claimed an unknown attacker wanted to see him dead and had threatened to kill him. However, when asked for evidence by the Crown, he failed to provide any proof. Several witnesses came forward and testified to overhearing George threaten to destroy the family home. Anything to keep his wife from claiming the property, they testified.

Even his best friend spoke out against him. Telling the judge how he'd changed and was consumed with hatred towards Hannah. George did not like to lose, he said. Several other witnesses agreed.

With the combined police evidence and witness testimony, the Senator was found guilty and sentenced to six months house arrest monitored with an ankle bracelet. He was also prohibited from possessing weapons. Hannah burst into silent sobs when the sentence was read. She'd thought her nightmare was over, but instead she was only getting a brief holiday. She had six months to work out what to do with her life. It was not just her anymore either. She had that baby to think about. I hurt for her.

After the judge read his sentence, I glanced over at George to gauge his reaction. He was staring hard in our direction. I gasped, recognizing the seething hatred in his soulless black eyes. He smirked at my obvious discomfort at being caught looking at him. I shuddered involuntarily. Hannah is absolutely right. There was something dangerous about this man. After sentencing, we fled the courtroom and I took Hannah home. She refused to speak the entire trip and went straight to bed when we got back to the condo.

I stayed another week, to make sure Hannah was okay. During that time I accompanied her to doctors and lawyer appointments. My once robust friend was now fragile and a shadow of her former self. I was worried about her and the pregnancy. After years of trying to get pregnant, she did not want to harm the baby. Even though keeping George from his child would surely send him over the edge, she was determined to keep it a secret. I was at a loss for how to help. Other than being a willing ear, there was little I could do.

Once the news hit that Connelly was convicted, the Prime Minister put out another press release. He was formally relieved of duties and kicked from the Senate. Dismissed and disgraced, George Connelly had hit rock bottom; he'd officially lost everything.

Meanwhile, Stephan was messaging me like crazy. When the story hit the national media, I was seen leaving the courthouse with Hannah in tow. The media painted a very different picture. Headings such as *Psychopathic Senator Gets Away with Attempted Murder* appeared on the front page of most newspapers. Not knowing the whole story, it was obvious he was worried.

"You know I worry about you, I certainly don't want you to think that you have to do absolutely everything alone, because I'm still here, and I'm not going anywhere," read one of his notes.

Despite his numerous attempts, I kept him at arm's length. It was difficult to allow him back into my world, when I'd made such a fool of myself. Deliberately ignoring my broken heart, I kept busy. Thanks to Debbie, joining the Pond had opened a doorway into a new chapter of life. After the trial, I threw myself into my social life. For once, I enjoyed myself instead of disconnecting from the world and hiding behind a computer screen. With Stephan out of the picture, there was no reason why I shouldn't try to move on.

I also had time to finish my magazine article. Using my personal experiences as research I completed my piece on online dating for *Exposed*. Much to everyone's surprise, the article was a hit. When the story hit the streets *TheFishPond*'s local membership increased by a few thousand local singles within a matter of days. For a city with a population of around 600,000 this was significant. People started emailing the magazine looking recommendations on what sites to join and tips to ensure success.

I even volunteered to help organise some of the weekly events. Local members of the Pond had many chances to meet other singles. We believed the internet was a great place to connect, but the real success came from meeting face to face. Monday's was pool night and on Wednesday's, we met for wings and beer. One of our favourite activities was meeting on Friday nights for drinks on the River Walk patio before heading to Wild Side for an evening of dancing. This was usually attended by at least fifty singles from all walks of life.

It was at one of these events that Stephan and I ended up back together. There was a party Friday night and rumour had it he was going to be there. As soon as Debbie told me, I decided I would show him that I had moved on.

When Friday night rolled around, I got ready with painstaking attention for detail. Since I needed a haircut, I got an appointment and updated my highlights. Taking an extra hour, I also got a manicure and pedicure. Finally, I headed to my favourite boutique and picked up a little black dress. I was not just dressing to impress; this evening, I was dressing for Stephan. I wanted him to see me as a woman, and as a potential lover. I wanted him to acknowledge that while I was more comfortable in denims and a T-shirt, I also looked amazing in a form fitting dress that left enough to the imagination. Spotting my reflection in the mirror, I stopped to do a little spin. The sweetheart neckline of the dress accentuated my full bust. With my hair soft-layered around my face, I looked feminine, and very sexy.

Satisfied, I headed to the club. Arriving early I headed to the bar and ordered a glass of Chablis. A light tapping on my shoulder distracted me from reaching for my glass. Spinning on my heel, I stopped. My bewildered eyes connected with sapphire blue, crowned by the longest lashes, my gaze traced his cheek to the trails of blonde curls framing his square jaw. His dimples deepened with his smile.

"I thought you were expecting me?" Stephan laughed at my startled reaction.

"I was, but I didn't think you would sneak up on me like that," I laughed, giving him a warm welcoming hug. His towering stature made me feel feminine and tiny. I blushed, surprised at the direction my thoughts were heading. Total erotic submission at his hands oddly appealed to me. I shook myself mentally. His thick muscles bulged as he reached for my beer.

"Let me help you with that," he palmed my drink, before I could react. Smiling, I turned away trying to crush the soft tingling between my thighs. Suddenly warm, I subconsciously fanned myself.

"You okay?" He asked.

Nodding, I pushed away from the bar, and started walking across the room. He followed closely as we searched for a secluded area to sit down. Finally finding a vacant table in a corner, we took our seats. From our vantage we could see everyone in the room, and watch the dancers.

"Care to dance?" Before I could reply, he took my hand and dragged me across the room. Giggling, I stumbled onto the floor after him. "You ready?"

"If I step on your toes, I apologize ahead of time," I laughed. The serious look on his face told me this would not be a normal waltz. Boy was I right. With a commanding gesture, he swept me into his arms; holding me tight for a few seconds. Then slowly and deliberately he began guiding me across the floor with expert ease. His right palm planted in the small of my back held me firmly against his torso.

"Did you have a safe trip?" I asked, trying to ignore my surprising reaction to his nearness. Swaying slowly in his arms, I inhaled deeply of his scent; an intoxicating mix of sweat, aftershave and a touch of cigarette tobacco. He smelled delicious to me and each whiff teased my senses. Something had taken place in the past few weeks, something I'd been oblivious to until he was standing next to me. For the first time in five years, since ending my marriage, I wanted to be with someone and it frightened me!

"Yes, I did; but I am glad to be home now," he said, before sweeping me into another wide spin. I gasped when he pulled me tight again. My heart raced at how effortless it was to follow his lead. Pressed flush against his firm torso, I could picture this man doing all sorts of delightful things to me. I could also imagine loving every moment. Moving in unison, I was blatantly aware of how his actions teased my senses. I needed fresh air before I embarrassed myself.

When the dance was ended, I headed outside for a cigarette. He followed closely behind.

"I missed you," he stated once we were outside and could hear ourselves speak.

"I missed you too." I shamefully admitted. I realized the truth. I had secretly counted the days until his return.

Weaving through the crowd of smokers gathered outside the door we headed round the corner. Needing a moment to catch my breath, I leaned against the wall and closed my eyes. He accepted it as an invitation and leaned in to take me into his arms. He wrapped me in his embrace and held me close. His breath teased the base of my neck, making me shiver.

"I've wanted to touch you since I spotted you earlier," he murmured huskily against my throat. I did not push him away. Instead my arms locked behind his back; ensuring he could not pull away. Encouraged, the tip of his tongue soon replaced his heated breath as he teased my throat. "Then why are we doing this?"

"Doing what?" I muttered back. I snuggled closer into his arms.

"Why are we denying that we want to be together? Listen, I screwed up. I just got scared. Things have been moving so fast lately. One minute I was single and miserable. The next minute I meet this amazing woman that makes me want to stop, and reconnect with the world. It's been a long time since I've felt this way, and it frightens me. But Emma, I want you to give me a chance."

My brunette hair draped over his arm, teasing him, and he buried his face in the tresses and inhaled deeply. Hearing him inhale stirred me. There was the beginning of tingling in my deepest recesses and my face burned with my arousal.

"You like this?" His deep voice rumbling against the lobe of my ear. His head lowered until I felt a light nip at the base of my throat. My world tilted, and I would have fallen if he hadn't been holding me up. Using his body to balance me, Stephan held me against the wall. We stood pressed together for a few moments, until my quaking reached a higher level.

"We need to go back to my place, now," he finally stammered. In full agreement, I let him hold my hand and lead me to his truck.

Back at his apartment, I was barely through the door when I was pressed firmly against the wall. Stephan's lips ravaged mine with desperate need. I melted into his waiting arms, as his mouth pillaged my face, then my neck and throat.

A deep groan escaped my parted lips when he bared my shoulders. Shaking with need, I allowed him to feed on my exposed flesh. Instinctively, my hands found his hair, grasping, tight as his lips blazed a trail across my heaving chest. He slowly unbuttoned me until full breasts bounced free of their silken traps. His hot tongue teased my aching mounds, flicking them lightly before encasing them within the scorching heat of his mouth. I would have collapsed if he hadn't been holding onto me so firmly.

Just when I couldn't stand his assault a second longer, he stood up. My breath came in soft pants, echoing loudly in the room. His eyes darkened as his mouth eagerly sought mine. His fingertips trailed my succulent thighs, reveling in the softness of my skin. His kiss swallowed my squeak of surprise as he suddenly hoisted into the air. My legs wrapped instinctively around his waist as he proceeded to carry me towards the bed.

"Please tell me you want me as much I want you," he whispered against my panting lips. I forced my eyes open to meet his intent gaze. My throat had suddenly forgotten how to work. His fingers still worked their magic, which made concentrating nearly impossible. Afraid to admit the truth with words, I answered the only way I knew. I let my body do the talking.

"So, now what?" Stephan asked, getting a spot on the couch beside me. We'd spent the rest of the night and following day cuddling in bed until finally dragging ourselves into the living room to enjoy a fresh coffee together. No longer naked and basking in the afterglow of our intense lovemaking, it was time to discuss the ramifications of what happened between us.

"What do you mean, now what?" I demanded.

"Well, I didn't exactly imagine that we would fall into bed like this," he began. "But now that we have, we need to talk about it."

"What is there to discuss? We are two adults, with needs." I volunteered. "There is no need to complicate things."

"I don't want to complicate things, but I want this to be a regular thing," he continued. *A regular thing?* I didn't know if I should be flattered or insulted. "What I'm trying to say is that I think that we should continue seeing each other. I want to find out where this will lead. I don't want this to be a one time thing."

"Well, you know I enjoy your company; and we are obviously compatible in other areas," I concurred. "I have no trouble giving this a chance if you want to."

"I do want to. As long as you understand that, I am out of town a lot. That won't change until some of these jobs we have are done. But when I am here, it's just you and me," he assured.

As far as I was concerned, once I opened up my mind and let Stephan in, things were exciting. For the most part we were compatible. We enjoyed many of the same things, music, comedy, and even cried watching the same movies. He was precocious, energetic and a delightful companion. His stories were animated and he made me laugh. As far as I could see, life was fabulous; Stephan was amazing.

Even Debbie was happy for me. Even though we had spent little time together in the past several months. Feeling guilty, I invited her over one afternoon for a dip in the lake. Slathered with oil, we baked our bronze bodies on the beach, our sangria glasses buried stem deep in the sand.

"You seem to have really blossomed. Stephan has been good for you," she marvelled, as she settled down on the blanket spread in the grass. "Is he good to you?"

"For the most part. He is attentive and sweet. He's also very handy around here," I confided. This much was true. Whenever Stephan came to the house, he puttered around and took care of things. A broken window, a plugged hose. He cut my grass. Having a man around was definitely something I could get used to.

"So when is he moving in?" Debbie chuckled.

"We've been talking about it, but he has a lease. I think it expires in two months," I admitted. "He hasn't really told me yet."

"If he's smart he would get rid of his apartment as soon as he can. No one likes living in the city and you have such a beautiful spot here," Debbie waved her arm around in emphasis. "He would be nuts to say no to living here."

"He definitely enjoys it here. It's the only time he seems to slow down. At his place, his phone is always ringing or he's on the computer. Sometimes, I feel invisible," I admitted. Debbie looked at me with mild surprise.

"Really? What does he do?" she looked puzzled. "How's the sex?"

Debbie laughed at my indignant snort. I should have known - no topic was off limits.

"The sex was - is wonderful," I quickly corrected myself, but I wasn't quick enough. Debbie caught it easily.

"Was?" Debbie perked up instantly. If she sensed relationship trouble, she was the first to butt in and try to repair it.

"For the most part, it's amazing," I shared. "Sometimes, I can't help but wonder though."

"Wonder about what?" Debbie leaned over on one elbow, offering her undivided attention.

"It's hard to put a finger on it. When we make love, he's absolutely amazing and he rocks my world. Then other times, it's like he can't be bothered," I blushed. Debbie knew I was not an insecure woman when it came to the bedroom. I loved sex, and the more practice I got, the better. For me, lovemaking was an art form and I gave my all.

"The other day, I got all dressed up and stood in front of him. He never looked up," I chuckled nervously. "I was wearing that cute little black number we bought together. I even put on thigh highs. I stood there for five minutes, until I finally gave up and went back into the room. It hurt my feelings."

"Did you tell him you were upset?" Debbie wondered.

"No. I figured my going to the room and changing into ugly pajama's would have given him the message," I laughed. I was desperately trying not to make it a big deal.

Debbie just smiled knowingly. I was immediately defensive and tried to assure my best friend of my genuine happiness. Then I realised that I shouldn't have bothered. She knew me better, and I could not lie. Instead, I gave voice to my concerns.

"I can't really explain it. Sometimes when I come into the room, he quickly closes his browser, or email. Other times he's texting. He tries to be discreet but it makes it look even more suspicious," I explained. "Maybe I am just being paranoid."

"You could be, but at the same time, I would pay more attention," Debbie suggested.

"Paying attention is one thing. I don't want to become one of those crazy suspicious girlfriends either," I admitted. Jealousy was new to me and I was not comfortable at all with it. Especially since I could not explain where it was coming from.

For the most part, Stephan was very attentive. Grant it, he was away a lot, but he made up for it is spades when he got home. He spoiled me rotten. Little surprises like roses and candy were common place. So was finding love notes and treats tucked away in my purse or briefcase. Text messages, emails, and greeting cards. There was never a moment when I was not aware that Stephan was thinking about me.

Everything seemed perfect.

Then, it suddenly wasn't.

CHAPTER FOURTEEN

The thing about betrayal is the impossibility to predict one's reaction until it actually happens. For years, my friends and I have pondered at one time or another what we would do if we'd been cheated on. There was no explanation or excuse that could make it okay. My first reaction, was swearing that I would simply kick the lying dog to the curb. It is exactly what I should have done! I didn't.

After discovering Stephan's active dating profile on AdultPlayBuddy, I grew determined to ascertain the extent of his sickening duplicity. While photos of him in a hotel room with two other women would be incriminating enough for most women, I was more interested in an explanation than actually analysing what I was seeing. It quickly became my secret obsession.

Unfortunately, Stephan was out of town at the time. I would have to wait until his return before any confrontations on the issue could come. But, patience was not my virtue, I could not wait a week. My overactive imagination started working overtime. My head pounded, threatening to burst forth with the volume of unanswered questions. I hovered between wanting to tear his eyes out, to wanting to hurt the women. Not knowing the full extent of his deception was driving me insane.

Fuelled by morbid curiosity, hurt and anger, I didn't worry about the consequences. I felt fully justified in taking whatever lengths I needed to expose the truth. If I had to, I would confront the women themselves. I felt that I was completely justified. We were talking about my life, my heart, and my sanity. This was not something I could just ignore and hope that it would disappear.

My investigative instincts kicked in and I did what came naturally; I went snooping. Even though I'd created a profile on the website, as a limited member I could not view the profiles of other members. While I couldn't see individual profiles, I could participate in other things, including the regional community chat rooms and talk "live" to other users. I logged on.

Any thoughts of sneaking into the chat room were gone within seconds. It may be a virtual world, but live updates clearly showed when new chatters joined the conversation or 'entered the room'. As a first timer, I was spotted fairly quickly. Within minutes of logging in, I received several private messages. Private messages caught user's attention by popping up in a corner of the screen. These messages were only visible to the sender and me. I ignored each one and silently watched over the room for a time.

As an observer, it did not take me long to figure out the chatroom action. Within half an hour, I quickly discovered that most of the men were looking for quick, meaningless sex. The balance of power lay in the women's hands as many of them played games the men seemed oblivious to. There was a sad desperation to the public interactions I witnessed. It became apparent that it was not all talk. A few married women were online bragging about their affairs. There was talk about meetings at bars, or private homes for orgies, threesomes and swinger's parties. The underlying implication made me sick to my stomach. Nothing seemed taboo to this group!

While watching people come and go, I continued to observe the room, looking for familiar names or faces. Each profile had a thumbnail sized photo attached. Most were shots of breasts or genitals but there was the odd face shot. I kept Stephen's public friend's list open in one browser so I could cross-reference it with the group in the chat room. Soon I was able to ascertain which members actually met other people and which ones were merely talking. It still wasn't enough. I knew there was more to discover and I was going to find it. I had to go into his secret accounts.

Searching his computer desk, I found a notepad tucked away in a corner. It looked harmless enough, but I was shaking by the time I flipped to the last page. I just got lucky. There, in Stephan's recognizable scrawl was a list of email addresses and accounts, along with websites and their corresponding passwords. He was definitely very organized. From this list, I found other accounts on several dating and 'instant sex' sites that he'd joined. I took very careful note of them. I would investigate them later in the privacy of my own living room.

Near the bottom of the list, I found what I was looking for - his APB login and password. I opened up a third browser and typed in the code. Holding my breath, I waited to see what would happen. My heart broke when his profile opened up before my very eyes. In seconds his entire Inbox was laid out before me. I never anticipated that it would be that easy. I stared blankly at the page while I tried to decide what to do next. It was one thing to want to snoop on someone and a very different thing when you actually do it. But in this case, I still felt justified. If Stephan was cheating on me, I needed to know both for my own sanity and safety. If he was meeting with other women, he could also be carrying a number of sexually transmitted diseases. For my own protection, I needed to know if I should be worried.

Stalling the eventuality of actually opening and reading his private Inbox messages, I took note of certain details on his profile. It stated that he was unmarried and had been created the account six years ago, long before we met. While that made sense, his last login showed he'd checked his messages within the last twenty-four hours; while on his business trip. That was odd because he told me there was no internet access where he was staying, which is why he didn't message me. Either way, it was obviously an active profile.

Then I noticed that he was a gold-member. According to the Signup page, gold-memberships were only available with a paid twelve month membership. Based on the renewal date, he'd renewed his membership only three months earlier. *It was not an accident or an oversight.* He could not tell me that he'd created the account and forgotten to delete it. I took a few screenshots for my records.

With each damning piece of evidence, my determination to expose his secrets escalated. Finally, I focused my attention on his Inbox. There were over two hundred messages, all read and mostly with replies. A few were casual in their response; "Hi, how are you?" messages. There was also a few extensive conversations between other women and a few couples.

This is how I discovered a woman with the username Jelly Bean. She was the woman in the incriminating photos. From what I could understand, they'd been talking for almost six months. He started the exchange by adding her to his friends list because he liked jelly beans. Apparently it worked. Based on her "Thank you for the photo and great body" response, he had responded by sending her a picture of himself.

There were a few more casual friendly notes between the pair, but there were also damning information. She thanked him for inviting her over for dinner. *When did he have time to do that?* She also told him how much she appreciated that he'd come to the door wearing nothing but a cowboy hat and a towel. That one hurt. I'd suggested stuff like that all the time, but he always made me feel like it was a stupid request. "I don't do role play" was his constant response.

The last message she sent rocked me to the core.

"Thank you for the wonderful morning. I am so glad that I got a chance to see you before you went on your trip. Sorry that your girlfriend couldn't drive you to the airport, but I am glad that I was able to be of service. It made me sad to see you get on the plane, but I knew it would be okay because you would be home in a few days. If you need a ride when you get home, don't hesitate to call me. I'll be waiting for your phone call. Hope you had a safe trip home. J"

I could not believe what I was reading. SHE was his ride to the airport? I was completely and utterly disgusted.

I remember vividly every detail of that day. Stephan was heading to Toronto for a few weeks on a business trip. The night before he left, the weatherman predicted an Alberta Clipper was heading our way. While I wanted to stay and spend one more night in the city with Stephan before he left, Belle needed attention. If there was a chance the power could go out, I didn't want her to freeze to death due to my carelessness.

As promised, we got nailed with a severe blizzard overnight. I awoke to find my car and driveway buried under a massive snow drift. I wasn't too concerned at first. Stephan's flight was scheduled to depart at 6 o'clock in the evening so I had plenty of time to dig out my car. What I didn't anticipate was that it would take all day. I spent all afternoon labouring under the heavy wet snow until I finally got both my car and the driveway clear. Once finished, I had two hours to get to the city, pick up Stephan and drive him to the airport.

Then I couldn't get my car started! Running into my shop, I grabbed the charger and connected the cables to the battery posts. Satisfied the battery was charging I dashed into the house to call Stephan to let him know what was going on.

"Hey babe," he said when he finally answered. The phone rang four times before it was picked up his end. I assumed he was packing.

"Hi Stephan," I panted into the mouthpiece. I was still out of breath from dashing around the yard.

"Are you okay?" he inquired. "It sounds like you've been running."

"Yeah, I am just having problems. I finally got the driveway clear, but now the car won't start." I said, fighting back tears of frustration. "I have the battery charger on it now, but it will take at least twenty minutes to charge up enough to turn over."

"That's okay, we still have some time. I am all packed up and ready to go," his calm voice sounded reassuring and I found myself growing less frantic.

"I am trying to get there as soon as I can," My voice cracked. "I genuinely want to see you off."

"I will be back in a few weeks," he laughed. "Don't cry; it's not that big of a deal."

"I know, but I want to send you off with a kiss." I said, feeling crestfallen. It may not have been a big deal for him, but I really wanted to be the one to put him on the plane; to kiss him goodbye and wish him a wondrous adventure. I was frantic in my determination to get to the City and see him off.

"No problem, do what you have to do and call me when you're on your way." He suggested. "Relax, it will be fine."

"I will do that." I hung up and went back outside. Unfortunately, my car had other plans. Despite my numerous attempts, I could not get it going. Eventually I reasoned that my battery must have frozen overnight. I hated to admit it, but I was stuck at home until I could get a replacement.

Reluctantly, I went back into the house and delivered the disappointing news to Stephan.

"I am so sorry, but I won't be able to take you to the airport," I told him once he picked up the phone. This time I lost control and burst into tears with disappointment.

"It's okay baby; I still have time to call a cab. I have to run, but I will see you when I get home. Love you." And then he was gone.

After he hung up, I collapsed on the sofa and sobbed. I felt like I had broken a promise. Even though he made it sound like a minor glitch, to me it was more. I wanted to be the woman that was always there for her man, who made promises and never broke them; who never left her man disappointed or wanting in any way.

Reading the incriminating emails between them, I could see Stephan already had a backup plan. I was crushed as the implications flowed over me. While I was heartbroken and devastated because I couldn't keep my promise, he had picked up the phone and found a replacement.

Thinking back to when I picked him up from the airport later on that particular trip, I was oblivious to any changes within our relationship. I was a typical love-struck female, waiting for my man to return from a trip. Breathless and excited as a teenager. As a matter of fact, everything seemed wonderful!

My hair was done, I dressed up to please Stephan and I was excited to feel his arms around me again. Three weeks seemed like an eternity. I was waiting eagerly at the bottom of the stairs when Stephan's plane arrived. Our eyes never parted as he descended the escalator and when he reached the bottom I ran into his arms. He dropped his carry-on and wrapped his arms round me.

"Welcome home," I was bursting with excitement.

"Hey baby, you look beautiful; you smell good too," he hugged me back. He looked worn out from the eight hour flight, but thrilled to see me. He squeezed me tighter when I tried to pull away.

"How was your trip?"

"Uneventful," he said, pulling out of my arms. "How was your week?"

"Too long; I was counting the days until you came home," I admitted.

"Well, I am home now; let's grab my bags and get out of here." He took my hand and we headed to the baggage carousel. He didn't let go until the luggage came around on the conveyer belt. Reaching out, he grabbed them and loaded them onto the waiting cart.

"Shall we get out of here? I can't wait to get home and take a hot shower. Then I plan to curl up on the couch with you," he grinned mischievously.

"Sounds like a plan," I laughed. Privately, I was looking forward to a relaxing weekend together as well. I even made arrangements for Belle with my neighbour before leaving for the airport. I want no spoilers, no interruptions.

When we got back to his apartment, I watched him unpack and started preparations for his welcome home dinner. While he took a shower, and supper cooked I tidied up his apartment. As I gathered his paperwork into an orderly pile on his desk, a yellow package caught my eye. I knew what it was immediately. It's an unopened condom. Dumbfounded, I picked it up and turned it over in my hand. I was totally confused. We'd stopped using condoms months ago. *Maybe he removed it while cleaning out his shaving kit before his trip?* I reassured myself. I was not going to go off half cocked over a stray rubber. Hearing the bathroom door open, I tossed the packet back onto the desk and gave the paperwork a quick adjustment.

"Dinner almost ready?" Stephan asked as he stepped out of the bathroom. Trying not to appear guilty of spying, I rushed over. The sight of his dripping body wrapped in a towel made my mouth water. When he wrapped his arms around me and leaned in for a kiss, I forgot about the condom.

After his shower we dined on sweet-and-sour pork chops, thinly sliced roasted almonds and carrots on a bed of wild rice. I even made New York style cheesecake for desert. The night was topped off with wine, strawberries and whipped cream, shared sensually by candlelight. It was the beginning of a wonderful 'welcome home' weekend.

Two days later, I went back to my place satisfied and happy.

Now, looking through his email, I noticed that after I went home Monday morning, Jellybean was invited over that same afternoon. Based on the email interaction, they'd made love in the same bed, we had shared together all weekend. It was not the first time, nor would it be the last.

CHAPTER FIFTEEN

It is kind of sad how we fail to see what is obvious until it is too late. Little signs that should have raised alarm bells in one's head. I let these all slip past unnoticed or ignored. Once I started digging into Stephan's activities a web of lies and betrayal surfaced. Some red flags I caught on to at the time and discounted, while others remained hidden except in hindsight.

There was the one night Stephan and I were settled in his apartment for an evening of pizzas and movies. When the pizza deliveryman arrived, I answered the door.

"Hey, how are you?" asked the delivery man.

"I am great, and you?" I responded, taking the debit machine from his hand. I punched in my password and we waited for the transaction to complete.

"I see that you have your cast off," he offered while we waited.

"My cast?" I asked in confusion. I had no clue what he was talking about. I hadn't had a cast on any part of my body in at least a decade.

"Last time when I was here, you answered the door with a cast on your leg," he continued with a puzzled expression. He was obviously convinced I was someone else, yet it made no sense to me. "If I recall correctly, you had a horse step on it."

"You must be mistaken." I responded. The debit machine beeped on my hand. Satisfied that the transaction was complete, I handed him back the machine.

"Maybe, it was someone else," he conceded. "Have a great night."

Dumbfounded, I shut the door behind him and headed back into the living room.

"That was odd!" I said, putting the pizza onto the coffee table and heading into the kitchen for napkins.

"What's that?" Stephan asked with mild curiosity.

"The pizza man must have thought I was someone else; he asked me about my broken leg." I continued while laying out plates and cups for pop.

Stephan stopped channel surfing, and for the briefest of seconds he looked guilty.

"He must have been talking about my neighbour; she had a broken leg a few weeks ago. It's not a surprise that he'd make a mistake. I am sure he does lots of deliveries to this building." Stephan offered before returning to clearing off the remainder of the coffee table.

It made sense, and I forgot about it.

While searching through his many emails during my investigation later, I found an email where Jellybean complained about how itchy her cast was. Turns out she wiped out and broke her ankle the racetrack where she worked as a groomer. She was off work for six weeks and bored as hell. That's when they had started to hook up.

"Could I come over for some loving?" she asked Stephan in an email message.

"Sure, I am sure we can figure out ways around the cast," was his response.

Based on her response the next day, they'd apparently figured out a way around the cast.

"Thank you for rocking my world; see you in a few days," was her message. I couldn't see his answer.

There was also the time I visited after one of his other trips. He floored me with the suggestion of bringing someone else into the bedroom. We'd been having a few drinks in the living room when he broached the subject.

"Remember that conversation we had once about you wanting to be with another woman?" He asked while we were curled up on the couch watching a movie.

"Yes." I hesitated, unsure of where this conversation was going. While I was notoriously heterosexual, during an evening of cribbage and drinking I had admitted to being curious about being with another woman sexually.

"I've found a friend who I've been talking to. She knows you and would love to have a threesome with us," he suggested. My head whipped up to look at him in surprise. This was not a conversation I expected. I could tell he was choosing his words carefully.

"Oh? Who did you have in mind?" I demanded. I was both curious and anxious. Suddenly I was terrified that this was going to be one of those conversations where the guy is going to give an ultimatum. Either have a threesome or we are done.

"Jade," his reply cuts into my frantic thoughts.

"You've been talking to Jade?" I was surprised. Jade and I had known each other for a few years. I considered her a good friend. We even successfully planned and hosted a major TFP Christmas event together. Over two hundred people from the dating site attended and it was a blast. The event packed WildSide. After that night, people were calling saying that we were the best hostesses ever! At no point did she mention she was talking to Stephan behind my back.

"Yea, she added me as a friend after the last pool tournament," Stephan admitted. "We were talking the other night in chat and she brought up the subject."

I was a little surprised that the topic of a threesome would come up in casual conversation. I didn't call him on it, though. While we were exclusive, we were also very open about certain things, so it made sense to me that this conversation would come up at some point.

"What did she say?" I demanded.

"That she thinks you are beautiful and if you are still looking for a first, she would love to be it," he offered. The casual manner he broached the subject reflected that he'd given this some thought before bringing it up.

My eyes narrowed. In all honesty, I was curious, but not that curious. I liked Jade, but I did not find her attractive sexually. She was not my type, not that I knew what my type of woman I preferred. Honestly, I never gave it much thought. I'd also knew several other men who'd found themselves in her bed, so I knew she got around. Not my idea of a good time. I have a little more class than that.

"Thanks, I appreciate the invitation, but I am not interested. If I decide to swing that way, I would prefer to take my own partner," I replied with irritation. "Besides, I don't sleep with friends."

"You slept with me," he laughed.

"This is, different; you're more than a friend!" I exclaimed in exasperation.

"Oh?" he looked at me intently. His eyes darkened as he explored my face for hidden meaning. I busied myself with pretended to straighten up the coffee table.

"Yeah, I could fall in love with you." I admitted. My eyes dropped in sudden shame, suddenly I regretted opening my big mouth. My heart had been hovering for months, and the more time we spent together the more I realized I really cared for him.

He sprang up from the couch, nearly knocking over the coffee table in the process.

"What do you mean?" he demanded. He sounded almost angry with me. He might as well have slapped me. I was quite taken aback by his hostile reaction.

"Never mind, I said too much," I responded. Taking the coward's route, I bailed on the conversation. Instead of following up on the topic, he shrugged and exited the room. By the time he returned from the bathroom half an hour later, my attention was back on the television and we went back to watch the movie as if nothing happened. Our earlier conversation was soon forgotten. Or at least pushed to the back burner for the time being.

A few months later, I discovered the truth while he was on another trip. This time he'd returned to England for his son's high school graduation. I promised him I would take care of the apartment while he was gone, and do bookkeeping for him in his absence. My work done for the day, I went to close out the accounting program when I found some deleted conversations in his Recycle Bin. Opening them up, I found a conversation between him and Jade. It didn't take me long to realise that there was more than chatting going on between the pair.

Instead of waiting when he returned, I decided to confront the source.

"*Hey Jade, how's your grandchild,*" I messaged her later that afternoon on MSN. Her daughter had recently given birth to a little boy and she was always online bragging about him. It was a safe way to start the conversation.

"*He's doing great! How are you?*" was her response.

"*I am going great! Stephan and I are together now and things are going great,*" I typed back. There was no point in beating around the bush.

"*You and Stephan are together? I didn't know that - congratulations,*" she responded after a pregnant pause.

"*Thank you!*" I sent back. Unsure of how to proceed, I decided to go for it. "*Can I ask you a question?*"

"*Sure,*" came her quick reply.

"How well do you know Stephan?" I demanded.

"*We've been talking for a while, but I did not know you were seeing each other,*" she replied.

"*Yeah, we've been seeing each other secretly for a few months already. We are thinking about moving in together,*" I lied. We hadn't had that conversation yet, but she didn't need to know. It took her a few minutes to answer. I started to believe she had exited the conversation.

"That's great, I am very glad for you. *Stephan is a great guy,*" came her reply.

"*How well do you know him?*" I asked again. I was not going to give up easily. I needed to know the truth, whatever it was.

"*We went out a few times,*" she admitted.

"*What do you mean, how long have you seen each other?*" I paused, feeling brave because this was over the internet and not face to face.

"*Since before Valentine's Day,*" she typed back. "*We've gone for dinner, we went to a movie; that kind of stuff.*"

I was not sure what upset me more, the movie or Jade's mention of Valentine's Day. My memory of that night consisted of putting together a picnic basket of sushi, chocolates, strawberries and other treats. Stephan eagerly invited me over and we enjoyed a picnic by candlelight. Instead of the night ending in sweet seduction, Stephan claimed a sudden migraine and he sent me home early. I offered to stay but he insisted that a dark room and complete quiet would be his only solace. I drove home at the end of the evening, stunned and disappointed.

"*You went to see him Valentine's Day?*" I hated what I was typing. It made me sick to ask, but I had to know the truth.

"*Yes, it was a late night. I got off work at 11pm and went over after my shift,*" she admitted. Rereading her words, I wanted to vomit, but I was not going to give in. Now was not the time to start being a coward, I chided myself.

"*A movie?*" I forced myself to ask. Here too, I was able to predict the lie before she answered my question. Stephan and I had planned a few weeks earlier to see the new Nicolas Cage movie. When I invited him to go with me, he admitted to already seeing it. The movie was already in the theatre for a few weeks, but he'd not said a word about going to see it. He finally admitted he'd gone to see it with a friend, who remained nameless. I dropped the subject. Going to watch a movie with a buddy is not a big deal in my books. I never thought of pressing him for further information.

"*We went to see Ghost Rider,*" was her typed response. WHOA! Until that moment, this was simply a conversation. I was fishing, but not expecting to see anything. Now it looked like I had a live one.

"What else?" I demanded. My face flushed with heat, as betrayal seeped through my veins. My fingers trembled uncontrollably where they hovered over the keyboard while I impatiently waited for her answer.

"*We hooked up a few times,*" she admitted.

"Define hooked up," I pressed.

"*We slept together a few times; at his apartment, at the theatre,*" she continued.

"*You're kidding, right?*" I replied. At the theatre? While watching the movie we were supposed to go see together? I was starting to seethe. I felt like such a fool!

"*Unfortunately, I am not. If I'd known you were dating him, I would never have gone out with him. But he never said anything, nor did he stop my advances,*" she typed back. "*I am really sorry Emma. I do not sleep with other women's boyfriends or husbands, but he never said a word.*"

Unsure of how to go forward, I decided to withdraw from the conversation. I needed time to think about what I had just found out. I needed the time to process the details and come up with a plan of action. Once again, Stephan was out of town and I would have to wait. I needed time to think.

"*Thanks for being honest with me*," I finally typed back. "*I really appreciate it.*"

"No problem and for what it is worth, I truly am sorry. *I won't see or speak to him again,*" she promised.

"*That isn't necessary. He can speak to whomever he wants.*" I volunteered.

"What are you going to do now?" she demanded.

"*I am not sure,*" I admitted.

"Well, if you need any assistance, let me know. *I will do anything to make this right,*" she assured.

"*Thanks, I will keep that in mind,*" I replied. I had no intention of asking her for help. As far as I was concerned, she was no longer my friend either. Despite her protests, I knew she was lying. She knew damn well I was interested in Stephan. After all, we attended the many meet-and-greets together. It was indisputable that something was going on between us, even if we hadn't announced it to the world. I believed that it was wrong to flirt with men my friends were interested in. In my mind, friends should hold themselves to the same standard. It was evident that my "friend" Jade was not. Our friendship was over.

Now I had to deal with Stephan and his deception.

I picked up the phone and called Debbie.

"I don't know what to do," I bawled after spilling out the sorted story. Debbie had arrived within thirty minutes of my call. That's the one thing I loved about her. When I needed her, she dropped everything and came to the rescue. Sometimes I believed it was just to get away from home and her houseful of teenagers. Whatever her reasons, it felt good to know I could rely on her, no matter what. I also knew she would never betray me like Jade did. She abided by the same code of ethics I did - boyfriends, husbands, and even exes were off limits between friends. Suddenly I realized how valuable and precious real friends were in my life.

"What are you going to do?" she asked once I finished pouring out all the sorted details.

"I don't know! I love him," I admitted.

"I know you love him, but look what he's done. He's been online meeting women, he slept with one of your friends, and do you really need more proof?" Debbie asked. I knew that she was right.

"I deal with facts," was my indecisive response. My words sounded as weak as I felt. I was gutted. It was one thing to speculate, it was another to hear or in this case, read the words. Thank goodness I had a copy of the conversation or I'd think I dreamt the entire thing.

"What kind of facts do you need? Do you need to catch him in the act? You got pictures, you have a lover admitting she banged him," Debbie pressed. I could hear her rising frustration. "What more do you need?"

"I don't know!" I felt defeated. My mind was playing the "what-if" game. What if I'd been more adventurous - not that I had many boundaries; what if I was skinner - not that I was overweight. Mentally, I was tearing myself apart. Instead of being angry at the lying, cheating bastard, I called a boyfriend, I was finding unfounded flaws within myself.

"What you need is a few days away. Stephan won't be back from his son's graduation for another two weeks. This is a conversation that will have to wait, but you can't sit here and destroy yourself. YOU are not to blame." Debbie put her hand on mine. "EMMA - snap out of it. It's not your fault."

"What am I supposed to do until he gets back?" I numbly asked. As far as I knew, I had fourteen days to torture myself. Stephan was not in the habit of picking up the phone while on his trips. Emails, chat messages and text messages remained standard means of communication. This allowed for spontaneity; we could send a quick message and not worry about time zones and interruptions. It worked for us. But in this case, a face-to-face was required. I needed to see his eyes when I laid out what I knew.

"Here, take these," she rummaged through her purse, then gave me a set of keys. "I have a room here, on standby. I will let them know you are coming. Check in for a few days, enjoy the spa, the pool, or the hot tub. There is even a country bar across the street."

"You have a motel room on standby?" I asked. I knew better than to suspect foul play. Debbie was not one to cheat on her husband, of this, I was positive.

"A friend of mine owns the place and he said I could stay there whenever I want; with or without my husband," she laughed at my accusatory look. "No, I am not cheating on Ron. He knows all about this place. Sometimes his mother watches the kids and we go there and pretend that we just met and are having a one-night stand. Our baby was conceived there."

I laughed. I should have known there was more to the story. Trust Debbie to have a backup plan for those days when the kids were just too much. That was one thing I knew about Ron and Debbie. He only had eyes for her. It was obvious in the way his eyes light up when she comes in the room. I bet she was surrounded with a halo in his eyes, he was so infatuated. I wanted that experience.

"I don't know..." I began to protest, but Debbie cut me off.

"No excuses. I will make a quick call and the room will be yours for as long as you need it," she said, taking charge. She was already dialing a number on her cell phone. "Go toss some things together - I will even take Belle home with me. NO EXCUSES!"

She waved me out of the room. Conceding defeat, I headed to my bedroom and grabbed a few clothes, my bathing suit and some toiletries. When I returned to the living room, Debbie was smiling with satisfaction.

"A room has been set aside for you at the Canterbury Inn. It's yours for as long as you like. Relax, go out and enjoy yourself. If you get bored, give me a shout and I will come join you in the hot-tub," Debbie was so excited, you'd think she'd just booked me a vacation to Cuba. "Just make me a promise."

"What's that?" I hesitated. Maybe she is sending me to Cuba? Nothing would surprise me anymore.

"Have fun, relax and forget about Stephan at least for a few days," she implored. "You need to get your head together and think about this rationally. So far, I've been impressed. Most women would have already charged out and slashed his tires. But no, you are still discussing this like a sane person. There is hope for you and you will come through, shining on top. I am not going to tell you what to do, nor am I going to tell you to kick Stephan to the curb. It has to be your decision, on your time. You will know when and what is right. When it's done, it will be done! I trust you!"

"It won't be easy, but you have a deal. Thank you for being my best friend." I pulled her in for a hug. I knew she was probably right.

She always knew what was best for me, even when I was wandering around clueless.

"Somebody has to take care of you," she laughed, hugging me back. "You know I love you. Now go play. I will grab the dog and lock up."

"You sure about Belle?" I asked, shrugging into my jacket and shouldering my bag as I spoke.

"Don't worry about the dog! We will get along just fine, now GO before I kick your ass," I had no choice but to obey as she pushed me out the door.

CHAPTER SIXTEEN

"There is no way that you can make that shot!" a voice demanded from behind me.

I was just lining up my next shot – a two-ball combo off the rag into the corner pocket - when the deep male voice cut through my concentration. Frowning in annoyance, I straightened and palmed the cue.

"I am getting along just fine – but thank you for your concern," I retorted briskly, before turning to face the source of the annoying interruption. As recognition hit, my mouth dropped open and words failed. Anything I could have said was lost as I scrutinized the figure leaning lazily against the wall with a smug grin on his face. It pained me to admit that before me stood the most beautiful male to cross my path in several days. Dominic!

Of course, leaving my room helped. Thanks to Debbie, I'd checked in a day earlier. She was right. The inn was a quaint little hideaway tucked within a pine-tree infused haven about an hour outside of the city. Intimate, cosy and relaxed. The seclusion was perfect for couples running away from home for a day or weekend. But I was not part of a couple on this trip. Instead, of being part of a couple and frolicking as a twosome, I was hiding away and nursing my wounds. It was not easy admitting that I'd fallen for another jerk. After a day of feeling sorry for myself, stir craziness set in. I could only sulk for so long.

Tonight, the small country bar across the street had beckoned. Finally able to admit I was bawling over someone not worth my tears, I grabbed my jacket and headed out. While a handful of people mingled and danced I was content playing pool alone. I was playing a game my uncle taught me when I was a teenager. To improve accuracy, he showed me how to place two balls at the entrance of each pocket. The goal was to sink all the balls without scratching in under twelve shots. I was trying to beat my personal best of sinking all the ball in eight shots.

I was busy working on my third game against myself and nursing a second Corona and lime when Dominic interrupted. Instead of taking my next shot, I leaned against the table and glared at him. Even standing straight and tall, I was compelled to lean back and look up to acknowledge the annoying man leaning against the wall. His casual stance oozed animalistic arrogance. Once I could focus again, my glare met dusky green eyes, topped with a mop of ash-blonde hair. His lips – *his sexy mouth* – was sexily rimmed with a neatly trimmed goatee. Realizing I was staring, my cheeks suddenly burned. My exasperated exhale sounded more like a hungry pant. I blushed crimson.

"Like what you see?" He drawled, obviously pleased with my appraisal. *Arrogant jerk.*

Unable to look away, I watched him take a deep swig from a bottle of sparkling water. I was startled, but I didn't even bother wondering why he was drinking water on a Friday night. He might mistake the question as a conversation starter and that was not what I wanted. I needed him to leave, and quickly.

"I was just thinking about cracking you with this cue," I snapped sarcastically. My words surprised me. *Where did that come from?* I blinked in surprise when he chuckled unaffected by my rudeness. *He's too dense to be insulted.*

"Mind if I challenge the winner?" He smirked. Is he mocking me? He knew damn well I was challenging myself. *Definitely a jerk.*

"Yes, I do mind," I countered before turning to take another shot; then cursed when I scratched the white ball. I did not come here to be picked up. Besides, what the hell was he doing here? We were more than an hour from the city. This was not a place you just happened to drop by. This was a planned destination.

"I am waiting for someone" It was a blatant lie.

"Are you waiting for Stephan?" he demanded. The question was innocent enough, but it annoyed the hell out of me.

"No! And I don't want to talk about him," I barked, as I collected all the balls out of the pockets and started to line them up again. He flinched and I briefly felt guilty for taking my anger out on him. He was just being friendly, I told myself.

"Touchy subject?" He pressed. Instantly annoyed, I took back any regrets about snapping at him.

"Let it go!" I firmly insisted. I turned and pointedly glared at him. "I do not want to talk about it."

"If you say so," he shrugged. "Want another Corona?"

I nodded yes.

"Be right back. In the meantime, rack'em up," he said before heading to the bar.

Conceding defeat, I pulled the balls together into the triangle and waited for him to return with our drinks. While I waited, for the first time I looked around the saloon. The room had filled up in the past hour and a live band was tuning up on stage. The log walls, and the old oak bar gave it a rustic lodge type atmosphere. Autographed 8x10's lined the walls, including head shots of country legends including Garth Brooks, Tim McGraw, and Emerson Drive. It was an astonishing collection of memorabilia.

"Flip to break?" He drew a coin from his pocket. I failed to notice Dominic's return. He placed another Corona on the table alongside his bottle of water. Maybe he was a recovering alcoholic? I stifled my curiosity. It was none of my business.

"Heads," I replied.

"Heads it is, you break." He wandered over to the rack along the wall and picked up a bag tucked into the back. I failed to notice until I spotted him deftly twisting it together that he brought his own cue. I was in serious trouble.

"Want to make it interesting?" He asked, while watching me chalk up the cue.

"I don't place bets," I retorted.

"Chicken?" he chortled.

"No, I just know better than to be hustled by you," I retorted. Refusing to take the bait, I lined up. *Crack!* I stood back and watched as the 12 ball spun into the corner pocket.

"Looks like you are high ball," he said, stating the obvious. "Let's see if you can make it two in a row."

In response, I cracked two more balls into the side pockets before finally missing my fourth shot. It was an easy one too; straight line to the corner pocket. Thanks to my overconfidence, I missed.

"Damn," I cursed.

"Oh, I see how it is. You didn't place a bet because you are going to hustle me," he laughed. *I thought, yeah right, uh huh sure. YOU'RE the one with a custom-made cue stick.*

"I just got lucky," I retorted. Grabbing my beer, I sat down at the lone table in the corner and watched him line up his first shot. I couldn't help but notice the way his jeans hugged taunt buttocks. His thighs bulged in the skin-tight denim. When he bent over, I could see a hint of blonde chest hair peeking over the top of his button-up denim shirt. A tattooed dragon played peek-a-boo beneath rolled up sleeves, cuffed tightly mid-arm. I was disgusted by my sudden urge to roll up his sleeve see the rest of his artwork. Thankfully, I was able to stifle the urge. That would have really been embarrassing.

"Like what you see?" He flashed me a cheeky grin. He noticed me staring and he wanted me to know that he noticed. *Bastard.*

I jumped up and tried not to look guilty. Nonchalantly I attempted to walk off my sudden nervousness. *What was wrong with me?* His amused look told me I failed. I downed the rest of my bottle in two swallows.

"So are you going to tell me why you are in the middle of nowhere and why Stephan isn't with you?" He tried once more.

"Why are you so interested?" I inquired. The beer must be loosening me up. The question did not annoy me as much at the moment.

"Because the last time I saw you, I was telling you to be careful. Based on your reaction tonight, I would hazard to guess that you learned the hard way." His voice softened with genuine concern. Even his eyes looked kinder. He was genuinely concerned. I fought the urge to spill the beans. I needed to talk, but he was still a stranger and did not deserve an explanation. Going back to the game, he got his shot and missed. "It's your shot."

I stood up and surveyed the table, trying to figure out my next move.

"Ok, I get the hint. You don't want to talk about Stephan. What do you want to talk about?" He tried once more.

"Thanks for understanding, but I am really here just to figure stuff out," I explained. Well, that much was true.

"Are you staying in town?" He asked, as I missed my next shot.

"Yeah, I have a room across the street for a few days," I admitted.

"That's cool. So do I." He said. "I am in room 5, where are you?"

"In room number 6," I replied. Gee whiz, we were right next to each other. When I checked in, I noticed the door to the adjoining room and hoped that some pervert wasn't on the other side of the wall. Now I am seeing that instead of a pervert, I had Dominic. *Yikes. That's way too close to home.*

"Why are you here?" I asked, not sure if I wanted to know the answer.

"I own the place." He took another shot and sank the 8 ball. "You win!"

I didn't even notice. My head was popping with questions. *He owned the inn?* No wonder Debbie had a standing invitation. She obviously knew him better than I first thought. Why the hell didn't she say anything?

"That's the game," I laughed. "I can't believe I just beat you."

"Just because I scratched. My turn to rack." He was already picking up the balls for a second game.

"Who says I want to play another game with you?" I stubbornly retorted. There was an unmistakable playfulness in my voice. The beer must have been kicking in because I was starting to feel relaxed and loosened up. Where I was once hesitant, I was now beginning to have fun. Nothing like some healthy competition to spice things up. *He was so damn sexy.*

"What else are we going to do?" he demanded. "Also, I am finding this banter quite entertaining."

I watched him rack the balls for the next game. The way he deftly arranged the balls inside the triangle made me wonder what else he could do with his fingers. *What the hell was that?* I took myself to task for allowing my thoughts to wander. *But damn, the man made me tingle.*

The slam of my bottle onto the table snapped me back to reality. Hell, Stephan was still out of town and had no idea what was going to happen when he got home. We had to talk, that much was clear. I had to tell him what I knew. I had a million questions to ask and then decisions to make depending on his answers. I should not be here with another man, no matter how innocent it was. And based on my thoughts, it was not going to remain innocent for long. Perhaps that is what scared me so much. The fact that Dominic seemed interested in me, and I was undeniably attracted to him. His mere presence left me unbent. *It must be the beer.*

"So how well do you know Debbie?" I wondered. Time to change the subject to something safer.

"We've been friends for years. Her brother and I went to school together." He explained. I tried desperately to ignore how sexy he looked, leaning against the table, arms crossed as he spoke. "I've known long before she was interested in boys."

I laughed at that; for as long as I'd known Debbie, she was boy crazy. Even married, she still flirted like a single woman. Her husband Ron was fine with it; their love was amazing and genuine. They were the most confident couple I knew.

"No, we have not, nor will we ever be lovers," he added. "Time to break."

I took hold of the cue and headed over to the table. I caught him staring at my back as I leaned over the table and lined up my shot. *Crack.* The balls moved around the table, but nothing dropped. When I came back to our side table, I noticed two more drinks had arrived. Taking the lime, I squeezed it into my bottle and pushed it in. Putting my thumb on the neck, I turned it upside down, then back upright without it foaming over and took a deep swig.

"You're a pro at that," he mused, watching me handle my bottle without making a mess.

"I learned how to manage that in Texas," I admitted.

"You've been to Texas?" He asked.

"A few years ago, I went down to Corpus Christi with Debbie. She was taking wedding photos for a couple who met in an online chat room. I went a little nuts in the heat. Debbie went home, but I stuck around. We spent a glorious month together," I confided. "I would have moved down there, but it didn't work out."

"Sounds like you are adventurous. Why didn't it work out?" he hedged.

"He was engaged before we met. She got pregnant, lost the baby and they broke up over it. When I saw her, I could tell they still had feelings for each other so I pointed it out. I suggested that they give it another chance. One thing led to another and they eventually got back together again. They are now happily married with two kids." I paused to take a breath. "I have no regrets."

"That's good. It is very refreshing to see a woman who admits that she is human," was his reply. He actually sounded impressed.

"What do you mean by that?" I demanded.

"Most women I know will deny they have needs; that they enjoy male companionship. Everyone is so afraid of what other people think or say. It is rare to find a female willing to admit that she found a man attractive and can just have fun," he continued. "Also, something tells me that you aren't the casual type of girl; that even if something doesn't work out, you still throw yourself into it and enjoy every moment for as long as it lasts. You don't just sleep around."

"That's a pretty bold assumption," I responded in annoyance. How had he deduced this in our few short meetings, I had no idea but I was impressed. "But it is accurate. I am a long term relationship type of girl, not a wham-bam thank you ma'am type."

"I kind of figured as much," he chortled. "Good to know I was right."

"Why aren't you drinking?" I asked, trying to change to subject. After having a few, I felt brave enough to broach the subject. I would do anything for a subject change, even if it meant offending him.

"I'm working," he answered. "Or at least I am for another hour."

"How are you working?" I was confused. At this point in the standoff, it didn't take much.

"I own this place too," he guffawed at the startled look on my face. "I have to stay sober for at least another hour. Security should arrive by then and then I can relax and have fun."

"You own the motel and the bar?" I was shocked. *Who the hell was this guy anyway?* So much for my assumption that he was a biker. Maybe he was a biker and this was a clubhouse? I glanced around the room. The band was playing country and couples were two stepping all over the dance floor. Nope, definitely not a biker bar.

"Yep, they are just a few of my investments. Just a little something to keep me going," he continued, before taking another shot. "All done, game over."

Turning my attention back to the table, I noticed only seven balls left on the slate - all low balls. So engrossed in the conversation,

I failed to notice him clear the table all in a single turn. The only shot I took was the break.

"Good thing I didn't post a bet," I laughed.

"Good for you, bad for me," he replied mischievously.

"Why?" I was afraid to ask.

"Because I was going to bet a kiss for each ball-in-pocket," he retorted. "You'd be making out with me at this very moment."

"Yeah, no kidding. That would not have been a good idea," I huffed.

"That's what you think," he replied. "Another game?"

"No, I think I'm going back to my room," I grabbed my beer and finished it in one swallow.

"Yeah, I better get back to work anyway," he replied. "Will I see you later?"

"We shall see. Thanks for the beer and the games. It's been fun. I needed this break and as much as I hate to admit it, your company was appreciated," I admitted, reaching for my jacket. Turning to leave, my speedy retreat was halted by his solid frame. It was like walking into a brick wall, but warm.

"Can I at least get a hug?" He asked. His dimples deepened as he grinned down at me.

"Really?" I thought he was joking. Giggling with amusement, I tried to squirm around him, but a tree-trunk sized arm came up to stop me.

"Really!" Instead of waiting, he pulled me close. I found myself engulfed in heavenly warmth. The scent of pine, aftershave, beer and cigarettes emanated off his clothes. He looked good and smelt delicious. I let myself melt into his embrace before catching myself.

"I have to go," I stammered, pulling myself away hurriedly.

"See you later 'gator," he called as I rushed towards the door. I paused long enough to toss him a grateful wave before heading out. The fresh air hit me in the face; making me shiver as I stepped onto the sidewalk. Making sure no one was following, I headed across the street.

Once I was sequestered in the safety of my room, I tossed my bag and jacket onto the bed and staggered into the bathroom. It was too late to get in the hot-tub room, but a hot bath was in order. Putting the plug in, I turned on the water full blast, tossed in a fragrant bath beads and went back into the bedroom. Opening the fridge, I reached in and grabbed the bottle of white wine chilling inside. After pouring a glass, I stripped off my clothes and walked back to the tub. Hovering less than daintily over the edge, I tested the water with a dangling toe. Satisfied that it was perfect I slipped into a sea of cinnamon and clove scented bubbles.

CHAPTER SEVENTEEN

"EMMA!"

Startled, my eyes popped open. The long chilled bathwater splashed onto the floor as I pulled myself upright. It took a few seconds for me to realise that I had blissfully dozed in the bathtub. The fresh air, wine and beer combined with the hot water must have snuck up on me.

Bang. Bang. Someone was pounding on the room's door loud enough to wake the dead. Glancing at the clock above the vanity, I could barely make out the time. *Who the heck was knocking at my door at three in the morning?*

"Emma? Are you in there, darling? If you don't answer the door right now, I am coming in," I heard Dominic yell from the hallway. He sounded scared.

Groaning, I tried to pull myself out, but slipped on the wet surface in my haste. Losing my balance, I fell back into the water with a *thud*. My head snapped against the ceramic tile wall on the way down. I yelped, then everything in the room dimmed.

In the distance, I could hear the sound a key turn in the lock, and then the door smashed against the wall as it was thrown open. Hurried footsteps made short work of the five feet between the hallway door and the bathroom.

"Shit!" Dominic exclaim as he barged through the bathroom door. His voice sounded far away. "You're bleeding."

My vision had returned, but my reflexes were still slow. I was not sure if it was the booze or the blow to the head. Before I could get hands up to stop his advance, Dominic was already reaching over and plucking me from the tub; oblivious of the water soaking his shoes, pants and the floor. With a clean swoop, he picked me up and carried me into the bedroom, then gently put me onto the bed. He quickly grabbed the corner of the bedspread and pulled it over my soaking wet body. I was too startled to respond, but grateful for the modesty. Everything seems to happen so quickly. I watched him turn back to the bathroom and return with several face clothes and the ice bucket.

"Here, let me clean you up," he said, placing the cloth against my forehead. When he withdrew it, it was covered with blood. "It looks like you hit your head pretty hard. Are you feeling okay? How many fingers am I holding?"

He waved a peace sign before my face. I frowned. *Smartass*.

"Two," I grumbled. I was having problems comprehending what happened. I remembered playing pool, I remembered coming back to my room and crawling into the bath. After that, there was nothing. "What are you doing here?"

"I just got off work and saw the lights still on in the room. Assuming you were still awake, I figured I'd pop in and see if you wanted to have another drink," he explained. His brow creased with concern as he rinsed out the bloody facecloth in the ice bucket. "Well, it looks like the bleeding stopped. I don't think you will need stitches, but you may have a headache in the morning and it won't be a hangover."

"Thank you," I weakly replied. "What do I owe you?"

He laughed.

"Not a thing Emma, not a thing. Unless you want to give me a kiss," he replied with a grin. "Can I get you anything else?"

Instead of responding, I tried to pull myself into a sitting position but I wobbled.

"Slow down, don't move. What do you need?" Dominic asked again.

"A shirt would be nice, I have to go pee," I snarled. Dominic looked up at me in surprise. I instantly regretted my rudeness, but this entire situation was embarrassing. Having him in my motel room in the middle of the night; knowing he'd only carried my sopping wet and naked body into bed, well it was too much for my brain to comprehend. "Sorry, I am not used to being treated like an invalid. All I did was slip in the tub and bump my head. Which I might add, would not have happened if you hadn't been banging on the door like the motel was on fire."

"Excuse me? I knocked on the door several times and you didn't answer. I thought something had happened to you," he replied. I watched him rummage through my bag until he found a shirt that he tossed onto the bed beside me. "You could have been dead!"

"Dead? Why the heck would I be dead? I was taking a bath you moron," I retorted. So much for my apology. The pounding in my mind was almost getting unbearable. I took hold of the shirt and pulled it over my head before climbing out of bed.

"Do you mind?" I sputtered, spotting Dominic staring at my naked bottom playing peek-a-boo under my shirt, just before I slammed the bathroom door shut. "I need a drink," I cried.

"I think you've had enough," was his reply. "And no, I do not mind the sight; not one bit!"

"Not if you're planning on sticking around much longer, then I am going to need a bottle," I muttered to myself. *Damn, he frustrated me.*

"I heard that," he called back. I slammed the door in his face, and then there was blessed silence.

I took care of business and washed up. Glancing in the mirror, I inspected the black and blue goose egg already forming on my brow. *That is going to leave a mark*, I muttered to myself. Exiting the bathroom I was surprised to find the suite empty. However, the door to the adjoining room was wide open. Curious, I wandered over and peeked in. It seemed empty. I casually glanced around. The room was a mirror image of the one I was staying in but definitely lived in. There were family photographs on the wall, and books everywhere. I could hear Dominic rummaging around in the adjacent bathroom.

"Do you live here?" I called into the other room. The suite was surprisingly neat. The kitchenette in the corner was tidy and the sinks were empty. He obviously cleaned up after himself or maybe he took advantage of room service. Either way, it was nice to see a man who knew how to keep everything in order. Even the bed was neatly made.

"For the most part. It is one of a few places where I stay," he called back.

"A few places?" I was suddenly very curious about the green-eyed Adonis hiding in the next room. I meandered around the room and looked closely at the photographs. There was one of him playing with a cocker spaniel on the beach. Another of him holding a little girl.

"Yeah, I have a few places," he whispered over my shoulder. I jumped, having failed to hear him sneaking up on me. "That is my niece, Sandy."

"Crap, do you have to sneak up on me like that?" I smacked him on the shoulder before moving off. I stopped short, having discovered that he was shirtless. His chest muscles rippled beneath a soft mat of blonde while he dried off his cheek with a hand towel. I dropped my eyes, only to pause when I reached the waist of his jeans where he'd left the button and zipper undone. I licked my lips subconsciously. I was blatantly staring.

"Boy, you sure get distracted easily," he guffawed, as I turned scarlet. His deep laughter snapped me back. "Do you like what you see?"

"NO!" I barked, before spinning on my heel to head back to my room. Any graceful exit I may have made was derailed with my next step. Not seeing the end table in my path, I tripped and began to go down. I may have hit the floor if he hadn't stepped forward and grabbed me at the last minute. We tumbled together in a heap on the sofa which dominated one side of the room. There was nothing graceful about our landing.

"That's two for two," Dominic chuckled into my ear. His breath was warm against my skin. His arms were still wrapped around me as he cradled me close. I became acutely aware that my bottom was pressed against his bare ABS. *I needed to get out of there.* He let go as I fought to sit upright.

"I think I am going to get to bed now," I stammered as I stood up, hastily pulling my shirt back down to where it was supposed to hang mid-thigh. "Thank you for taking care of me; although if you'd left me alone in the first place, I would not have needed to be taken care of."

"That might not be a bad idea," he concurred. "If you don't mind, I am going to leave the doorway between our suites open for the remainder of the night. That way, I can check on you. You hit your head pretty hard and one can never be too careful."

I frowned. Was this man ever planning to leave me alone? All I wanted to do was crawl into bed, turn out the lights and sleep until the world seemed perfect again. It looked like that was not going to materialize any time soon.

"Don't worry, I will stay in my room if you stay in yours," he promised. "I'll even let you sleep in through the morning."

"Gee thanks, that is so kind of you," I replied sarcastically. "Thanks again."

I forced a smile before turning to go back to my room. I started to close the door behind me, but one look back at his face stopped me cold. The warning in his eyes was clear. If I locked the door behind me, he was going to kick it down. Deciding not to push it, I conceded that he was right and crawled back into my bed. Once I was safely tucked under the blankets, I pulled my shirt over my head and tossed it onto a chair in the corner. Just because he was in the next room, did not mean I was going to change my sleeping habits. I was born naked, I slept naked and if I had my way, I would die naked.

"I saw that," I heard him yell from his room.

Jerk! Ignoring him, I switched off the light and rolled over. Within minutes I was fast asleep.

The insistent beeping of my cell phone woke me up the next morning. It first went off several hours earlier, but I chose to ignore it. Reaching up to brush the hair out of my face, I cringed when I touched the goose bump on my head. Everything that happened the night before came back with vivid clarity. Ugh. I did not want to deal with it. Groaning, I leaned across the bed and grabbed the offending contraption. Ten new text messages - all from Debbie.

"*Where are you? Are you okay? I haven't heard from you in days!*" A slight exaggeration, but hey, Debbie was known to be a little dramatic. I quickly messaged her back, assuring her that I was doing fine and enjoying the hotel suite.

"*Have you seen Dominic yet?*" was her reply.

"You knew he'd be here, didn't you," I demanded.

"*Yep, what are you going to do about that?*" she typed back.

"You will find out when I get back," I promised.

"*Belle's fine,*" she added. "*Have fun *wink. But not too much fun *wink.*"

"You awake?" I heard Dominic ask. Looking up, he was standing in the doorway watching me typing frantically into my phone. "Is everything okay?"

"Just Debbie, being a concerned and annoying friend," I laughed. "Is that coffee?"

"Yep, freshly brewed. How do you like it?" he asked.

"With a little cream would be fine," I replied. He retreated back into his suite and I used the opportunity to clamber out of bed. I just finished pulling on a shirt and shorts when he returned with coffee in hand.

"Here you go. Nice legs," he added, handing me the steaming cup. "How's the head?"

"I could definitely use a few Tylenol; I feel like someone clubbed me upside the head," I admitted begrudged.

"I am sorry, but I was really worried about you. We may be in the middle of nowhere but you never know who's come into town. That's the trouble with small towns that are popular pit stops along a major highway. Too many drifters and not all are savoury," he continued while making himself a space to sit on the bed.

"Sure, make yourself comfortable," I muttered under my breath. Taking a sip of the coffee, I admitted it was the best I'd had for a while. "Good coffee; thanks."

"Are we going to do this again?" He laughed. "And you're welcome."

"Do what?" I feigned innocence.

"I say something and you respond sarcastically. Are you always this sassy or do I just bring it out in you?" he smirked. I wanted to smack it right off his face.

"You just happen to bring it out in me. What are you doing here anyway?" I retorted.

"I live here."

"You already told me that," I snapped back. "Why are you bothering me?"

"Because Debbie told me to," he admitted.

"Debbie told you to?" I was confused. What was she up to? *Why was she setting me up like this?*

"She knew I could help you," he continued, taking a swig of his coffee.

"Help me what?" I was confused. How could Dominic help me, other than to provide me with a place to stay?

"I have certain accomplishments," he slowly replied. "Skills that can aid you greatly in this situation."

"What kind of skills?" I demanded. What kind of skills was he talking about? Maybe he knew people, or maybe he knew more about Stephan than he led on in the first place. Now, I was really curious. What else could a man who owned an inn, a country bar and drove a motorcycle do? Maybe I was wrong; maybe he was in a motorcycle gang. Either way, this man was a walking contradiction.

"I heard you were experiencing problems with Stephan," came his matter of fact response. "There are things that I can do to help you."

"Such as?" I asked again. His avoidance of the question fed my curiosity.

"I can follow him, I can hack him, I can make him disappear." His eyes never wavered; he watched me intently as if to gauge my reaction. To be honest, I didn't know how to react. This was something I was prepared to deal with on my own. The thought of having help was not something I considered; of course that was before I knew who to ask.

"Well, I don't want him to disappear, but I would love to know what is going on," I admitted. "But who says I need your help?"

"There are things I can do. I promise I won't hurt him," he tried to reassure me. "As much as I'd love to break every bone in his body for hurting you, I will refrain from bodily harm. Unless, of course, he throws the first punch. Then, all bets are off."

"What do you know about things?" I asked. "How much as Debbie told you?"

"Actually, she didn't have to tell me anything. We happen to know many of the same people, and people like to spill the beans. There are rumours circulating about him. Remember? I warned you about him. But it looks like it goes deeper," his voice grew quieter. I remained quiet, waiting for him to continue.

"What do you mean?" I inquired when he failed to go forward with an explanation. *What was he not telling me?*

"I would prefer not to say anything more at the moment. I have no solid proof yet. But once I have it, you will be the first to know," Dominic promised. "IF you give me permission to snoop. I will not do anything without your permission. As much as it may surprise you, I like you and don't want to see you destroyed by somebody who isn't worthy to lick your boots."

"Can I think about it?" I demanded. *He told me he liked me too?* As much as the comment intrigued me, now was not the time to well on the possibilities.

"Sure, but don't think about it too long. The longer you stay in this relationship, the harder it will be to get out of it later. You should know this," Dominic responded with exasperation. "Now, I need to get out of here for a few hours. Are you going to be okay by yourself? How's your head?"

"It will be fine when you leave." I retorted. I regretted it immediately. He actually seemed hurt and I felt guilty for sounding so curt. "I am sorry; thanks for your help."

"You're welcome," he replied, already pulling himself off the bed. "See you later?" He asked hopefully.

"I will be here," I assured.

"Great, then enjoy the day. Don't forget the check out the pool." he added before turning and exiting the room. This time, he closed the door between our rooms. I plopped down on the bed, and let out a big sigh before falling backwards onto the mattress. I had a feeling the peace experienced during the first day at the motel were over. The rest of the week would be spent verbally sparring with Mr. Stubborn from next door.

I pondered if I should pack my things and head back home, but I knew that I would just spend the next ten days moping over Stephan or rehashing the many questions plaguing my thoughts. At least here, I had a change of scenery. Besides, something told me that if Debbie knew I had run back home, she would be very upset with me. That annoyed me more than anything else did. She was only trying to help and while it was obvious she was meddling, I did not want to make her angry. Nope, I would be a big girl and suck it up. The inn was lovely, and otherwise abandoned. Where else could I enjoy a mini vacation without getting very far?

Not willing to dwell on things any further I slipped into my two-piece bathing suit, grabbed a towel and headed towards the pool. A few hours by the water was just what the doctor aka Dominic had ordered. Might as well enjoy it, right?

CHAPTER EIGHTEEN

It was another two days before I heard from Stephan.

"How was graduation?" I asked when he finally called.

"It went really well. Derek graduated near the top of his class. Looks like he can get into Oxford!" he told me with pride. "Wish you could have come with me."

"That's awesome! You must be very proud of him," I replied, stating the obvious. In all honesty, I didn't know what to say. This was the first time I have spoken to him since finding out about Jellybean and Judy, and I had so many doubts. But I forced myself to hold my curiosity. I was not ready for this confrontation, and it should not be done on the telephone.

"Where are you? You sound different," he demanded. He sounded so oblivious. If I didn't know better, he sounded like the typical devoted man who missed the love of his life.

"I am at a hotel about an hour from the city," I admitted. "Debbie thought I needed a holiday so she found me a room at a little place her and Ron frequent."

"Sounds nice - glad to hear that you are relaxing for a change. I worry about you; you tend to work way too hard and when I am not around I am afraid you don't take any time off," he interjected. It all sounded so sincere.

"Yea, I still have three weeks before I have to get my article in, so the timing was perfect to get away. I've been chilling by the pool, cooking in the hot tub; enjoying good food and drink," I responded with forced cheerfulness. While this much was true, he did not need to know the full story.

"Anyways, I better let you go. International calls are not cheap. Speak to you in a few days?" He sounded so hopeful. If I didn't know otherwise, I would have been bouncing off the walls with lovesick excitement.

"Yes, I should be home at the end of the week," I replied.

"Oh, you're going to be gone for a few more days?" he asked. "Hang on." The telephone receiver crackled briefly and I heard him shout to someone "hang on, be right there."

"I have to go, we have dinner reservations," he stated when he came back onto the phone.

"Not a problem. I actually love it here; between the spa, massages, pool and hot tub, I am in no rush to get home," I answered cautiously. I didn't want to give him any clues that something was up or someone else may be more deserving of my attention. While things between Dominic and I were innocent, there was no point, giving him any ammunition to toss back in my face when we finally had our chat.

"You better run; it was nice to hear your voice," I managed to say,

"You as well. Love you," he answered. With a click, he was gone.

Putting the phone onto the night stand, I sighed with relief. I was actually very proud of myself. It was a brief conversation, but I managed to keep my mouth shut. I was nervously waiting for that 'first call' and now that it was over, I felt nothing but relief. It was a test, and I had passed with flying colours.

It was still early in the day, so I decided to hit the pool for a couple of hours. So far I had been miraculously lucky. Other than Dominic and I, the place was gloriously empty. He'd already told me that normally, during the week the motel was quiet but on weekends, the party crowd invaded. I still had two days left before that happened. The other bonus, if I desired, I could lock the door and have the pool to myself. This allowed me full freedom. As I said, I enjoyed being nude. That was the whole point of having my private swimming hole at home. An opportunity to be one with nature.

I hadn't seen anyone check in yet, so I decided to take a chance. I wandered over to the doorway and snapped the locking bolt shut.

Heading back to my chaise lounge, I spread out the towel before heading to the pool. I started to shrug out of my shirt when I realized, what the hell. No one was around, so why bother with a bathing suit. My clothing was soon cast aside into a careless pile on the recliner. Without a second thought, I wandered to the edge of the pool and jumped in.

Coming up, I gasped at the change in temperature on my bare skin. It briefly took my breath away. I stood nearly chest deep in water, with my wet hair dribbling water down my back, allowing my body to get used to the temperature. My hands instinctively rose to my swollen breasts. The pool was heated, but it was still cooler than expected. The water hardened my nipples almost painfully. Once I caught my breath, I lay back and let the water carry me.

Strangely enough, I can fall asleep while swimming on my back in any water. I have scared a few people doing this, but for me, it was easy and natural. Once my ears were below the surface of the water, I'd listen to my breath, and allow myself to rise. The more I practiced, the easier it became. Dozing off is a real hazard.

Confident that I had the pool to myself, I surrendered to the water's gentle seduction. The gentle current, caused by the waterfall at one end of the pool teased my nipples, as they protruded through the surface. The water caressed my thighs, teasing me further. I was in absolute heaven. And there was no one there to disturb me.

After a while I switched positions. I rolled over onto my stomach, then stood up in the water. I lay back, allowing the water to hold me up and swam backwards across the surface. When I made it across the pool, I stood up to shake out my hair.

"What do we have here?" said a distinct male voice from someplace behind me. I cried with surprise, and ducked under the water while I searched the room for the source of the voice. At first I didn't see Dominic is standing in the shadow of a gigantic banana tree, until he stepped forward and moved closer to the pool.

"Are you following me?" I asked, as I ducked beneath the surface so he couldn't see that I was naked.

"Too late for that darling, I've already seen what you're trying to hide," he laughed, taking a few steps closer to the water. I stepped backward, and tripped. Losing my balance, I tried to keep from falling. But I had nothing to grab, so my effort was in vain. My head slipped below the surface, and I came up sputtering.

"Are you okay?" He asked, attempting to muffle his laugh. He failed miserably. "I see you're taking advantage of some alone time in the pond. Glad to see someone enjoying it."

I rose quickly, then regretted it immediately when I noticed Dominic was no longer looking at my face. His eyes had settled on my naked breasts and it did not look like he was going to turn away any time soon. I stifled a growl when he licked his lips.

"Do you mind?" I snapped, suddenly desperate for some sort of cover, I decided to head deeper into the water.

"Where are you going?" He asked after me. I looked over my shoulder in time to see him enjoying my naked retreat. Irritated, I dove in until nothing was exposed other than my head and shoulders.

"Are you running away from me?" He asked again. All I wanted was for him to go away, but I was not going to admit it. Bad enough that I thought he was the sexiest thing around, but to have him so close, and find me naked as a jaybird in broad daylight - in HIS pool - was a tad unsettling.

"Maybe – aren't you supposed to be at work?" I demanded, hoping to remind that he had other obligations.

"I saw you heading this way, and I thought I'd see what you were up to." He looked too smug at his admission.

"Well, you found me, what do you want?" I was becoming irritated. I wanted to enjoy my swim, alone.

"You!" Even from a distance I could see his eyes blazing.

Any response that I started to sputter faded away as he began to unbutton his trademark denim shirt. I gasped when his broad chest was exposed. His muscles rippled with every move. His tattoos added colour to his otherwise bronze flesh.

"What are you doing?" I demanded. His actions, both frightened and fascinated me.

"What does it look like," he replied as his boots hit the deck, followed by his socks. When he reached for the zipper in his pants, I spun away in sudden shyness. His intentions were no longer a question and the eventualities were intimidating yet highly stimulating. My lips clenched with annoyance, more at my reaction than anything else.

"What's the matter, I am just going to go for a swim," he laughed. The sound irked me. How dare he interrupt my day just to mock me. Turning on my heel, I swam further into the deep end.

When I turned around to glance at the pool deck, he was no longer there.

"Oh come on, don't be like that," I spun around when he finally surfaced in front me, mere inches separated us. My hand came up instinctively and I pushed hard against his chest. The firm push sent him backwards in surprise.

"You are a sneaky bastard, aren't you." I sputtered in surprise. He moved towards me with a peculiar grin. I started to step back, but remembered what happened the last time.

Watching him, I suddenly shivered. I blamed the trickle of cold water dripping onto skin previous warmed by the sun beaming down through the glass roof. He must have noticed, because his arms reached out for me. I shut my eyes in anticipation of his caress, but it didn't come. Instead, his fingers deftly flicked at a strand of hair plastered against my chest providing me some modesty.

"That's better – now I can see your glorious breasts," His hazel eyes twinkled when he smiled. My eyes fell to his lips, surrounded by his goatee. They look so soft and sweet. I would have stumbled if he hadn't reached out to grab my arms, pulling me towards him until we were pressed together. Naked flesh against naked flesh.

I could feel the heat of him hardening against my thigh. Alarmed, my eyes rose to meet his gaze. Our eyes connected, and his face came down towards mine. My knees buckled when our lips finally connected. The coldness of the water was soon forgotten in the warmth of that single kiss. Our tongues were soon battling, as he devoured my mouth in ownership. This was the kiss of a man taking his prize.

Tearing his lips away from mine, his tongue traced the curve of my face to my earlobe. He nibbled gently, making me shiver. His fingers found my hair, and he firmly grasped a handful in his fist. I gasped in surprise as he pulled my head back, exposing my throat and shoulders to his mouth. A moan escaped as he tasted my skin. As he alternated his tongue, lips and teeth, my body succumbed to uncontrollable shakes and I twitched in anticipation.

Bang. Bang. Bang.

"Shit!" Staggering, I pulled myself away. Someone was knocking on the glass door leading to the pool. Thanks to the many tropical trees, whoever it was couldn't see us. I thanked God for the interruption. A few minutes longer, I would have been no better than Stephan; a liar and a cheat. I pushed away from Dominic guiltily.

"Hey, don't leave," he reached out and tried to stop me, but I was already pulling myself out of the pool and reaching for my towel. I could tell by the splashing closing in behind me, he had followed me out of the pool.

"Emma!" he gasped.

"Sorry, we can't do this Dominic. I really have to go now. " I answered, purposely ignoring him while I pulled the towel around my body, and grabbed the remainder of my things. I didn't even bother getting dressed. I was on the brink of tears. I needed to get back to my room before I lost all restraint.

I unlocked the pool side door and let the maid in. I ignored the puzzled look on her face as I rushed past and dash down the hall to my room. Shutting the door behind me, I slipped in the deadbolt and chain. Content that I was safe behind closed doors, I slide down the door until I was parked on the floor and lost control. I was overwhelmed with pity for what almost happened. With my arms wrapped around my knees, I broke down and sobbed. My heart was breaking inside. I felt like such a fraud.

"Are you okay?" Dominic's concerned voice filtered through my tortured thoughts. I snuffled deeply, not willing to open my eyes and acknowledge that he'd come in through the adjoining room door. Maybe if I ignored him long enough, he would go away.

"Emma? Here, wipe your eyes." He was attempting to push clean tissues into my clenched fists. I turned away, still refusing to respond.

"Come on Emmy, he's not worth it," he murmured. I sensed him move to sit alongside me, and lean backwards against the doorway. I did not struggle when his arm came over my trembling shoulders and gently pulled me against his chest.

"I am sorry; I don't know what came over me," he stammered. "Just to be clear, I am sorry that you are upset. I am not sorry for trying to kiss you, nor am I sorry for trying to make love to you."

I snuffled in response.

"Listen Emma, I am not sure about what is all going on, but I get the feeling that Stephan has done something unforgivable and you are torn on how to handle it. It's simple - if he hurt you, I am going to hurt him," he assured.

"Do you think that will help?" I stammered through my tears. "Do you really think getting back at him is the answer?"

"Do you love him?" he asked hesitantly. I could tell it wasn't the question he wanted to ask.

"I believed I did, now I am not so sure I can," I acknowledged.

"How bad is it?" he asked. "What has he all done?"

"I don't know." It was the truth. I truly did not know the profundity of his deceit. I had bits and pieces, but I knew there was more to the puzzle. I just had to dig a little deeper.

"Tell you what; if I promise to help, will you allow me?" he begged.

"Are you going to hurt him?" I sniffled into the tissue. The one thing I hated about crying was what it did to my sinuses.

"Not unless you want me to," he chuckled. He leaned closer and whispered, "Do I detect a trace of interest?"

"What do you have in mind?" I drew back and looked upwards at him. He reached over and brushed a strand of hair off my face, dislodging it from where it was stuck to my tear soaked cheeks.

"Leave it up to me; if he is up to no good, I will find out. And no, I will not touch him. I will let you know what happens with him. I can promise you that much. You have to get me one promise, though," he appended. "You have to make an educated decision before you can move on."

"What is that?" I asked hesitantly.

"I want you to promise that if things don't work out with Stephan that you will give me a chance; that you will give US a chance," Dominic pressed.

"Pardon me?" I was shocked. His request insinuated he was interested was more than a passing fling.

"I am serious! You have fascinated me since the minute I set eyes on you. I simply want to come to know you better. But I realize now is not the time for anything more than friendship; and I AM a friend. Can you give me a chance for more should the time arise?" His green eyes darkened as he searched my face. "If you can't, I understand that as well. My timing sucks."

"Yes, it does." I concurred. His timing did suck. If he'd said something three years ago, then maybe things would be different. But then again, perhaps not. He hadn't made a great impression that night at the club that much I remembered.

He laughed, and then surprised me by setting a tender kiss on my brow. It was all the encouragement that I needed.

"I promise that when and if this turns out the way I believe it will, I will get naked with you and not run away this time," I replied sarcastically. I had to lighten the situation or I was going to have another meltdown. As I spoke, I realized that given the chance, I honestly believed that Dominic could be good for me. I quickly stifled that thought. Right now, I needed a friend not a lover.

"Deal!" He answered with a cheeky smile. "Shake on it?"

I hesitated, and then took the hand thrust in my direction, all the while hoping I hadn't just made a deal with the devil.

CHAPTER NINETEEN

A telephone call from Debbie a few days later cut my trip shorter than anticipated.

"Emma? Were you expecting someone?" Debbie asked when she finally got me on the telephone. "By the way, you need to empty your voice mail. I couldn't leave a message."

"No, I wasn't. Why?" I replied.

"I came to grab some things for Belle, and I found Hannah here. She says you gave her a key," Debbie explained.

"She's there now?" I asked. I had given her a spare key if she needed it, but I was not expecting her.

"Yes, she says she's been here for a few days. She's tried calling you but you've had your phone turned off. Is everything okay?" Debbie asked, her voice full of concern.

"I was just taking a break from technology," I admitted. After my chat with Dominic, I decided to turn off my phone and not check emails for a day or two. I felt awful screening my calls, but it was easier to clear my head without distractions. Between the pool and hot tub, I'd managed to alleviate a lot of stress. I was more than ready to return to reality and take on whatever life through my way.

"Is everything okay there?" I asked.

"She needs a place to go and this was the only place she could think of on short notice. She tried calling your cell phone, but she didn't know you were on a holiday," Debbie sounded apologetic. "I am sorry, but you need to come home."

"I will leave right away," I promised. Debbie sounded relieved when she hung up. Understanding the urgency, I quickly packed and headed back to the cottage.

As expected, Hannah and Debbie were waiting when I arrived, sharing a pot of tea at the kitchen table, laughing like old friends. I felt relieved to see they were getting along. Not that I expected differently. Everyone like Debbie. She was a sassy mother hen. In a time of crisis, she never lost her head. But if she felt that anyone she loved was in danger, sweet little Debbie became a lioness protecting her cubs. Knowing the Hannah's situation, I was sure that Debbie had spent the majority of their visit assuring the formerly abused bride.

"How was your trip?" Debbie smirked knowingly in my direction. Something about her attitude made me steer clear. She had that "I know something that you don't want me to know" look on her face. Or maybe it was guilt over the near miss with Dominic. There was no way she could know, I assured myself.

"What are you doing here?" I asked Hannah, choosing to ignore Debbie.

"George is having his bracelet removed next week. I need a place to stay for a few days," Hannah replied. Her eyes shone with worry. "I hope you don't mind."

"His sentence was done already?" I felt foolish asking. I'd been so involved with my own drama, I neglected to look at the calendar. His release date was marked with a bright red X on the front of my fridge.

"Yes, and he's going to come looking for me," Hannah continued quietly. I watched her fidget by stirring her tea without pause.

"Why now?" I asked, while pouring myself a cup of tea.

"The insurance company is suing him now and he is pissed. After the explosion, they paid me out on the policy. According to the divorce everything would have been fifty-fifty. But his attempt to destroy the property in his greed, gave me the advantage. Now the insurance company is going after him for the money. Plus, he's not getting anything in the divorce. The only way he could possibly get a dime is if I am dead. And honestly? The way he's been? That would not surprise me at all," Hannah confided. Tears of fear flowed down her cheeks as she spoke.

Debbie and I sat in shocked silence.

"What are you going to do?" Debbie gently asked.

"I am going to take the money and buy a place. I just don't know where to go next. I keep thinking he will find me wherever I go. Debbie says she knows somebody who can help me disappear," Hannah continued. She accepted the box of Kleenex I offered with a grateful smile.

"I told her about Dominic. I am convinced he will help and not ask any questions," Debbie interjected.

"Why Dominic?" I turned to Debbie. *Why was she getting him involved?*

"I just know he can help, or at least he will know someone who can be of assistance. He knows a lot of people, particularly in law enforcement. His brother's a cop," Debbie explained. "If anyone would know anything about safe houses, Dominic would."

Hannah got up and started pacing. I watched her absent-mindedly rubbing her hands together as she worried.

"Do you think we can really pull this off?" She stopped in the centre of the room and looked at both of us. Terror blazed in her eyes. "I am not overreacting. I need to hide!"

"Hannah, calm down. It's not good for you to be upset like this," Debbie tried to calm her down. "Come, finish your tea. I have already contacted Dominic and he's on his way down."

"He's on his way here?" I blurted, looking at Debbie with surprise.

"Yes, I called him after I spoke to you. He left about an hour after you. He should be pulling in the driveway soon. I told him to call if my directions sucked," Debbie confessed almost sheepishly. "Sorry, I forgot to tell you. Besides, what does it matter?"

"Things got a little awkward," I conceded sheepishly.

"Define awkward," Debbie giggled when I blushed. She recognized my guilty expression. We'd been friends far too long.

"He kissed me," I moaned at Debbie's reaction.

Debbie hooted with glee.

"No way! That sneaky devil. I told him to leave you alone. I probably should have known better though. To him, hands off mean exactly the opposite," Debbie babbled with mirth. "Wait until he gets here. I am going to kick his ass."

"If you're so mad, why are you laughing?" Hannah innocently asked.

"When you meet Dominic, you will see why. He is a sexy hunk of a man. Unfortunately, I've known him way too long to see him other than a brother, but still. Vin Diesel could be his twin."

"Oh, I understand! Now that is a sexy piece of manliness," Hannah snickered playfully.

I knew they were teasing, but suddenly, I felt like the butt of everyone's joke. I was still ashamed of my wanton behaviour in Dominic's arms. I acted like a shameless hussy.

"Wait, this is where she gets really guilty looking," Debbie giggled harder. I knew she was teasing but I still wanted to smack her. "Admit it Emma, he is very sexy, and you like him."

"Like who?" came an unmistakable voice from the doorway.

"DOM! I see you found it," Debbie squealed, flying across the room and into his arms. "Thank you for taking such good care of Emmy this week. She looks happy and refreshed."

"She does? It was nothing I did - trust me," he looked pointedly at me and winked. Debbie gave him a playful swat before turning her attention back to my houseguest.

"This is Hannah, she needs your help," Debbie interjected, bringing the seriousness back to the table. She quickly filled him in. Unable to stay still, I poured Dominic a cup of tea and set it down on the table to his right. He smiled gratefully before turning to the matter at hand.

"Well, it will take me a few days to set something up more permanent, but she can come and stay at the hotel. I have a few empty rooms. She will be safe there," Dominic suggested. "What do you think Emma? She should be comfortable, right?"

My gut churned. Hannah was cute, and single. She may have a crazy ex on her tail, but she was definitely someone I could see catching Dominic's eye. Her petite frame would be the perfect accent to his chiselled arms. For some reason, that really pissed me off! Realizing I was jealous, made it even more maddening; I had no right to be upset. It really was as simple as that.

"Yes, Hannah, you should be safe there," I begrudged admitted.

"Are you sure? You don't sound too happy with the prospect," Debbie teased. I growled at her and she laughed harder.

"Did I miss something?" Dominic inquired, looking at each of us with confusion.

"Oh, nothing much. Emmy has been telling us about her stay at your hotel," Hannah giggled. Great, she was following Debbie's lead. Now both of them were picking on me.

"What did she tell?" his eyebrows lifted in question. He watched me with an amused look on his face. I pointedly ignored him.

Debbie turned her mockery in his direction.

"Actually, she didn't tell us anything. She was starting to when you walked in. So wipe that guilty look off your face. At this moment, your secret is still safe - whatever that secret may be," she chortled as he squirmed under her scrutiny. "For a moment you looked nervous. What did happen?"

"Nothing!" we both replied in unison. I wished the floor would open up and swallow me.

Debbie threw her head back and howled with laughter. She was enjoying our discomfort way too much.

"Anyways, what are we going to do about Hannah?" Debbie asked again, trying to bring our attention back to the matter at hand. I was grateful for the subject change. Time to get down to business.

"I will take her back to the hotel, and set her up there. I will contact a realtor friend in the morning and she will set up some appointments to look at property. Do you have your things?" he turned to Hannah.

"I have everything I need. Anything else, I can buy on the way," she replied.

"Would George know where you are now?" Dominic pressed.

"No. I don't think so," Hannah admitted. "However, he does have resources available."

"Not legit ones," Dominic said. "The only people who will unite with him now, are people who are just as crooked as he is. No one wants to be associated with a known wife abuser."

"How do you know?" Debbie asked. "You sound so confident."

"Hey, when you asked for my help, you got it. I don't do things half way," he muttered. "I was already keeping an eye on things. When I heard Emma was writing the story, I did some research on my own. I come prepared. Knowledge is power and right now, we have the power!"

While he spoke, Hannah disappeared into my room, presumably to gather her things. It was then I realised there was something really different about my friend. I stood up and followed her.

Walking into my bedroom, I found Hannah placing a blanket over an infant car seat.

"Hang on," I gasped. "You had the baby?"

"Two weeks ago. This is Liam Connelly," she smiled down at her tiny son. The infant tucked into the seat looked like a doll. His porcelain soft face was topped by a tuft of blonde hair. He was a delightful little peanut with the chubbiest of cheeks. While I preferred puppies and kittens to babies - they were less work - I accepted that he was quite adorable.

"How come you didn't call me when you had him?" I asked, helping her pack Liam's things into a diaper bag. The baby cooed and farted in his car seat. We both giggled and he cooed louder.

"I couldn't take the chance. Once I went into labour, things went fairly quickly. I had a midwife so Liam was born quietly on the down low. Since he was born, I never take him out publicly. Even bringing him here today involved a degree of mystery. A friend brought an empty basket to my home and left with Liam safely inside. Only then did I feel it was safe to come here," Hannah explained. "I know he is safe here. I am not being paranoid, I know someone is watching. George cannot find out about Liam. Thank you; you have no idea how much this means to me. I can never repay you for helping me."

"You'd do the same for me," I politely responded.

"Would I? I sometimes wonder if I would have your courage," Hannah sheepishly admitted. I watched her fiddle with the receiving blankets she was folding.

"Honey, you're the one with courage. Let's not forget about Samantha. Giving up a child takes ultimate courage. Leaving George took courage too. Never think otherwise," I declared. "Never cut yourself short Hannah. Don't let George take that away from you too."

"I won't," she promised. Giving me another quick hug, she grabbed the baby and swept out the door.

An hour later, Hannah and Dominic left for the hotel. The cottage was quiet for all of five minutes before Debbie started questioning me.

"So, what are you going to do about Stephan?" Debbie asked once the coast was clear.

"I don't know what to do. I haven't even talked to him yet, other than a few email messages. He does not know what I know yet," I admitted. "That is a conversation I do not know how to start."

"I can see what you mean. As far as he is concerned, you should have none of this information. Some of it, grant it, was legitimately sent to you. The rest, you got on your own. He is not going to be happy you went through his stuff," Debbie reminded me.

"I know. He's going to be pissed; but does it really matter how he feels? He gave up that right when he decided not to wait for me. He decided to lie, to keep secrets, to literally live a double life. Why should I care if he's pissed?" I blurted defensively. I knew that Debbie was right. Snooping was wrong. But I felt justified and I needed her to acknowledge that fact.

"Hannah," Debbie replied. "Need I remind you that she thought she was with Mr. Perfect and he turned out to be hell on wheels?"

"No, you don't. Stephan would never...."I started defensively, but Debbie cut me off.

"Stephan would never what? Hit you? Hurt you? Try to kill you? I bet Hannah said that once too! I am beginning to realise that anything is possible in this day and age. Relationships can become volatile in moments. Depending on how good of a liar, someone is. An evil personally can't remain buried forever. Unfortunately, it can turn up when you least expect it. When you blow the lid off this can of worms, you better expect shit to hit the fan," Debbie continued. "Listen, I am not trying to frighten you, but you have to be careful."

"Emma, you are not a coward. Look at Hannah. You've been incredible with her. You held her hand during the toughest part of her life. That is a bond you cannot break. She will be okay, with your help. And you know damn well, that with our help, you will be ok too." Debbie promised. "You will see."

"So what's first? Hannah is in capable hands, and it's just me and you. What do you really want to do now? Or can I suggest something," she smiled mischievously. "There is only one way to get a beast and that's with a well-baited trap. We need to lay a trap."

"How are we going to manage that?" I asked. Knowing Debbie, I was almost afraid to ask.

"That's the easy part. You've seen his profile. Make a fake one. Find pictures of some really hot girls, create a profile and set the trap. If he is really out to cheat, he won't be able to resist. Especially since you recognize his triggers. He will think he's died and gone to heaven," Debbie continued. "Make her irresistible to him."

"Then we set up a meeting. Either I can go, or you can go. Either way, we catch him in the act. There is no way he can talk his way out of it," Debbie continued.

"I can't do that. I can't be with him and pretend that everything is okay, while waiting for the trap to snap. He's going to get suspicious. And if he takes the bait, I don't know if I can be quiet while we wait for the actual meeting to take place. I am going to want to kick his ass," I explained.

"Then give us permission to do it. Dominic and I will do it. All you need to know is that we set something up. The rest, we will keep to ourselves until you say otherwise. You can even pretend that you didn't know," Debbie suggested. "Hell, we won't tell you anything until he agrees to meet with us. If he doesn't meet then everything should be fine."

"And what if he does show up?" I asked.

"Then you kick the lying, cheating dog to the curb! No questions asked." Debbie stated empathically. She made it sound easy. "Now let's get to work."

For the rest of the afternoon, Debbie and I worked to create an enticing online profile. This is where we got creative. Our lovely bait was not one - but two buxom blondes. They were best friends and eager to please. Debbie even logged into the chat room and arranged for a full friends list by adding most of the people she already knew. This was when I discovered that many of the people looking for relationships on TheFishPond were secretly looking for friends with benefits on AdultPlayBuddy. So much for the legitimacy of online dating!

The profile was an immediate success; within two hours our friends list had expanded to over three hundred acquaintances. If Stephan actually read the profile, there was no way he would recognize it was not legit. Debbie logged off after sending Stephan's profile a friend request and a personal Inbox message.

"Hey sexy; My friend and I think you are hot. We would love to hear from you. Would you like to meet? XOXO"

"Are you sure that's enough?" I asked, before Debbie pressed send. I was partially eager to see if we could actually fool him. The rest of me worried about the consequences of his actually taking the bait. I told myself not to worry about it until we actually received a response. IF he responded.

"Without a doubt! I've attached a private photo for his consideration. If he's the dog I think he is, he will fall for it," Debbie replied, then showed me the picture. There were our lovely girls, sprawled out on a bed together. They were topless and enticing. Unless the viewer was homosexual, there was no way he could resist. Debbie was good; our fake bait girls were hot!

"Now we wait," she stated, closing out the browser window. "Do you still have the key to his apartment?"

"Yes, why?" I asked.

"Hold onto it, we may need it yet," Debbie replied.

As it worked out, neither of us had to sneak into Stephan's apartment undetected. Later the same evening, he called from England to ask a favour. There was a blueprint laying on his desk, and he needed me to go scan it and email it to his office. I agreed to get on it right away, and picked Debbie up along the way.

As Stephan had explained, the blueprint was exactly where he thought it would be. I quickly scanned it and sent it off. Meanwhile, Debbie was busy looking around the apartment.

"What is this?" Debbie suddenly asked. When I looked up, she was waving a piece of paper. Not recognizing the document she was holding, I shrugged.

"It looks like Stephan's lease," she went on.

"Oh?" I inquired inquisitively. I had totally forgotten about the lease. Stephan and I had discussed moving in together instead of signing for another year. That was several months ago. I presumed it was merely a small detail and the issue was resolved. He'd just not had time to tell me yet. I had every reason to believe he planned on packing and moving in after he returned from England.

"It looks like he signed it for another year," Debbie said as she read the document. She looked up when I yelped in shock.

"You're freaking kidding, right?" I stammered. *He signed it and didn't say anything? When had he planned on telling me? Or was he going to tell me.* My head was beginning to ache with this overload of information.

Just then, we both heard a beeping coming from under a stack of papers on the coffee table. Debbie searched the pile and pulled out Stephan's cell phone.

"Stephan forgot his cell?" She asked, looking at me questioningly. I was still standing frozen and mute in the dining room trying to comprehend the lease. I shrugged. When he travelled overseas, he'd usually pack his Tablet. As long as he found a WIFI connection, he didn't need his cell phone and it was cheaper.

"Yeah, I guess he did. Maybe he didn't want to worry about roaming charges?" I reasoned. I glanced up when it beeped again in Debbie's hand.

"Looks like he has a text message. Maybe it's important," she said, already flipping open the cell phone. Her forehead creased as she read the message. "What's this?"

"What is it?" I inquired, suddenly curious. The colour had drained from Debbie's face as she read the message. That was definitely not a good sign.

"Um, I don't know. It looks like an automated message, but it makes no sense," she replied, then handed over the phone. I read the incoming message; it was previously unread. It said: This is to confirm your advertisement on Craigslist is now active; Please confirm your email TopFun4U@your.email.com.

"What's Stephan selling?" Debbie asked. Her expression of confusion mirrored mine.

"I don't know. He never said anything to me about it. Did you see the email address?" I hesitantly asked. For me, the implication of clear. I just wanted to make sure that Debbie read it the same way.

"TopFun4U? What the hell?" Debbie shouted after rereading the message out loud. "You can't think Stephan is trolling for gay sex on Craigslist?"

Her bellowed words hung in the air, unanswered. That is exactly what I was thinking. The blood drained from my face and I felt physically ill. First, there were women and now there are men? Did I ever really know who or what Stephan really was? How could I have been so blind and foolish. This could not be happening to me. All I tried to do was be a good girlfriend and meanwhile, he was playing me. Even worse, I fell for it! I thought I was smarter than that.

"Wait, there has to be a valid explanation," I tried to reason. My mind was jumping to every conclusion possible. None of them were useful, or reassuring.

"Emma, are you blind?" Debbie insisted angrily. She was getting angry with me. She looked like she was going to hit me. "There is no sensible explanation."

"It's only an ambiguous message. We don't know that anything ever came of it," I insisted. Debbie walked over to where I was standing, forcing me to look at her. I got ready to duck in the event that she started swinging.

"Emma, get your head out of your backside. I love you, but you are being blind. I know you love Stephan, but this is not something that you can just shut your eyes to and forget. He may be sweet, and spoils you rotten, but you now have reason to believe that it is all a cover," Debbie stared me down as she spoke.

"What should I do?" I asked. The answer was obvious, but I needed to hear someone else say it.

"You still have his email password right?" Debbie asked.

"He gave it to me so I could send him the blueprint," I admitted.

"Did you look at his email messages?" Debbie was already heading to the computer.

"I didn't think of it," I sighed. This was getting ridiculous.

"It's time to think about it," Debbie insisted, sitting down at the computer. "Let's see what Stephan has really been up to."

I sat down beside her and held my breath while we waited for the page to load. When Stephan's Inbox was finally laid out before us, I felt myself start to fall. Thankfully Debbie's hand firmly grasping my arm kept me from hitting the floor.

"Holy shit!" Debbie gasped.

CHAPTER TWENTY

Two weeks later, I picked Stephan up from the airport as previously planned. As I sat in my car and waited for him at the front of the airport, I played out various scenarios in my mind. Accusing one's boyfriend of cheating could lead to any assortment of complications and reactions. None of them was positive. It was nearly impossible to predict what would happen.

For a brief moment, I felt guilty for blindsiding him with the decision to end our relationship on the way back to his apartment. Unfortunately, it had to be done. One thing was clear, I could not live another day pretending everything was fantastic. The past few weeks had already been hell. There was nothing worse than attempting to pretend everything was all right when it wasn't. Besides, I was not a very good actress.

Debbie was furious that I chose to honour my commitment to pick Stephan up from the airport, but she also understood my need for closure. I could not simply walk off without looking back. I had to deal with the situation and ensuing complications.

It had not been difficult to avoid Stephan's many attempts to reach me during the remainder of his trip. I had numerous email messages and voice mails. He always sounded cheerful and chipper so it was difficult to differentiate if he ever caught on to the fact I was screening his calls. Watching him walk from the doors of the airport to my waiting vehicle, it was obvious he was oblivious.

"Emma! You're looking beautiful! Baby, I've been missing you so much. How have you been doing lately? Where have you been?" he raved. Before I could react, he dropped his bags onto the sidewalk and swept me into his arms. I allowed him to hug me, but remained stiff in his arms. He didn't even notice. I twisted my head precisely in time to avoid his lips on mine. He set me down and grinned at me. "God, I missed you! I can't wait to take you home and ravish you."

Instead of replying, I twisted away and opened the trunk.

"Did you have a good flight?" I asked before grabbing his bags and tossing them into the back. He stood and watched as I loaded his things, his gaze openly appreciative of how I looked. "You've gotten hotter in my absence baby. I can't wait to see what you have under that dress."

Ignoring his flirtatious comments, I got into the car. He promptly followed suit. I shifted the car into gear and pulled out of the parking spot. Pretending to shift gears, I managed to avoid his hand reaching for mine. Consumed with happiness to be home, he failed to note my continued indifference.

"When we get back to my apartment, I want to take a shower and tonight, we are going out someplace special for dinner. I heard the revolving restaurant recently reopened. I can call and make reservations. Doesn't that sound lovely?" Stephan enthusiastically suggested.

I listened quietly and nodded. It was getting harder to keep my emotions in check. From the second I set eyes on him, I wanted to shout, holler and kick. I wanted to scratch his eyes out, but I sat there, silent. Listening to him spew romantic bullshit. Knowing all the long, he was a lying dirt bag. I was having impulse control issues.

It wasn't until we left the airport parking lot and hit the main streets that he realized I was still silent.

"You have no idea how glad I am to see you," he said, clasping my hand in his. I cringed inwardly when he brushed the back of it with his lips. "Is everything all right?"

I swallowed hard again and shook my head. It was becoming difficult to keep my mouth shut yet at the same time, all I wanted to do was verbally lash out. The confused and slightly innocent look on his face was my undoing. How dare he act like he had no idea what was going on? His reaction made me even more furious! I was about ready to explode. I made my decision quickly. It's now or never for me. Time to quit being such a coward. At the next intersection I deliberately pulled over to the side of the busy highway and put the car in park. Stephan was now watching me quizzically, but he did not open his mouth.

"You need to determine where we are going?" I finally blurted.

Startled, Stephan turned and looking at me questioningly.

"What do you mean?" he demanded. He blinked with confusion.

"You need to determine if we are going to your apartment, my place or to the next walk-in clinic," I finally blurted. It was the most difficult sentence I had to put together in a very long time. I almost gasped in relief when I finally put voice to my opinions.

"Excuse me?" he was beginning to look worried. I nearly felt guilty for playing this game. Almost.

"I have reason to believe that you have put my health at risk. We need to get to the doctor right away and get tested for sexually transmitted diseases," I blurted out in one breath. Okay, that was the second hardest sentence I had to say. I looked at him square in the face as I spoke. He looked like I'd slapped him. Then he fell silent again and looked out the passenger window. There was no denial, no excuses, no "what the hell" - just silent acceptance. Like his secret was out. There is no reason to hide anymore.

"What are you talking about?" he quietly asked.

"Do not pretend to not know what I am talking about," I angrily retorted. Now that I'd opened my mouth, the weeks of anger, disillusion and disappointment came bursting out.

"I don't know what you are talking about," he insisted with frustration.

"Oh please, do not do this now! I know everything," I insisted. "I saw your emails!"

He looked up with surprise, then realization began to set in. After my admission, he visibly crumbled under the weight of defeat in the passenger seat. For a second, I wished I dealt with the matter with more tact, but it was too late now. He knew there was no point in maintaining this ruse.

"I was careful," he weakly replied. I barely suppressed the impulse to slap him.

"I do not believe you!" I retorted. "You are naive to think I'd believe anything you say. You owe me that much. I don't think this one requires an explanation. I want to know that I am not going to die because you are a selfish prick."

"I am sorry," he whispered beside me. I looked over and he looked close to crying. I felt brief shame for humiliating him with this confrontation. But the bitterness in me won, and I wanted him to feel a little of the pain I'd suffered in the past few weeks. How dare he waltz back into my life after a wonderful vacation while I stayed home and anguished over the secrets I'd unearthed. It was simply not fair. Then put into perspective, they were his secrets. Secrets he'd carried in his heart - if he had a heart. Who was I to judge and to hurt him. He was more of a mess than I ever could be.

"Listen Stephan, I do not desire to hurt you. However, we both need to get to the doc," I asserted. "I'd like to believe you've been careful, but please understand when I say, I can't believe you right now. I think you owe me that much. Afterwards, we will deal with us."

"Us?" he demanded. The hopefulness was clear in his eyes. I knew there would be no us, but I couldn't tell him that yet. The risk of him refusing medical testing was too high. I had to lead him on a little longer.

"Yes, I am a rational woman and we are going to deal with this rationally," I went on. The vehicle fell into silence. Neither one of us really knew what to say next. I had so many questions, but I was afraid to ask. Then there were the countless questions that I was afraid I'd ask, when I should have kept my mouth shut. To play it safe, I kept quiet - period.

"I want you to know that I never did it," he softly began to explain.

"Never did what? I have pages messages back and forth; private conversations. I read them word for word. Don't tell me it was not genuine," I returned. How dare he try to refute the physical evidence I was capable of producing. I'd kept copies of everything on my tablet, in the event he tried to deny my accusations.

"It was all talk. I never met anyone," he insisted.

"What about Jade? What about Jelly? Try to convince me that you never met them! I even saw the pictures," I retorted with disbelief. Stephan's head snapped upward in surprise.

"Photographs?" he demanded. His eyes frantically searched my face. I was afraid to meet his gaze.

"Yes, the photographs of you and Jelly in the hotel. We had a date night planned. Are you going to deny screwing her in your bed?"

I accused. Frantically I dug out my tablet, pulled up the photographs and showed him the screen. His face dropped and his shoulders sagged. Simultaneously, there was a hint of relief. Was there something else that I missed?

"Where did you find these?" He asked, glancing quickly at the photograph I produced on my tablet. He blushed red with shame. With the evidence laid out before him, he knew it was over.

"Someone emailed them to me. They heard me talking about us moving in together, and thought I needed to be warned. Why do you have an active dating account on *TheFishPond*? What about *AdultPlayBuddy*? Has this all been a game for you?" I blitzed him with a barrage of questions.

He sat in uncomfortable silence instead of replying.

"Don't you have anything to say?" I demanded again. His silence infuriated me, but I managed to hold in my anger.

"Let's get to the clinic," came his stony response.

Recognizing that he was done with the conversation, I put the car into gear and pulled back out into traffic in search for the closest medical clinic.

A half an hour later, Stephan and I were sitting in a crowded walk-in clinic waiting for blood work. I nervously played on my tablet, while he sat next to me feigning sleep. When the nurse finally called my name, I went into the examining room alone. It was humiliating telling the nurse why I was there, but there was no point being dishonest. She was sympathetic and so was the doctor. I can't say that Stephan's examination was as painless. Later on, I noticed him rubbing his arm where blood was taken. Something told me the nurse forgot how to be gentle when it came to his testing.

The worse part of the entire experience was having to list my previous sexual encounters. The nurse said the list would remain secret unless I tested positive with something serious like Hepatitis C or HIV. Then the public health act required that former lovers be contacted and told to visit their doctors as soon as possible. Her assurances did not make it any easier to write. Gratefully, my list only comprised of one - Stephan - but on the off chance that I had taken more lovers in the past year or so, let's say the reality really hit.

I wondered if Stephan had the same response. How many people had he really been with? I knew of two for sure, but I surmised there were more. Based on the numerous private conversations found in his APB account, he'd met with at least two couples. He'd even had sex with the wives while the husbands watched or participated. The actual messages between the parties were vague, but the implications were very clear. He'd been doing more than travelling. There was even evidence in his email, that proved he'd met up with past flames on his many trips to England. There was one woman, he'd promised to meet at her ranch. Apparently she'd built a new barn and he wanted to try out the hayloft with her.

One thing was very clear - the Stephan I discovered cavorting on the Internet was NOT the man who shared my bed. For the most part, our relationship seemed pretty strong. He claimed an interest in my household and took charge of it as if it was his own. Without my asking, he loved to play handyman. I never had to ask for wood to be chopped, the dog to be walked, or for supper to be prepared. It was done before I even knew it. There were roses, chocolates, surprises here and there. He was perfect in every way.

Then there was the side that confused me. Unlike every other man I'd ever met, he seemed completely immune to my charms. More often than naught, my attempts to kiss him were brushed off. Our love life had decreased in both quantity and quality. It would be days, sometimes weeks before he'd attempt physical contact. I'd call him on his behaviour, but he always had an excuse. He just happened to be stretching, have an itch, or he was suddenly thirsty.

He was a walking contradiction when it came to stereotypical males. Instead of jumping me when I tried to seduce him, he acted like I was doing something wrong. Despite his uncooperative behaviour, I continued to try to rekindle the initial heat on our relationship. I tried wearing lingerie, only to get turned down, yet I still tried. Even coming home from work one afternoon to discover my cleaning the apartment in a sexy maid costume, thigh highs and stilettos failed to get the desired reaction.

I was often left frustrated and agitated, but it was easy to make up excuses. Both of us had busy lives. He had a physically and mentally challenging profession. Mine was mentally draining. It was easier to blame life than to look at the real issues. Unfortunately, his selfishness forced me to look at the issue in a very real way and address it - at a medical clinic.

We went back to his apartment after leaving the clinic without any answers to the big questions. It would be another week before we'd get the results of our blood work. The wait would be excruciating but there was nothing we could do to speed things up. Our lives would remain hold until the lab finally called. Neither us knew what to say, so the ride was long and silent.

"I am sorry," Stephan said again, when I finally pulled up in front of his apartment building. I ignored him, refusing to grant absolution.

"I think I should come in and grab my stuff," I replied instead. Over the previous months, I'd started leaving personal items behind. Having a few items on hand always made it easier for Stephan to convince me to spend the night.

"Okay, that would be fine," he conceded, finally getting out of the car.

I followed him upstairs. In his apartment, he sat down on the computer chair and watching me gather my things.

"I am really sorry, I can't say that enough. I hope you will forgive me for this one day," he weakly implored. Unable to respond, I pretended not to hear him while going from room to room making sure I was leaving without a trace. Finally, I'd collected two cardboard boxes of personal items. I didn't realize I'd moved so much over.

"You can come fetch your stuff from my place later," I volunteered. It was only fair that if I could go away with my stuff unmolested, I extend the same courtesy. At this point, I felt like I was moving around in a semi-traumatised state. This day was the last day of a particularly harrowing part of my life. Realizing that, I was more than ready to move on.

I looked at Stephan, curled up and pathetic in the chair, and realized that yes, he was miserable. He was the one who failed to see the wonderful relationship he was in. He failed to appreciate the woman I was. It will be his loss. Not just mine alone. I was just glad we hadn't moved in yet. It would have been harder to cut the ties.

Taking a last look round, I carried my boxes to the threshold. Stephan followed slowly behind. Reaching out to open the door, my hand was stopped. He quickly stepped between me and the only way out, successfully preventing any further retreat.

"Emma. Please, don't stop talking to me," he begged. "Don't leave like this!"

"What is there to say? You didn't value us, or this would not have occurred. It's done, it's over with. You made your choice," I responded sadly. Now that I was packed and ready to walk away, the tears of finality threatened to spill over. As much as my heart hurts from his betrayal, it was painful to walk away. I loved him. I cared about him deeply. I'd thought that we were the exception. Just because we'd met in an unconventional manner, I'd believed we could make it. Now, the only thing I discovered was that he was an amazing liar; and I was a fool to believe him.

Thank goodness for my close friends! They'd help me pick up the pieces, there was no doubt about that.

"I am sorry Stephan too," I whispered. Then quickly I dove in for a hug. His arms came up around me and tightened. He refused to let me go. As I tried to pull away, I picked up a slight sniffle over my shoulder. When he finally let me go, I caught him discretely wiping away tears.

I straightened in defiance, refusing to acknowledge his show of emotion and remorse. It was too little, much too late. Fighting the urge to cave, I opened the door, and picked up the boxes. I walked out the door without looking back.

He accompanied me into the hallway and followed as I walked down the hallway. I half expected him to chase after me, but I refused to pause. I nearly ran down the three flights of stairs and out the front door of the building.

As I left, I picked up a soft tapping from above. I looked up and spotted Stephan standing in the third floor landing window. He raised his hand and gave me a final wave. I nodded slightly in acknowledgment before turning away and walked to my car.

Fighting my tears, I finally pulled away from the curb and headed for home. It took every ounce of strength I possessed not to look back.

CHAPTER TWENTY-ONE

"Have you heard from Emma?" Debbie asked Dominic the next afternoon. He'd just called to give her an update on Hannah's situation. He'd found an affordable house for her. Apparently the mother and child were settling into their new home just fine.

Hannah ended up staying a week at the hotel before Dominic found her a safer location. No one knew where she was, and it was supposed to stay that way until further notice.

"No, I haven't heard from her in over a week. What's up?" he inquired into the receiver. He'd picked up the telephone to call Emma a few times but refrained. He knew she felt bad over what went on in the hotel, and he felt awful for pushing things. But what was he supposed to do? He was a hot-blooded male and she was a very sensual woman, even if she neglected to see that herself. He knew she was tormented over Stephan and while he wanted to help, he didn't want to get in the way. The last thing she needed at the moment was him complicating things.

"Stephan got back into town yesterday. She was supposed to collect him from the airport, but I haven't heard from her. I didn't want her to go pick him up alone. I told her to walk away and never look back. But she insisted on confronting him," Debbie blurted out her fears. It felt good to finally release all her pent up anxiety and worry. Dominic knew their friendship. He would understand and not think she was being worrisome for nothing.

"She picked him up from the airport? That takes balls," Dominic whistled. "I am impressed. Have you tried her cell?"

"Over and over; it's dead or turned off," Debbie replied hysterically. "What if he didn't take things well? What if he had more invested in this relationship than she thought? What if he hurt her?"

"Why would he hurt her?" Dominic barked, suddenly concerned. Without further explanation, the hair stood up on the back of his neck. "Has he done something?"

"No, but look at Hannah. Who ever expected George to be such a nut job?" Debbie admitted. "I don't know if you know, but Emma was going to break up with Stephan when he got off the plane."

"She broke up with him?" Dominic was all ears again. Did this mean he finally had a chance with her? He tried not to be hopeful. It made him feel like a predator.

"I don't know if she did, but when she went to get him, she was going to take him to the doctor to do STD tests. She was adamant about that aspect of the trip," Debbie confided. "She is fairly positive that he was cheating on her - not with one person but with several."

"Do you suppose he went?" Dominic was starting to get concerned again. Forcing a man to a doctor's office for STD testing was treading on dangerous ground. Some men were adult enough to comply, but most would put up some kind of fuss. While Stephan did not appear to be the type of cat who'd get nasty, anything could happen given the proper conditions. Every man and woman has a breaking point.

Emma had obviously got to her breaking point, Dominic thought proudly.

"Something tells me that he went without argument. One thing I could tell is that Stephan cares about Emma. Once he realizes how much she's hurt, he's going to do the right thing. Besides, he's English. They are bred to do the correct thing. His honour won't let him." Debbie tried to sound confident, but internally, she was worried sick. It was extremely unusual for Emma to vanish without giving her the heads-up first.

"If he had the honour, he wouldn't have been poking other women. Emma is simply incredible. How could he have hurt her that way? It makes me want to hurt him," Dominic fumed. Imagining his fist pulverizing Stephan's face made him smile to himself.

"Dominic!" Debbie started laughing.

"What?" Startled at her sudden levity, Dominic stopped his rant long enough to listen.

"You're falling in love with her!" She snorted with satisfied glee. The phone line remained silent, making her giggle harder. "That is amazing! You are perfect for her."

"I don't know about that," Dominic admitted after a significant pause. "I will admit, that given the opportunity I would love to make her happy."

"Well, I am sure you will get that chance, but first we have to find her," Debbie interjected. While she was thrilled Emma had a champion, finding her missing friend was the immediate priority. "Would you come to the Stephan's apartment with me? He's the last person to have seen her. Maybe he knows something. If she's not there, we may have to send for the police."

"What about her editor?" Dominic asked. "Have you called the office yet?"

"I already called him. He hasn't heard from her in days. It's still another week until the deadline so he isn't expecting to hear from her for another few days at least," Debbie said. "He promised to notify me immediately if she contacts him."

"Ok, I will come and pick you up. We will do it together. Who knows, maybe she changed her mind and we will find her naked in his bed," Dominic reluctantly suggested. As he spoke, the thought of Emma laying naked with another man made him physically ill. He wanted to be the only man to lay naked alongside her, enjoying her luscious curves. Stop, he mentally scolded himself. Now is certainly not the time to be thinking about this.

"Alright, see you in half an hour," Debbie's agreement interrupted his thoughts. "I will wait for you by the gate."

"See you in a bit," he replied and hung up.

An hour afterwards, Debbie and Dominic converged on Stephan's doorstep. Unsure of what he drove, neither was able to determine if he was home or not. It didn't matter, they were on a mission. Outside the apartment door, Debbie pulled out the key and slipped it into the keyhole. The door unlatched and quietly opened.

Dominic pushed her away and stepped inside first.

The television turned on but abandoned in the living room while soft music streamed from the bedroom. Mixed with the music came the sound of heavy panting. Clothing is strewn everywhere.

"Crap, he's home?" Debbie mouthed to Dominic. He nodded slowly. Suddenly feeling like burglars, the duo tiptoed down the short hall to stand outside the chamber doorway. From the open doorway they could clearly make out two naked bodies, thrusting against each other in the middle of the bed.

"What the hell?" Debbie blurted, unable to remain silent a moment longer.

Stephan's head popped up first, accompanied by a second, brunette cropped mop. It was obvious the lovers were stunned by the interruption. No surprise there; they had basically broken in.

"Damn it!" Dominic cursed loudly, glaring at the guilty looking male who was obviously busy playing with Stephan under the blankets. It was obvious what they'd snuck in on.

"Oh. My. God!" Debbie sputtered. She struggled to articulate another word. It didn't really matter. It was Stephan's turn to react to the intruders.

"What the hell? How did you come in here?" Stephan yelled, getting up from the bed, dragging the sheet along with him. "Get out of here before I call the police."

"Wait," Debbie yelled, putting her hand up to stop Stephan's angry advance. "Have you seen Emma? She is the sole reason why we are here."

Stephan had stopped dead in his tracks.

"No, not since yesterday. Why?" He suddenly looked concerned. Then he realized they'd broken in and got angry again. "How did you get in here anyway?"

Both Debbie and Dominic ignored his question and his rage.

"She never arrived home last night," Dominic interrupted. "As far as we know, you were the last person to see her. What happened?"

"She picked me up from the airport, we talked and she left," Stephan replied defiantly.

"That's all?" Debbie asked. "We know you were banging other women. There is no point in keeping that from us. We know more than you realize so tell us what happened?"

"FINE! She split up with me, took her things and left," he sobbed. Overcome with emotion, he plopped back down on the couch. He looked visibly distraught.

"I see you really missed her," Dominic retorted angrily, pointing towards the bedroom where Stephan's lover still cowered under the covers. *How dare this snivelling cheater pretend he cared about Emma?*

"How long did you wait until you checked Craigslist and started answering e-mails? Was Emma even in her car yet?" Dominic snarled.

Stephan did not answer. Rather, he had the decency to look worried, having noticed his adversary subconsciously pounding a fist in his opposite hand. Briefly, he worried Dominic was imagining the empty palm was actually his face.

"I swear. I watched her leave," Stephan replied with renewed earnest. It was obvious neither Debbie or Dominic would leave until they had some answers.

"Did you watch her get into her car?" Dominic demanded.

"No, but it's not on the street either," Stephan went to the window to double check. Sure enough the parking space was empty and her car was nowhere to be seen. "See? She was parked right there and now she is gone."

"Where the hell did that woman go?" Dominic barked at no one in particular. Debbie jumped and Stephan snivelled. The man who was sharing his bed, was still hiding the bedroom. He was smart by staying put.

"Sorry for barging in on you," Debbie apologized awkwardly. "We've wasted enough time here and need to start looking. Call us if you hear anything."

"I will, I swear!" Stephan promised. He looked relieved when they both got up to leave. He went with them to the door.

"Oh, here, You might want this back," Debbie said, moving around to pass him the key. "Sorry for barging in on you. By the way, in case you are wondering, your secret is safe with us."

"Before you leave, can I ask a question? Does Emma know...about this?" Stephan asked, waving his arm towards the bedroom. Even he was unable to put into words what they'd just witnessed.

"Yes, she does," Debbie reluctantly admitted after a significant pause. Dominic looked down at her with surprise.

"She does?" Stephan and Dominic asked in unison.

"Yes, she found several messages in your email while you were in England. You had replied to some ads on Craigslist before you went away. You should have seen her face when she read your notes. It's hard to tell what hurt her more; reading you talk about needing to be discreet because you're in a relationship. Or asking other men to allow you to poke their arse. If you desire to be with men, that is your business. Might I suggest that you not be so selfish next time. Ever consider staying single? Don't use a woman to cover your real wants. You're not only lying to her, but to yourself," Debbie replied coldly.

Stephan looked both ashamed and devastated at Debbie's words. He realized quickly that Emma could have made their breakup nastier. Instead, she handled it with poise and kept the worst of the allegations to herself. Any other woman would have flipped out after finding out their lover was not only sharing his bed with other women, but seemed to prefer men. He'd underestimated her and ultimately her love for him.

"Wow; she never gave it away," he reflected in awe. "She had every reason to get nasty with me and she didn't!"

"Emma is not the type of woman to toss your mistakes in your face. She may have seemed harsh hauling you to a doctor, but under the circumstances you can't blame her," Debbie continued. "All she wanted to know was that you did not put her health in danger. That's all that mattered."

Stephan nodded in understanding.

With nothing left to say, the couple turned to leave.

"Thanks. I will let you know if I hear from her," Stephan promised as they exited the apartment. "And if you see her first, tell her I will be over to grab my things in a few days,"

"Consider it done," Debbie replied.

Downstairs, Dominic and Debbie climbed back into the truck. He put the key in the ignition, but did not turn the key.

"Have you gone to her house yet?" Dominic turned to Debbie and asked the obvious.

"No, but I tried calling numerous times. The answering machine kept picking it up," she admitted. "Hang on, I will try again."

While she dialed Emma's cell phone number for what seemed like the fiftieth time, Dominic deftly guided the truck out of town towards the cottage. There was still no answer.

"It simply keeps ringing," Debbie said, before disconnecting the call. The same thing happened when she tried the house phone.

"Maybe she wanted some time by herself. Maybe, she's outside, enjoying the fresh air. Not answering your phone does not necessarily mean you're missing. If that was true, I'd be reported missing at least once a week," Dominic barked in frustration. The more complicated the story became, the more patience he lost. "Seriously woman?"

"Well, let's go look then. If she's there, we will find her," Debbie replied calmly. "Don't get mad at me; we are both worried."

"We should have done that first, before we humiliated Stephan," Dominic added. Despite the circumstances, he felt horrible barging in on the man.

"Don't tell me you feel sorry for him," Debbie replied in disbelief.

"Actually, I do a little. Put aside the fact that he cheated on Emma, he's not in a great place. If he is secretly gay, that is a huge secret to carry," he concluded. "Our generation was taught that man on man love was wrong. Sure the youth of today are sexual explorers, but for men like me, coming out of the closet is very difficult. There is still such a stigma attached."

"I can understand that; but if he was confused, he should not be trying to be in a relationship," Debbie considered. "His mistake was dragging someone else into it."

"I won't argue," Dominic agreed. "I hope Emma's okay."

When they finally arrived at their destination. Dominic deftly steered the truck down the lengthy driveway into Emma's yard. As they drew closer to the house, they spotted Emma's sports car parked behind the house. It was slightly hidden in the trees.

"That's odd. She doesn't usually park there," Debbie mused. A dog barked persistently from inside the house. "Sounds like Belle's at home. Emma can't be too far away. She would never have left the dog without letting someone know."

Dominic was no longer paying attention. Something outside the cottage had caught his eye. He tried to ignore the prickling discomfort of the hair standing up on the back of his neck. Most of all, he tried not to alarm Debbie.

"Hang on, something not right," Dominic interjected, putting his hand up to stop Debbie from leaving the vehicle. He parked the truck and got out. Debbie watched as he walked over to the deck, while carefully inspecting the ground on the way.

"What do you see?" Debbie called, having rolled down window.

"Blood spatter," Dominic mumbled low enough so only he could hear.

"WHAT?" Debbie exclaimed.

"Shush up woman!" Dominic yelled, but it was too late. Debbie was already out of the vehicle and flying towards the back door. She skidded to a halt, then reached up and grabbed a piece of paper attached to the door. An arrow shot through the centre of the page held it securely in position. She ripped the paper off the shaft and handed it to Dominic, unable to read it for herself.

"What does it say?" she gasped impatiently, fighting back tears. Now that she looked around, Dominic was right. There were several tiny droplets of brownish red dried up on the surface of the wood.

"Hang on; calm down," Dominic said as he tried to piece the torn scraps of paper together so he could read the handwritten note.

"Let's make a trade ~ Woman for woman. You have 24 hours," he read loud enough for Debbie's benefit.

"What the hell is this supposed to mean? Woman for woman? Who the hell would want..."Dominic's voice trailed off. "Wait. Have you heard from Hannah today?"

"Hang on!" Debbie said, already dialing Hannah's cell number. She picked up after two rings.

"Hi Debbie, what's up?" Hannah asked. She sounded like she'd just woken up from a nap. Liam could be heard gurgling happily in the background.

"Are you okay?" Debbie asked. She was relieved to hear Hannah's voice.

"Sure, why wouldn't I be?" Hannah asked, slightly alarmed. "Has something happened?"

"Have you heard from Emma lately?" Debbie carefully asked. She didn't want Hannah to freak out unnecessarily in the event that Emma had already made contact.

"Not for a few days. Why? Is everything okay?" Hannah persisted. She was starting to get worried.

"She's been missing since yesterday evening. We found a note attached to her door. Somebody used a bow and arrow to fasten it to her doorway!" Debbie was trying to be gentle but she had to find the answers she needed and fast. Emma's life might depend on it. "Do you know who could have done that?"

"She's missing?" Hannah gasped. This was not the news she expected to hear.

"We found a note, suggesting an even trade. Hannah, I think George has her," Debbie suggested cautiously. "I think he's going to hurt her if we don't' tell him where you are. Don't worry, we won't tell him. But Hannah, we have to find her!"

Hannah burst into tears.

"I can't believe he would take my friend. Why would he do that?" Hannah bawled. "We have to find her!"

"Because he knows how to hurt you. You will do anything for your friends. Even go to him. Promise you will stay put," Debbie insisted. "You have to keep Liam safe!"

"I will stay here. Where would he hide her?" Hannah asked, then she thought of something. "Wait, there is a mobile home; out in the bush, along Fireguard 75. He calls it his hunting cottage, but it's kind of tough to find unless you know where to look. That was one of his demands when he bought the place. You should look there."

"How do you get there?" Dominic asked loud enough so Debbie did not need to repeat it over the telephone.

"Tell him I will email you a map with co-ordinates. I have the coordinates bookmarked in my GPS. Why would George do this?" Hannah wondered.

"It's simple. He wants you and he is trying to flush you out," Dominic grabbed the phone from Debbie's hand. "Listen. Look under your mattress. There is a handgun there. I put it there the night you moved in. Don't argue. The bullets are in the shoebox on the top shelf of the closet. Load it and keep it close. It sounds like he's desperate."

"Do you think he knows where I am?" Hannah asked fearfully.

"If he did, I don't think he'd have taken Emma," Dominic pointed out.

"Hang tight, I will have the map to you in ten minutes, " Hannah promised, and then she hung up.

While they waited for the email, Dominic made a few phone calls, while Debbie inspected the cottage. Everything appeared in order, except that Emma was not to be found. When he finally returned to the kitchen table he was sombre and worried.

"I just got off the phone with my man in Baudette. George got his monitoring bracelet removed a few days ago," Dominic explained carefully. "Last night, he went out for a few beers and somehow gave us the slip. I don't know how to say this, but as of last night, we have no idea where he is."

Debbie looked startled.

"This is not good," Debbie replied. Her eyes were frantic with worry.

"No, it is not! We need to find that cabin!" Dominic agreed.

CHAPTER TWENTY-TWO

It was dark out when I woke up shivering. Groggy and disoriented, I fought against the darkness for a few minutes before realizing it was futile; I was wearing a blindfold. I forced myself to calm down and listen intently for some clue to where I was. Once I calmed down, the only sound in the room was my own breath, panting in fear. Fighting the panic clutching my heart, I drove myself to focus on my breathing - in and out; in and out. With each exhale, I feel myself relax further and my pulse slowing.

I tried to move, but it was impossible to budge. Ragged rope pinched my flesh where it bound my ankles and my wrists. Whomever had tied me up had also stripped me bare. As I shivered uncontrollably, I was grateful for the thin sheet I was allowed. I wiggled some more, but the only thing I achieved was to dislodge the sheet. I realised quickly that if I wiggled around too much, I would be totally uncovered. I reluctantly gave up struggling. I had no idea how long it would be until someone checked on me so modesty and warmth became priorities. Better to be safe than be sorry. I recognized neither the scent or sounds surrounding me. I had no choice but to wait to see who would show up.

After a while my arms ached and I tried to readjust. By turning my head from side to side, I was able to work the loosened blindfold off my face. I was briefly blinded by the sunlight, which bathed the tiny room. My prison appeared to be an old mobile home, but there was nothing familiar about it. Looking around, I could make out the shape of a workbench, sofa and TV. A kitchenette sized table and two chairs sat in the corner. An empty coffee cup was abandoned on the table. Someone has been here recently. There were still coals smouldering in the blackened wood stove tucked into the corner. It appeared to be the only source of heat in the tiny room.

Unable to do anything other than wait, I strained to recall the events leading up to my waking up, naked in an unknown location. Some of the details were kind of fuzzy.

After I left Stephan's apartment, I decided to head directly home. All I wanted was to get within the comforting familiarity of my haven, lock the door and deal with the events of the day uninterrupted. I required a mental time-out. After feeding Belle, I decided to enjoy a nice hot bubble bath. I'd just stopped filling the bath when my cell phone rang. At first, I was going to ignore it. It rang four times, then proceeded to the answering machine. Just when I started to forget about it, the phone started ringing again. Whomever was calling was persistent, so I finally answered it.

"Hello?" I asked, when I finally plucked up the phone. I didn't recognize the number on the call display.

"Emma? It's Hannah!" said the voice. I was puzzled, it sounded like Hannah, and yet there was something odd about her voice. I couldn't quite put my finger on it.

"Hannah? Are you okay?" I asked. "I was not expecting to hear from you for a few days."

"Emma, You need to come here. I need you," she said, completely ignoring what I'd just asked. "I need you to come now."

"Where is here?" I asked, suddenly alarmed.

Instead of a response, the phone line went dead.

Getting the phone number off my call display, I tried calling Hannah back several times, but I kept getting the operator. *The cellular customer you have dialed is away from the phone or out of the service area. Please try again later,* said the robotic voice message. Her cell phone must have been either dead or turned off, I concluded.

I didn't know what else to do. Glancing at the time, I realized there was no one available to accompany me. Debbie is still at work. I tried calling Dominic but his phone was turned off too. *What the hell?* No one is ever around when you need them, I swore.

"Damn it," I yelled into the empty cottage. Startled, Belle barked, then ran off to hide in the bedroom. I grabbed my bag and headed to my car. I continued trying to call Dominic. He was the only one who could give me the exact directions to Hannah's safehouse. In the meantime, I was going to at least hit the road.

I tossed my purse onto the passenger seat and climbed in. I was reaching to put the key in the ignition when something moved to the left side of the vehicle. Before I could search out what I'd seen out of the corner of my eye, shards of glass sprayed throughout the car as the driver side window shattered. My head burst with sudden pain; then everything faded to black.

The next thing I knew, I was waking up naked, tied to a mattress wearing nothing but a dirty sheet. When I opened my eyes next, the shadows on the wall had changed positions. I must have dozed off for a while. The vibrant oranges glowing on the wall mirrored a glorious sunset. It would soon be dusk. I couldn't feel my arms and the need to relieve myself was becoming urgent. I should have been panicking, but something told me that whomever was responsible for my current state of affairs would eventually come back. There was a reason why I was like this, and being left to die alone was not one of them.

The crunch of rubber on gravel filtered through the walls. Someone was driving up to the trailer. I stilled and pretended to sleep. Meanwhile, I mustered all my strength to control my rising terror. My breathing came first. I concentrated, until my head hurt. A vehicle door slammed in the distance. Footsteps on gravel grew closer to the cabin. I clenched my eyes tightly shut. *Come on Emma, relax. Breathe. Pretend to be sleeping.*

The door screeched as it slowly swung open on rusty hinges. A huge shadow was cast on the wall as whomever entered blocked the sunset from the room. I held my breath and waited. The footsteps moved closer. I could feel someone peering at me in the semi-darkness. I fought the urge to squirm.

"I know your awake sunshine. You can stop pretending to sleep," came a slightly familiar voice. Keeping my eyes tightly closed, I tried to recognize the speaker.

"Come on, sit up and eat something," he barked. Then he had started to laugh. "Oh, I forgot, You're tied up. You can't even sit up on your own. Would you like me to fix that?"

I felt fingers lift away the blindfold the rest of the way. I shook my head, unable to remain still a moment longer.

"See? I knew you were awake," he said with smug satisfaction. I turned towards the voice and faced my captor for the first time. I blinked in shock.

"You!" I tried to shout. In my mind, my voice screamed but nothing came out I was parched. I stared straight into the face of my captor and stuttered. "George!"

"Here, have something to drink. It will help," he said, handing me an open bottle of water, ignoring my shock. "Don't worry, I didn't put anything in it - yet. Oh wait, you can't hold that either."

Realizing I couldn't grab the bottle due to my restraints, he reached over and the cut the ropes attached to my feet. Then he cut the ropes to my right wrist.

"There, you can eat now," he said. Putting his hands under my armpits, he pulled me upright into a sitting position on the bed. The sheet fell down, revealing my bare breasts to his piercing eyes. His face dropped and I nearly vomited when his mouth fell open with appreciation before blurting, "You have gorgeous tits."

Mortified by his visual inspection, I hastily pulled the sheet over myself as soon as he helped me upright. He smirked at my obvious discomfort and fear.

"Thank you for untying me," I said, reaching gratefully for the water. The coolness refreshingly soothed my parched throat. My empty stomach rumbled as liquid filled the aching void. It had been over twenty-four hours since I last ate or drank.

"I got you some soup and a sandwich," he said, setting a takeout bag on the bed beside me. As hungry as I was, I refused to touch it.

"Can I use the toilet? Please," I begged. The need to relieve myself was bordering overpowering. He got up reluctantly, then cut off the remaining rope. Pulling out a pair of handcuffs from his back pocket, he slapped them onto my left wrist, then attached the other loop to his wrist.

"Okay, let's go," he said, roughly pulling me off the bed. The sheet slide to the floor. My attempt to reclaim it and cover myself was stopped as George yanked me towards the toilet. I forced myself to stand straight and tall despite my nakedness. I was vulnerable and terrified, but I was not going to let him take my dignity. At the bathroom door, he politely stood outside while I relieved myself. When I was done, he helped me wash my hands and handed me a towel.

"Thank you," I said, heading back to the bed, grabbing the sheet to wrap around me before I climbed back onto the dirty mattress. I was not going to let him know how terrified I really was. He unlatched the cuff from his wrist and reattached it to the bedpost. I was once again confined to one location. Content that I was unable to escape, George returned to the fridge and grabbed a beer. I watched in terror as he brought a chair from the kitchen and placed it beside the bed. He straddled it, sat down, then guzzled down his beer in silence. Then he poured a double whiskey shot and poured it down his throat in one gulp.

Instead of cowering, I remained still and watched his every move.

"What do you want with me?" I quietly asked, breaking the silence. His contemplative silence was unnerving. Since he was not speaking, I figured there was no harm in questioning his intentions.

"Don't speak to me," he finally replied gruffly. All the earlier kindness was gone in a flash. His eyes blazed with wrath. He was seething inside and it wouldn't take much to set him off. *I was being kept hostage by a ticking time bomb.*

"Where is Hannah?" He leaned forward and waited for a response. I refused to be intimidated. "I know you know where she is hiding!"

"You ordered me not to speak to you," I yelped as my head whipped back as he backhanded me viciously across the cheek.

"There is no need to be sassy," he spat angrily. He poured himself another shot and swallowed it. He was getting drunk fast. "Do not lie to me! Where is she?"

"I don't know!" I insisted. I was just telling the truth. Dominic didn't have a chance to tell me where he'd moved her. Nor had he replied to my texts, which was a good thing. My cell was in my purse and I assumed that George that it hidden in the trailer someplace.

"I don't believe you," he replied matter-of-factly. "It doesn't matter anyway. I know I will soon enough. As soon as your friends show up, I will have Hannah and you can go home."

"Who says they are coming for me?" I asked. I made another attempt to gather the sheet around myself. This time, he did not stop me. Still ignoring me, he got up and grabbed another beer from the fridge before consumed it in three swallows. Then he unwrapped one of the sandwiches he'd picked up at the store.

"What are you going to do to me?" I demanded bravely. It was making me hungry watching him eat, but I was not ready to look into the bag he'd brought for me.

"I am still thinking about it," he replied gruffly, looking up from his sandwich. He grabbed the second one and offered it to me. "Eat something."

Giving in to the hunger pains in my gut, I forced myself to take a bite of the ham and cheese sandwich. I was famished and soon, I made short work of it, along with the homemade cabbage soup.

"Feel better now?" George asked after watching me swallow my last bite of the delicious concoction.

"Yes, a lot better. Thank you," I answered after wiping my mouth with the sheet.

A grunt was his only response. Meanwhile, I noticed that he was attempting to appear relaxed but he kept glancing at his wristwatch. There was something familiar about that timepiece, but I could not place my finger on it.

"Are you waiting for something?" I demanded. Maybe someone was coming to get me. I tried not to appear too hopeful.

"Quit asking me questions," he bellowed angrily in reply. I instinctively scooted backwards across the mattress until my back was pressed up against the wall. Desperately trying to put as much distance between us as I could. I was not sure what to expect at this point. He noticed me cowering in the corner. "Come here!"

I shook my head no, refusing to budge.

"Come here!" He shrieked. This time when I refused, he lunged in my direction. I lurched away and he missed my wrist; his hand grabbed the sheet instead. With one deft movement, I was naked once again beneath his drunken stare.

"Fuck your hot," he slurred drunkenly. He reached out before I could react. I flinched as his hand grabbed my right breast roughly. I stifled a yelp as he squeezed. "Yep, nice breasts too."

"You don't want to do this," I stammered in an attempt to reason with him. I fought off the urge to cry. He's already hurt me physically, and appeared to enjoy it. I was frightened of what he would do next. However, I was not going to let him think that I was completely helpless. I intended on fighting back with every ounce of energy I could muster.

"Are you still thirsty?" he asked, surprising me by changing the subject. Once again, I was baffled; one moment he was screaming and angry with me; then he'd offer a hint of kindness. I decided it would be safer to play his game.

"Yes, I'd love a drink," I acknowledged, taking the bait. My mouth was parched from thirst. I watched him pour me a drink. When he came back, I grabbed it gratefully and drank it greedily.

"Feeling better now?" he asked with a sneer, taking the empty glass from my hands. I started to nod, but I was having problems with movement. Then it hit me; he'd put something into the water. In shock, I tried to focus on his face, but the room swam before me. I blinked several times, trying to clear my vision, but it didn't help.

"Emma?" I heard someone call my name from a distance, but I was unable to respond. Then there was nothing.

The next time I opened my eyes, I was once again tied to the bed; this time spread out like a naked starfish. My hands were shackled to the headboard with metal cuffs. He was kinder with my legs. This time, instead of the ragged old rope, there was a number of knit scarves wrapped around my ankles. Admittedly, they were softer on my skin and would not chafe me. I was grateful for the kindness. My ankles were already ringed with angry purple welts from earlier in the day.

Gauging the darkness within the room, the sun had set hours earlier. The only light in the chamber was the glow emanating from the blaze crackling in the wood stove. Lifting my head up slightly from the mattress, I looked around. I was not alone. George sat silently by the fireplace smoking a cigarette. The glass clutched in his other hand was full of amber liquid. I assumed it was pure whiskey. Hearing movement coming from the bed, he spun around in his chair and found me watching him. He stood up immediately and staggered over to the bed.

"Hello sleeping beauty," he slurred, leaning over until he was mere inches from my cheek. I flinched with distaste. His breath reeked of rye and stale cigarettes. He chuckled sadistically. "Look what I did to you."

Obediently, I glanced down at my restrained body. The sheet was once again gone and I was fully exposed. I conducted a mental examination of my body and knew he hadn't violated me while I was unconscious. I squirmed uncomfortably when I discovered the way George was ogling my body.

"You will be happy to know that I made a decision while you were taking your nap," he sneered, oblivious of the drool dripped onto my cheek. I shuddered with disgust and turned away in an attempt to avoid his rancid breath. "I am going to screw you! I am going to hurt you until you tell me what I want to know. I know you and your friends are hiding my wife and by the time I am done with you, you are going to tell me where she is."

I clenched my eyes shut and tried to wish him away, but it didn't work. Tears streamed down my cheeks, soaking the dirty pillow he'd been kind to stuff under my head. My frightened eyes met his and I could view the sincerity in his expression. He was not trying to scare me, he was actually informing me of his intentions.

"You don't want to do this George, you can't take it back," I sobbed, trying to reason with him. He turned back to me and shoved something against my mouth. My eyes widened in panic as he forced my lips apart and shoved in a gag. "Shut up bitch! You're making way too much noise."

Forced to be quiet, I was no longer able to remain calm. Tears poured down my cheeks as I struggled desperately against my bounds. George laughed sadistically. It was then I noticed the bottle in his hands. I gagged behind the muzzle as he poured baby oil along my bare belly. Slipping his fingers into the puddle of oil on my skin, he proceeded to smear my entire body. I sobbed as he rubbed the oil over every inch of my skin, not missing a single spot. My arms, my legs, my thighs and my breasts. I felt like a dirty, slippery mess.

"Why are you doing this to me?" I tried to whimper. My words were barely audible behind the gag. He reached over and moved it aside.

"Because I know you are hiding that bitch! This would never have happened if it hadn't been for you!" George snarled. "This all started because she had to find that kid. Do you know how many years we tried to get pregnant? My spiteful father tells his friends I am impotent! He expected us to have a son within the first year of our marriage. Then to find out that she has a kid? With someone else? My father would disown me if he knew what a whore I married."

"Hannah is not a whore!" I sputtered, in my friend's defence.

"She's a whore; only a whore would throw away a child," he spat venomously. He was consumed with hatred towards Hannah. Now I understood why she fled the way she did. He was insane over this. "I am going to hurt you until you tell me the truth."

"I am not lying. She relocated, but never told me where she is," I argued, but my words fell on deaf ears. Instead of listening, he was already focused on his next move. I nearly passed out when he shoved greasy fingers between my thighs, taking his time to massage my bottom. I yelped in pain and humiliation. The more I squirmed and tried to get away, the harder he squeezed. It was obvious my pain was his pleasure.

I sighed with relief when he finally moved away, but my relief was short lived. He pulled away long enough to unzip his pants. I lay in absolute terror when he grasped his exposed swollen member and started stroking. I closed my eyes tightly and tried to block out his next intention. Within moments, he grunted with animalistic satisfaction and finished himself all over my chest.

"Much better now," he grumbled with satisfaction before tucking himself back in and zipping up his pants. Disgusted by his actions, I started retching in horror. He laughed and cruelly grabbed my breasts. "Sorry, it's been months; I am sure you understand."

Eyes wide, I shook my head and fought against his touch until I could fight no more. He just laughed and continued. At one point, I watched with relief as he walked back to the woodstove. I made the mistake of thinking he was leaving me alone. Instead, I heard the distinct clank of metal on metal.

"What are you going to do?" I tried to scream in protest.

"I am going to make you hurt like *she* should have," he growled. He placed the poker inside the coals, then sat down and waited.

"What do you mean?" I insisted. My mind was already working overtime, trying to figure a way out of this situation. I was starting to panic. "I already told you, I don't know where Hannah is!"

"I know your lying and you know more than you are saying. I am going to get it out of you, one way or another," he barked. "I am going to burn you, like I was going to burn her."

"Burn her?" I asked with a strangled sob. *Was he about to confess to trying to kill Hannah in the house explosion?* For a moment, I forgot the immediate danger I was in. If he admitted to his actions, I could testify against him in a new trial. He may have done time for arson, but attempted murder charges could still be pressed against him.

"If that stupid bitch had shown up like she was supposed to, you and I would not be having this conversation," George sneered venomously. "But we are, and now you have to deal with it. You know more than you are saying about this entire situation. From day one, you've known about the baby, you were friends for god sake."

My heart sank. He'd obviously done his research.

"I was wondering who you were when we got to court, and what your role in all this was. Do you think I am stupid? I'd never laid eyes on you before, and suddenly there you were, protecting her, keeping her away from me," George rambled on. "Then I saw you leave the courtroom together on television. I waited to see the article you would write but when the bare minimum appeared in your monthly rag, I knew you were not there as a reporter. She's obviously smarter than I ever expected."

"What do you mean smarter?" I asked, fishing for more information. Despite my precarious position, I was still hopeful that with a distraction, I'd be able to defuse the situation and leave unscathed.

"The only way Hannah would have been able to disappear so thoroughly was to ask for help from people outside our inner circle," George continued to rant. "None of our mutual friends would have helped her."

"Why do you want her so bad?" I asked.

"Because no one makes a fool of me and gets away with it," he barked angrily. "The only way anyone can leave me, is if they die!"

He got up quickly, grabbed the poker from the fire, and turning towards me. His eyes glowed menacingly in the firelight, nearly matching the sinister red glow of the poker. It took only moments for me to realize his intent.

"What are you going to do?" I gasped in renewed terror.

"I am going to do to you, what I was going to do to Hannah," He replied. Before I could reply, he roughly forced the gag back into my mouth. My eyes widened with horror as the glowing red tip moved towards my delicate flesh.

"Where is she?" he yelled. "Tell me where she is hiding!"

Unable to respond, I shook my head no, tears of dread flowed down my cheeks. Ignoring me, he roughly pulled my legs apart and exposed my tender thighs. Before I could blink, he pressed the hot poker against my skin. I screamed, but it came out garbled and ragged. The pain was excruciating. I fought for air as the scent of burning flesh filled the room.

"WHERE IS SHE?" he yelled again. I shook my head harder. Through a fog of sheer agony, I hear George laughed sadistically as he forced the poker between my inner thighs a second time. The burning pain between my legs was unbearable. I saw stars as I tried to scream in vain. My skin sizzled as it cooked. Tears flowed unchecked down my cheeks.

"You like that, bitch, don't you," he kept saying, ignoring my tears, then he cruelly pressed the poker against my flesh again.

I tried to scream but it came out a strangled gargle. Unable to catch my breath, started to choke on saliva and bile. I fought in vain for air, then everything went blessedly black.

CHAPTER TWENTY-THREE

It was still pitch dark when I regained consciousness a few hours later. My body screamed in agony and I was afraid to move. As I listened to the sounds of the night, a sudden flash of bright light flickered across the walls through the windows from outside cottage. In that brief moment, I could barely make out George passed out on the floor. I assumed he drank himself into a stupor. I held my breath.

Someone was outside and so far, he had not stirred. I exhaled quietly with relief. I tried to scream out, but couldn't. The disgusting gag was still stuffed in my mouth. I was a helpless mess. At this point, I didn't care that I would be found nude and violated. I simply desired to be found alive. I waited, breathing softly.

George remained undisturbed, snoring loudly on the floor. Otherwise, the night remained still and quiet. I whimpered in disappointment, thinking whomever as outside either left or I was hearing things. Either way, my rescue was an illusion. I started sobbing softly, not wanting to wake up my tormentor.

The door suddenly burst open and crashed against the wall. Startled I jumped as shattered wood shards flew across the room. My eyes flew to the door. Seconds later, Dominic came flying into the cabin, Debbie was right on his heels. Awakened by the ruckus, George sat up on the floor dazed. The booze dulled his reflexes. While he rubbed the confusion out of his eyes, Dominic jumped onto him and knocked him over with a single punch. George tried to fight back, but failed. They grappled back and forth briefly.

Dominic grabbed a handful of hair and smashed his face onto the corner of the table. George's head bounced, then he collapsed into an unconscious heap on the ground. Dominic grabbed the discarded rope still lying on the floor and quickly tied him up like a calf.

Meanwhile, Debbie was already climbed onto the bed with me. As soon as she'd spotted me laying in the shadows, she ran over and pulled me into her arms. She grabbed the sheet and pulled it protectively over my shivering body. I sobbed with relief when she finally pulled the gag off my face.

"Emma, Oh my God Emma. What did he do to you?" Debbie asked, even though she didn't have to. She quickly surveyed the damage. My body and face was covered with blood and bruises. The baby oil made the abuse look even worse. A broken and bloody broomstick lay on the side of the bed. I had no recollection of its use.

"Dominic, we need to get her to the hospital, immediately," Debbie cried. Her voice thick with worry. That was when Dominic finally turned and spotted me laying on the bed.

"Emma!" he bellowed, and with two large steps, he closed the gap between us. Debbie struggled to untie me, and I was still cuffed to the bedposts. He growled when he lifted the sheet and found me still restrained. Flying back across the room, he picked George unceremoniously off the floor and shook him. The keys fell onto the floor, and Dominic dropped him just as roughing onto the floor then scooped them up. Dashing back to my side, he quickly unlatched the cuffs. As he unlocked each shackle, he softly rubbed the circulation back into my fingers, then lightly kissed the black and blue welts left behind by the tattered rope.

"Emmy, I am so sorry for leaving your side, are you okay?" Dominic asked, still kissing my fingertips. Then, realizing my legs were still bound tightly, he swiftly pulled out a knife from inside his boot and cut them loose. Once again, he massaged each ankle and kissed each as he did. His tenderness warmed me, despite the trauma.

"We need to get her to the hospital," Debbie repeated loudly. The urgency in her voice grew. Leaving Dominic beside me, she searched the room for a clean towel. Unable to find one, she grabbed a package of moisturizing towelettes from her purse. Dominic put his hand out and stopped her.

"She's bleeding and we need to take her in right away. She's a mess," she argued, trying to push him aside.

"We can't clean her up; you know that. We don't know what he did to her and her body is evidence now," Dominic gently reasoned. He reached out and took the moist wipes away from Debbie. "You can't wash her; I am sorry, but we have to call the police. All the physical evidence points to him assaulting her. He's got to go to jail for this."

"I've already called the police," Debbie interjected. "They should be here soon.

She returned to my side and pulled me back into her arms. I gratefully curled up into her lap while she attempted to rub the circulation back into my fingers and toes. I attempted to speak, but no words formed. All I wanted was human contact and comfort. I let her hold me, while she patted my head like a child and assured me that everything would be fine.

Ten minutes later, the cabin was swarming with police detectives. In the distance a helicopter could be heard coming in over the trees to finally land in a tiny clearing outside. Everyone sighed with relief that backup had arrived. I was oblivious that the cabin was so far into the bush, it was inaccessible by ambulance or larger vehicles.

Paramedic rushed in and quickly covered my gaping wounds. Content that I was stable, they put me onto the stretcher and covered me with warm blankets. Once I was loaded into the waiting Medi-Vac helicopter, I was flown to the nearest hospital. Debbie never left my side. At one point I started shivering uncontrollably and everyone began moving quickly around me in the tight space.

"What's happening?" I could hear Debbie call my name in the distance, but I was unable to respond.

"She's going into shock," the medic called to the pilot. I tried to focus, but failed. The pounding routers overhead faded and I felt woozy. I didn't care. I just wanted to sleep. Halfway to the hospital, the world went black.

When I next opened my eyes, it was under the bright lights of a hospital emergency room. A number of tubes were attached to my arm; an intravenous line was started in my left arm. I tried to ignore the throbbing ache in my shoulders and legs, but it was impossible. I tried to sit up. That was when I noticed Debbie curled up in a chair in the corner. Movement on my left startled me. I nearly sobbed in relief when I turned to find Dominic leaning forward. He took my hand.

"Hey sunshine; how are you feeling?" he softly asked. His voice was unusually gentle and his eyes welled with concern.

"I hurt like hell," I replied honestly. My voice cracked from lack of use.

"Do you need something for pain?" he asked.

I tried to move, first lifting each arm, then wiggling my legs beneath the warm blankets. For the first time in forty-eight hours I felt warm to the core. While the majority of my body felt sore, but whole, my legs felt heavy and awkward. Everything hurt, but nothing compared to the unbearable burning sensation from between my legs.

"The doctors have bandaged up your thighs," Dominic started to explain. He paused when a nurse swept into the room carrying a tray. Debbie woke up and stretched, as the nurse approached the right side of my bed.

"Good afternoon Emma, how are you feeling," she asked. Her eyes were kind and sympathetic. "My name is Shirley and I am your nurse this evening. How is your pain? On a scale from one to ten, with ten being the worst pain you've ever had."

"Depending what part of my body you're talking about; some are about a three and others about an eight," I admitted. Shirley put down the tray and turned her attention back to me.

"Well, I can give you a shot to help with the pain," Shirley offered. Without waiting, she injected a clear liquid into my intravenous tube. Within moments I could feel the pain relief seeping in. I smiled gratefully.

"That better?" she asked, while moving around and recording the readings off various machines surrounding my hospital bed. I nodded. "Good! Now I am going to check your dressings."

I watched quietly as she pulled aside the blankets and exposed my legs. Both thighs were thickly bandaged. Very carefully, she started to loosen the medical tape.

"What's wrong with my legs?" I asked, watching Shirley peel back layers of white gauze.

"Do you not remember?" Dominic asked, unable to hide the surprise in his voice.

"I remember bits and pieces, but not everything," I responded with confusion. "I am sure he drugged me at one point."

"Your blood work will confirm that," Shirley interjected, while gently unwrapping my thighs. I tried to pull myself up to get a better view. Dominic attempted to stop me.

"What?" I asked, starting to get alarmed. "What are you not telling me?"

"That's just it, we don't know how to warn you," Debbie stated, having come over to take my other hand. She held it tightly, absently rubbing her fingers in comforting circles across the back of my fingers.

"Emma? This is going to hurt a little," the nurse softly interrupted. "Are you ready?"

"As ready as I will ever be," I replied, then gasped as I felt the gauze peeled away from my injured flesh. I bite back a scream of sheer agony. Debbie and Dominic each grabbed my hands tighter, and tried to calm me down. Their words were blocked out as I tried to manage my pain through concentration. Vaguely, I could hear them speaking softly in my ear, but I could not make out their words.

"Emma, it's okay. We are here. This has to be done," Debbie persisted. Finally her calming voice penetrated the cloud of physical agony I was experiencing, and I tried to focus on her actual words.

"Deep breathes baby, it will be over soon. That's it, breathe in, breathe out; calm down baby," she muttered over and over. When I finally was able to breathe through the pain, I decided to steal a look at the damage. Glancing down, I could see my thighs were covered with patched of raw flesh. The jagged edges of skin were lightly charred, and each wound was swollen and inflamed.

"What the hell?" I screamed in both surprise and agony. "What did he do to me?"

"He branded you," Debbie whispered into my ear. "He branded you with a hot poker."

"You're doing great," the nurse interjected. She was now gently cleansing the open lesions with water, then applied a thick white cream over each wound. Content that they were sufficiently covered, Shirley prepared my legs for rewrapping. "We have already called in a doctor; they are going to try to fix this so you won't have too many scars. You might need some skin grafts."

"What else did he do?" I was nearly hysterical. I was not sure what was worse. The fact he'd branded me or the fact that I did not remember what he'd done.

"We completed a sexual assault kit and, other than finding semen on your chest, you showed no other sign of sexual violation," the nurse continued. My heart swelled with relief. At least I did not have to worry about being raped. Not that being held hostage is any less traumatic, but I felt lucky.

"The police will fill you in when you are ready to talk," Dominic added. "They are waiting outside to question you. They are going to need a statement. George is already in jail, but they cannot charge him fully without your testimony."

"I couldn't tell him anything," I suddenly babbled. "He kept asking where Hannah was, but he didn't believe I didn't know."

"He's been watching you. He knows you went to the house after the explosion," Dominic continued. "We found an entire wall board of photos; he even found Hannah's daughter."

"Is she safe?" I looked up with worry.

"Yes, the police contacted her parents and they are aware of the situation. As far as they know he has not tried to contact her or interfere with her life," Debbie added. "Hannah is also safe. She is very worried about you and feels horrible. She was hysterical when we told her what George did to you."

"What's going to happen now," I asked, trying to ignore the nurse who was busy wrapping my legs. Talking was distracting me from the pain, at least for now.

"George is going to go to jail for a very long time," interjected a voice from the doorway. We all looked up as Chief Alexander entering the room.

"Hey Chief," I welcomed him. As if on cue, Shirley quickly double checked the dressings and turned to leave.

"If you need anything, just press the call button," she instructed, while gathering up the pile of discarded dressings.

"Thank you," I replied, giving her a weak smile of appreciation. She smiled back, then left the room as quietly as she arrived.

"Do you mind if I ask you a few questions?" Chief Alexander asked, coming up alongside my hospital bed. "How are you doing?"

"As well as can be expected I guess," came my honest reply. "What do you need?"

"Hey Dominic," said the chief, instead of answering my question right away. "Long time no see."

"Hey Graham; how's the investigation?" Dominic replied. I looked from one man to the next in confusion.

"You know each other?" I asked needlessly.

"We go way back; we've worked a few cases together," Chief Alexander replied. It was obvious from their tones their relationship was based on mutual respect and admiration.

"A few cases?" I pushed. Catching the furtive glances between them, it was obvious I would not get a real answer.

"Yeah, he's a private investigator," the chief continued. "He has been helping us with this case - unofficially that is."

"How unofficial?" Debbie interjected. Her confused expression matched mine.

"So unofficial that only he knew what was going on; then when all hell broke loose, he invited the real cops to the party," the chief laughed. Dominic shrugged.

"Hey, someone had to protect these women," he chuckled unapologetically.

"You were always good at that," Chief Alexander marvelled, before turning his attention back to me. "Can we talk?"

The next hour was spent recounting the little details I remembered. For the most part I managed to get through the ordeal without incident. However, whenever my voice cracked or I appeared on the verge of a breakdown, Dominic and Debbie had my back. I don't think I could have managed if they hadn't stayed with me. When I was done, I signed my name on the bottom of the statement and pushed it away. It was officially on record.

"So what did you all find at the cottage," Dominic interrupted.

"We searched the entire place and gathered enough evidence to put George away for a very long time," confirmed Chief Alexander. He added that an intensive search of the mobile home was still underway. Officer's had bagged and tagged mountains of evidence, he added.

"In a crawl space under the trailer, we found a hidden room," Chief Alexander explained. "The walls were covered with countless photographs of Hannah. There were also several of just Emma. He'd obviously been following both women for awhile."

"I warned you," Dominic chimed in. Chief Alexander flashed him a look of forewarning and continued.

"Based on our findings, it looks like George hadn't completed his horrific plan. We uncovered a well drafted scheme, including detailed diagrams on where to plant explosives throughout the family home. If the police had gathered this information in the first place, his trial would have ended very differently," Chief Alexander continued. "We also found a number of insurance documents and a will for Hannah, all naming George as the sole beneficiary."

"Oh. My. God." Debbie gasped in shock. "He really wanted to get rid of Hannah."

"Apparently," agreed Chief Alexander. "We found a cardboard box containing a number of Hannah's missing personal items stashed under the bed. Under the kitchen floorboards, police also found a cache of unregistered weapons. By the end of the day, investigators will have everything they need to put the former senator away for years. This time George will go to jail for a very long time."

"Do we know why he was after Hannah with such intensity?" Debbie asked.

"We are still trying to piece things together, but George is not talking," Chief Alexander replied. "What is really weird, is that he still has not asked for a lawyer. Usually that is the first thing suspects do; they lawyer up. When I left the station, he was pacing his cell ranting and raving in a drunken rage. We are going to try questioning him again when he sobers up more."

Closing his notepad, Chief Alexander prepared to leave.

"Thank you Emma; you are a very brave woman," Chief Alexander praised me before heading to the door. He stopped on the threshold and turned back to address the three of us. "By the way, we got the test results back. There were traces of Rohypnol - otherwise known as the date rape drug in your system. You may never remember all the bits and pieces of what happened to you."

"That might not be a bad thing," Debbie reluctantly admitted. I nodded with agreement. Maybe it was a blessing that I would not remember everything.

"Either way, we are going to make sure you talk to a professional," Dominic stressed. "You will need some type of debriefing."

"I will mention it to her doctor," Debbie agreed. "I will make sure that counselling is part of her discharge plan."

"Wait a second; I am perfectly capable of making my own decisions," I interrupted their discussion. While their concern was welcome, it annoyed me how they were both making decisions about my care, as if I was not in the room.

"Really?" Dominic and Debbie both replied in unison. They made it worse by starting to giggle at my exasperated frown.

"I think you both can go now, I am feeling tired," I replied drowsily, then yawned for emphasise. Truthfully, I was exhausted. After speaking to the police, I was ready for a good night sleep. For the first time in days, I felt warm, comfortable and safe.

"You are right, we should leave you alone for now," Debbie reluctantly agreed.

"I am not going anywhere," Dominic staunchly argued. I sighed with exasperation.

"Dom? I think we should let her sleep. You can come back in the morning," Debbie suggested. I smiled at her gratefully.

"Nope, I am not leaving here until she is discharged; I will sleep in the hallway if I have to," Dominic remained steadfast with his refusal. I shrugged, too tired to argue further. Debbie looked at me, and recognized my acceptance. Half-heartedly she conceded defeat.

"Fine, do what you want; you will anyway. I have a husband waiting at home. Are you sure you are okay Emma?" she asked with concern, before leaning over to kiss my forehead. Heavy-eyed, I nodded

"I will be fine after a good night sleep," I murmured sleepily, giving her a hug back. "Thank you for being here. Go home and I will see you tomorrow."

Exhaustion and the pain medication was making it difficult to stay alert. Finally I succumbed to my body's need for a healing rest. I nestled deeper into the semi-comfortable hospital bed, and closed my eyes.

I was asleep before Debbie and Dominic left the room.

CHAPTER TWENTY-FOUR

Sometime in the middle of the night, a soft rustling sound woke me up. Startled, I opened my eyes and peered into the shadows, but I was momentarily blind. Eventually the darkened hospital room came into focus as my eyes adjusted to the lack of light. I scanned the room to no avail. *I must be hearing things again.*

As I gingerly turned onto my opposite side and nestled back into the warm bed, I spotted movement in the corner of the room.

"Hello?" I demanded, still unable to make out the figure standing in the shadows. I started to sit up. "Who's there?"

Initially there was no answer. Frightened, I slowly reached for the call button pinned to my pillow and prepared to scream. When the shadow stepped into the light trickling in from the hall, I hesitated. My heart just about hit the floor. Stephan!

"What are you doing here?" I loudly whispered, unable to conceal the intense shock in my voice. He was the last person I expected to find standing in my hospital room in the middle of the night. After our last visit, I never expected to see him again. "How did you know I was here?"

He ignored my questions and moved closer to the bed. I gasped audibly. In the dim hallway light, his face looked alarmingly different. I'd never seen Stephan so emotional. Even when I dragged him begrudgingly to the doctor's office, he'd shown more restraint. For a brief second, I considered his odd behaviour was remorse over our separation. Or perhaps the doctor had delivered bad news about his blood work.

"Stephan, are you okay?" I asked, suddenly worried. Regardless of our breakup, we could revert to friendship. It was not uncommon for exes to remain friends. Just because I called it quits on the relationship did not mean the door was closed on friendship.

His next words blew that theory out of the water.

"He's dead," Stephan snarled unexpectedly. I blinked in surprise. At the same time, I was immensely relieved. The simple statement meant his emotional state had nothing to do with our breakup.

"Who's dead?" I inquired, totally bewildered. *Had something happened to his son?* There was something not right about this situation, and yet, I could be overreacting, I reasoned. Unsure about raising the alarm, I decided to wait.

"George is dead and it's all your fault," Stephan scowled. *George? He knew George?* My confusion was mounting. Perhaps the nurse gave me too much pain medicine. I had to be hallucinating. It was the only explanation that made any sense.

"What are you babbling about?" I pressed. "What do you know about George?"

"You are going to pay for this," Stephan replied, deliberately disregarding my questions. He moved quickly, until he was standing beside my bed, alongside the IV stand. It was then I spotted the tiny syringe in his fingers. My mouth dropped open and I prepared to scream, but he moved quickly and covered my mouth with his free hand.

"Don't you dare open your mouth," Stephan threatened. My gaping mouth snapped shut, and I frantically scanned the vicinity to find something to utilise as a weapon. Or at least something to knock onto the floor that would make a racket. Disappointed, I sagged back into the mattress. There was nothing within reach.

"You are going to pay for this," he growled threateningly. His sneering face was inches from mine. I instinctively recoiled. This was a side of my former lover, I'd never caught sight of before. Stephan fumbled for my intravenous in the dimness with one hand, while keeping his other palm plastered onto my face. When he finally found the tiny clear line, he brought the needle up to the injection site. My eyes widened with horror.

"Don't worry, this will be fast and painless," he assured. The hum of voices outside my hospital room door stopped his next movement. He removed his hand off my mouth and pressed an index finger against his lips in warning. Then he stood quietly and listened carefully. He was still frozen in that position when the overhead lights popped on and the room was flooded with fluorescent.

"What the hell?" snapped Shirley, when she spotted the complete stranger standing beside my bed. "Who are you and what are you doing in here?"

Her questioning gaze switched between Stephan and I. Recognizing the panicked look in my eyes, her stance changed subtly. She realized instantly that my late night guest was not welcome. Focusing her attention back to Stephan, the nurse spotted the syringe still dangling in his fingers.

She shrieked, "What are you doing?"

She'd barely screamed when Dominic came flying in from the hall. Hannah came charging in on his heels. Stephan looked up with dread, having spotted the towering giant heading in his direction, murder clearing written in his eyes. He tried to scramble away, until he spotted Hannah. He instantly froze, having noticed her standing in the doorway with Liam sleeping in her arms. He looked like he'd just seen a ghost.

"Hannah?" Stephan hesitantly asked, looking at the frightened woman with recognition. It was apparent he was surprised to catch her in my hospital room. When his eyes finally settled on the infant, his behaviour changed. He bristled visibly.

"That is George's son!" He declared loudly, panting in disbelief and astonishment. Four pairs of eyes swung towards Stephan questioningly. He never noticed because he was occupied with the child. His face glowed with both awe and mortification. Within seconds, his bravado vanished. He started blubbering and sobbing. "He never knew he had a son."

While the women stood and watched the nearly hysterical man with bewilderment, Dominic wasted no time jumping in and questioning the interloper.

"What the hell is going on here," Dominic demanded. "How do you know George?"

Without waiting for a response, Dominic moved forward quickly, closing the distance between the doorway and Stephan. Before he could retreat, Stephan was grasped firmly by the front of his shirt. He did not fight back. Rather, his attention remained fixated on Hannah and the still sleeping infant.

"Is this why you were hiding from your husband?" Stephan softly asked. He tried to step forward, but Dominic maintained his firm grip. That was when he spotted the needle, still hanging loosely in Stephan's fingers. He snatched it away deftly and handed it to Shirley.

"I am going to go bag this and call the police," she stated, taking the offending instrument away from Dominic gingerly, before flying from the room. "I will be right back."

"Why are you asking me these questions," Hannah finally managed to respond to Stephan's questions once the initial surprise wore off. "I don't recognize you! Who are you?"

"George and I go way back," Stephan sneered. "We are...old friends."

"What kind of friends," Dominic replied. He already had a vague idea, but he needed something more definitive than just suspicions.

"What do you think?" Stephan glared back defiantly. He tried to pull himself up to meet Dominic eye to eye but failed. His adversary was about a foot taller and solid like a brick wall.

"What is he talking about," Hannah asked with rising alarm. She looks pointedly at Dominic. "How does he know George?"

"I can beat it out of him," Dominic offered hopefully. Before anyone could answer, the sound of someone clearing their throat drew everyone's attention to the door.

"I think we can refrain from taking such drastic measures," replied Chief Alexander, who'd just entered the room. It was the second time he'd snuck up on the group. His left hand was sitting loosely on the butt of the holstered gun strapped to his waist. The Chief was ready to draw his pistol just in case. "Don't move Stephan!"

The order was useless. With Dominic's firm grasp still clutching Stephan, he was not going anywhere. Besides, his rapt attention was still fixated on Liam. He was oblivious to everyone else in the room.

"How'd you get here so fast," I gasped, addressing Chief Alexander directly. Everyone finally turned to look at me in surprise. It was as if they'd forgotten the drama was taking place in my hospital room. "What is going on here?"

"I was already on my way here to speak to Emma when I received the 9-11 page from the nurses' station. I have some news," Chief Alexander replied, addressing everyone in the room. Then he walked over the Hannah's side and softly asked, "Can I talk to you in private?"

"Whatever you have to say to me, you can say in front of everyone here. They've looked out for me and are my family," Hannah replied with dread.

"Fine; I will have to tell you all anyway so I might as well do it all at once," Chief Alexander reluctantly agreed. "I have some bad news. There has been a surprising development. Due to circumstances we did not foresee, we will not be pressing charges against George."

Everyone in the room gasped with shock. Stephan let out a strangled sound and sagged in Dominic's hands. I glanced at him in surprise, then returned my attention back to Chief Alexander. *What the hell happened?* My guts churned with both fear and disappointment. I couldn't even believe what I was hearing.

"Hannah, I regret to inform you that George is dead," he softly continued, addressing Hannah directly. Amid gasps of shock, Hannah sank to the visitors chair in the corner and succumbed to tears of both relief and sorrow. The officer moved quickly and grabbed the baby before the distraught woman dropped him in her grief. Liam remained asleep and the chief placed him carefully back into the infant seat.

"He's dead?" I finally managed to rasp. As I spoke, my eyes welled with tears of relief and disappointment. Glancing over at Hannah crumpled and sobbing on the floor, I felt helpless. I could not imagine what she was going through. The chief looked unsure of how to respond. It was the first time he was surrounded by a room full of weeping women - and a weeping Stephan.

"What happened Graham?" Dominic asked, seemingly oblivious to the hysterics surrounding him. "How is George dead? He was in jail; it's impossible!"

"He killed himself in the jail cell," Chief Alexander carefully resumed his explanation. "Somehow he managed to tie the bed sheets together and string himself from the top bunk. The deputies were having supper when they heard a commotion in the back. They cut him down and performed CPR, but it was too late. He was already dead. There will be no criminal charges. Neither one of you have to worry about him coming after you again!"

Chief Alexander kneeled down and addressed Hannah directly.

"Hannah? That means you and the baby are safe. You do not need to hid anymore," Chief Alexander consoled. She ignored him and continued to sob quietly to herself.

The room fell into a stupefied silence as we all sought to digest this sudden twist of events. We'd all played out various scenarios in our minds on how this would end, but George's suicide was never a consideration. He did not seem like the type who'd take the coward's way out.

"It's entirely your fault," Stephan suddenly screamed. Enraged, he vainly attempted to disengage himself from Dominic's firm grasp. "He would never have killed himself if he knew he'd had a son."

Furious, he attempted to lunge towards Hannah again, but this time Dominic stopped him with a single slug in the face. While Stephan staggered from the blow, Chief Alexander jumped in, and shoved him forcefully up against the wall face first and quickly slapped handcuffs on him. Grabbing him roughly, he pulled him away from the wall. Stephan was forced to stand upright and face the room.

"What is your problem dude?" Dominic demanded. There was obviously a piece of the puzzle still missing. Stephan's erratic behaviour failed to make any sense. "Why is this so important to you?"

Realizing escape was futile, Stephan sagged in the officer's arms, defeated. However, he remained stubbornly silent.

"Wait a second," I interposed. While I sat and watched the heated interchange between the men, I scoured my memory for something that made sense. I knew I had the answer, I'd just not stumbled upon it yet. Then it hit me. I started to tremble.

The watch. I suddenly knew where I'd seen it before.

"George was the mysterious photographer," I blurted out excitedly. Everyone stopped talking and stared at me with astonishment.

"Photographer?" Dominic asked. "What photographer?"

"The pictures; the pictures that someone emailed to me a few months ago. The one's taken in the hotel room, with Jelly and the other woman," I proceeded. Based on the blank expressions of those in the room, no one knew exactly what I was talking about. I ignored them and continued my frantic explanation.

"Some time ago, I was emailed photos, of Stephan. He was cheating on me with two other women. In one picture, there is an arm pointing at the naked threesome from behind the camera, as if to give them directions. It was along the edge of one of the photos," I hurriedly explained. Everyone continued to watch me, baffled. Except for Stephan. He had the decency to look guilty.

"While George held hostage, I noticed his watch. There was something familiar about it, but I could not place it at the time. He kept checking the time and I wondered if he was waiting for someone. I even asked him about it but he never answered. He was waiting for you," I accused. Stephan looked guiltily down at the floor while everyone's attention turned back to him.

"Wait a second! This was all a setup," I gasped with sudden realization. "You knew damn well who I was and my connection with Hannah before we even met. You tried to use me to get to Hannah! I found your dirty secret, but I still kept it to myself. When I broke up with you, I could have told you that I knew you were sleeping with men, but I didn't. I decided that I would have taken it to the grave."

Stephan had the decency to look embarrassed. Everyone else was staring at me, shock clearly visible on all three of their faces. Undaunted, I kept going.

"I figured if you wanted to use women to cover your true sexual inclinations, that was your business. I was just not going to let you use me anymore. Now everyone is going to know - everyone is going to know that you and George were lovers. That's what this is truly all about," I raged on. I'd had enough and there was no stopping my tirade. It felt good to get all the secrets off my chest. "How long were you willing to pretend you were in love with me?"

Dominic, Hannah and Chief Alexander still stood in stunned silence, glancing back and forth between me and Stephan. It was obvious they were contemplating all the accusations, however they were unsure how to respond.

Stephan's next words confirmed my suspicions.

"George was afraid the world would learn that he was gay. His father knew he preferred men, and made his life miserable every chance he got. His father was a homophobic bastard. He told him to get straight or he would never get a dime," Stephan blurted. "He had a wife, and all he needed was a kid to get the old man off his back. George would never have killed himself if he knew about the boy. His son would have been the golden ticket. Now he is gone."

Stephan's voice broke and he succumbed to tears while we sought to digest his shocking confession. Chief Alexander was the first to snap into action.

"Stephan, you are under arrest for conspiracy to commit kidnapping," barked the Chief. He grabbed Stephan by the arm and started to lead him out of the room. "We will figure out the rest of the charges once I bring you into the office and we start talking."

"Wait one second," Hannah interrupted. It was the first time she'd spoken since first coming into the room. Everyone stopped in their tracks. "Are you telling me that you and George were 'together' as in lovers?"

Stephan nodded yes, but remained mute.

"For how long?" she asked, her voice betrayed disbelief.

"We've been together for a few years," Stephan admitted. "We met in college. Long before you were married."

"When?" Hannah pried. "When did you have a chance to get together?"

"Whenever we possibly could meet," Stephan replied with a sigh of pure despair.

Unsure of what to say next, Hannah remained silent, pondering what she'd just learned. Everyone waited, but it was clear the conversation was ended. Chief Alexander started to leave with his prisoner then stopped in the doorway and turned to address Hannah.

"You will be all right now," he attempted to reassure her. "We will talk later."

Hannah smiled back sweetly and silently nodded. Taken aback at her response, I glanced at Dominic, who was also watching the exchange. He looked at me and winked.

"I think someone is smitten," he lowered his voice and grinned. He looked pointedly at the Chief who was scowling in their direction.

"Do you think so?" I whispered back.

"I know so!" He said. "Wait and see; those two are going to be an item yet."

"You could at least wait until I leave the room," Chief Alexander barked over his shoulder. "I am going to run this dirt bag to the station, then I will be back for the rest of the story. Get some rest Emma."

Turning, he pushed Stephan roughly out the door and down the hall.

"Are you okay?" I asked Hannah, who was now busy collecting her things.

"I guess I will be. Dominic? Can you give me a ride home? I don't think I can drive," she asked, quietly. There was something in the tone her voice that concerned me, but I shook it off. Under the circumstances, I understood the shock she must be experiencing. We'd both just discovered we were pawns in someone else's game. It was a lot to digest; and it was even worse for Hannah. One day she will have to explain to Liam who and what his father was. "Is that all right with you if I steal Dom away for awhile Emma?"

"Of course! You've just experienced a shock. You are in no shape to drive," I agreed wholeheartedly. "That's all right with you, isn't it Dominic?"

"I hadn't planned on leaving, but I can drive Hannah and Liam home," Domini consented reluctantly. It was obvious he did not want to leave the hospital. Hannah also looked concerned about me.

"Will you be okay?" Dominic insisted, still clasping my hand tightly in his. I squeezed it back gratefully.

"You know what? I am exhausted. It has been an emotional couple of days. I should be safe now; George is gone; Stephan is in custody. All I need are some pain medication and I will sleep like a baby," I attempted to reassure them both. Turning to Dominic, I smiled weakly.

"I think you should take Hannah to Debbie's for the night," I suggested. It may be the middle of the night, but I knew Debbie. Once she heard what happened tonight, she would want to assist in whatever way possible. One thing was clear; Hannah was going to need all our support during the upcoming days. Under the circumstances, planning George's funeral and dealing with his family was going to take all the reinforcements she could get.

"I already thought of that. I will give her a call shortly," Dominic agreed, then moved aside so Hannah could approach the bedside. "When we leave, I will let the nurses know you are ready for some more meds."

Hannah leaned over and put her arms around me; I returned her embrace. Dominic remained in the shadows while we held onto each other for a few minutes. Once again, we had a shared experience. Only this time, it was me in the hospital bed.

"Emma, I don't know what to say other than thank you. You put yourself on the line to protect us. There are no words..." she whispered into my ear. Her voice broke with emotion. "Thank you from the bottom of my heart; from both Liam and myself."

When we finally pulled apart, we were both in tears.

"Hey, it's okay," I replied, reaching up and wiping her cheek. "You and I will be okay; we are both strong women and we will get through this together - I promise!"

Hannah nodded and smiled, then returned her attention back to Liam, who was beginning to stir in his car seat.

Taking advantage of her distraction, Dominic returned to say goodnight. He leaned over to kiss my forehead, then thought better of it. Before I could react, his warm lips covered mine. Lightly at first, then he deepened the kiss for the briefest of seconds. I was left gasping in surprise when he finally pulled away.

"Sweet dreams Emma," he stated as he reluctantly straightened. "I will see you in the morning."

"I will be here," I chuckled, suddenly eager to be left alone.

"I will tell Shirley to come check on you," Dominic promised. When I nodded, he turned his attention back to Hannah. "Ready to go?"

Hannah picked up Liam and headed to the doorway.

"Good night Emma," she called, then headed into the hallway. Dominic grabbed the diaper bag and followed. I listened to their receding footsteps until they were no longer audible. With my friends were gone, the hospital ward was once again silent.

"Are you ready for some pain relief?" Shirley asked when she swept into the room a few minutes after.

"More than ready," I agreed gratefully. I watched her slip the needle into the shunt, and press the plunger. I closed my eyes and waited. A few minutes later, the ache in my shoulders and arms started to melt; and the burning in my thighs began to ease.

"You should be able to sleep within a few minutes," Shirley promised, as she dimmed the lights. "By the way, we have security at the end of the hall now. No one will be allowed onto the floor without some sort of identification or a valid reason for being here. You are finally safe. Have a good sleep, and buzz if you need anything."

"Thank you Shirley. Good night," I replied sleepily.

Sapped of energy, I allowed the medication to work its magic. My eyes were already drooping and my vision blurred. Instead of fighting the medications, I succumbed to their sweet seduction. Within minutes I slipped into the first dreamless sleep in weeks.

CHAPTER TWENTY-FIVE

Two days later, I was discharged from the hospital. Thanks to the wonderful care of the doctors and nurses the poker burns on my thighs were healing beautifully. Alas, there would be some scarring, but thankfully the injuries were in a forgiving location. They could also be covered with the right clothing.

The thick layers of gauze made it difficult for me to move and the doctors did not want me to be alone. Debbie was gracious enough to invite me to recover at her house, but I refused. I wanted to sleep in the comfort of my own bed. Besides, I was sure that Belle was fit to be tied. This was the longest I'd ever stayed away from her.

I also didn't want to a nuisance to my friend; Debbie already had a full house. Hannah and Liam were still camped out in her spare room. They planned to stay until after George's funeral.

For Hannah, dealing with his family had turned out to be a disaster; thank goodness Debbie was around to help. His father freaked when he discovered George killed himself, and why. They refused to believe he'd committed suicide. Initially they accused me of making up the entire affair. They backed off when the police evidence gave credibility to my story. Finally, they turned their misplaced wrath on Hannah, especially when they found out about Liam.

Fortunately, being sequestered in the hospital kept me out of the immediate picture. I was not a coward, but I had my own issues to deal with. I'd been held hostage, tortured and nearly raped. I'd believed I was in love, then found out that my lover was secretly homosexual and using me to sniff out my friend. My entire world was moving around on its axis. It's a lot to adjust to.

The worst part, was as much as I wanted to return home and be in my own space, I was also frightened to go back to the cottage. It was where George found me and took me hostage. I did not know if I'd feel safe there ever again. However, I was strong and stubborn. The only way I would get over this trauma was to face it dead on. I needed to go home and get my life back. I would not allow recent events to dictate the rest of my life.

"Are you ready to go home?" Dominic's voice intruded on my thoughts. I paused amid gathering up my personal effects, and looked up.

"Yes, I was just going to ask the nurse to call me a cab," I replied.

"Why would you not call any of us?" He asked in surprise.

"Everyone puts their lives on hold enough before of me. It's time for me to get back to regular life, and work. Enough of feeling sorry for myself," I admitted, in a feeble attempt to stubbornly stand up for myself.

"I would not say you are throwing a pity party. I'd suppose you've been to hell and back," Dominic corrected. "It's going to take time to get over this; and you will. We will all be here to help you as well. Anyhow, I am here to drive you home."

"You don't need to do that," I feebly argued. "You've already done enough."

"Don't argue. It's already done," he replied. Looking round, he spotted my bags. "These ready to go?"

"Yes, I am all packed. I am just waiting for a box for all these flowers," I replied, then waved my arm across the room. Dominic looked around and whistled softly. Get well wishes from friends and fans filled the tiny hospital room. Every counter, table and windowsill was covered with colorful bouquets of flowers and tokens of affection.

"Do I need to rent a delivery truck?" He teased. "Be right back; I will see what I can find."

Five minutes afterward he came back with several strong boxes and carefully packed each bouquet away. Once the boxes were loaded, he began to carry things down to his truck, while I waited patiently for my discharge papers. By the time he returned for the final load, the nurse had come and gone.

"I am ready now," I replied when he eventually came back with a wheelchair. I smiled gratefully and sat down. "We can go."

"Okay, let's get out of here," he stated, then he wheeled me outside for the first time in days. I breathed in deeply, savouring the fresh air and sunshine. It felt so good to be alive.

"Are you okay?" Dominic asked, pausing for a moment after helping me into the truck.

"I am wonderful," I responded truthfully, giving him a grateful grin once I settled into the passenger seat. "I want to go home!"

"Your wish is my command," he laughed, before closing the door and climbing into the driver's seat. Before long we were heading out of town in the direction of the cottage. I tried not to dwell on my anticipated reaction to coming home. I'd never been attacked on my own property before. I expected to experience some fear. I should have known I'd wasted time worrying for nothing.

When we pulled into the driveway, Debbie's car was already parked beside mine. As we drew closer, I could see the smashed out the driver side window on the car. My vehicle was wrapped in police tape. Someone had covered the gaping window with plastic to keep the vehicle's interior dry.

"Once I was mobile, I will have to visit the insurance company," I blurted upon seeing the car. "Thanks for covering my window."

"No problem, how did you know it was me?" Dominic asked.

"Debbie would never have thought of it," I chortled. "It would never have crossed her mind."

"Good point!" Dominic laughed. "Speak of the devil."

I looked up and spotted Debbie and Hannah waiting on the deck. Belle was dancing about in circles in excitement as well. I giggled at her antics. Crazy little furry dog. She knew her mama was home.

"EMMA!" Debbie squealed with excitement. She jumped off the deck, dashed across the yard and threw open the passenger door. She was gushing with happiness. "Honey, I am so glad you are home. How are you doing? Let's get you inside."

She was already helping me out of the vehicle.

"Hang on," Dominic interjected. Walking over, he gave me a quick smile of apology. Before I could question his intent, he swung me up into his arms. I squealed in surprise when he drew me tight. I blushed slightly. It felt oddly safe being nestled in his firm arms.

"Hey look Emma, you have a he-man," Hannah laughed. Debbie joined in.

"Glad you guys are enjoying this," I grumbled. They all laughed harder.

Once inside, Dominic placed me gently onto the couch.

"There you go. That is where you are going to stay for the next two weeks," Dominic stated. "Doctor's orders."

"Oh?" I was puzzled.

"Dominic's going to stay with you for a while," Debbie butted in. I looked up. "Don't argue; it has been decided."

"Whoa. I have no say in the matter?" I asked in surprise.

"Nope, he's got to remain here until we are assured that you are all right," Hannah interjected, sitting down on the couch beside me. "You've been through a traumatic ordeal."

"So have you," I responded sympathetically. I grasped her hands, and kept them close. Tears welled briefly as we shared a moment. This experience was both of ours. She's the one who was mistreated, then bravely left. Choosing Liam's life over her own showed inner strength as a woman. I on the other hand, had bravely stood up for her and refused to reveal the little I knew. Even while enduring extreme torture. We'd both be moving forward in life with scars; most invisible to the naked eye.

"I am going to be at your side tomorrow," I sniffled. Hannah would be burying George the next afternoon. We were all surprised by her decision to plan the funeral as if nothing had happened. However, without a finalized divorce, she felt compelled to plan his memorial service despite what everyone said or felt.

"How have George's family been?" I asked.

"They are devastated. The media has not been kind. Once word got out that George and Stephan were lovers, and he'd resorted to kidnapping to protect his secrets, anything left of his reputation was destroyed," Debbie explained sadly. "There was no way they could hide the suicide, which made things worse."

"It was Liam who nearly sent them over the edge," Hannah continued. "When they discovered he had a son, George's old man threatened to sue for custody. I even had a goon show up and threat me! There is no way I am going to give him up. Liam is also my son.

I will teach him about George; I am not certain if I will ever tell him the truth."

Debbie and I nodded.

"When the time comes, you will know what to say," Debbie reassured. "That's the one thing I have learned about parenting. Somehow you will find the words and Liam will be okay."

"I will be happy when tomorrow is over," Hannah admitted. "Is that bad to admit? Pretended to be the mourning widow is going to kill me. Don't get me wrong. I am sad that George is dead! I would be heartless to think otherwise. However, it was his choice. He made his decisions, and while we have to deal with the ramifications, it was HIS choice!"

"Well, like I said, I will be there at your side. You are not going to do this alone," I offered in consolation.

"We will all be there Hannah," Debbie added. It was obvious the two women had bonded over the past few days. I was thrilled that both my friends were getting along so well.

"You're going to have to get used to having me under foot," Dominic butted in changing the subject. I looked up and watched him place a box of flowers onto the dining room table. "I am moving in!"

"What?" I roared. "You're joking!"

"No he's not," Debbie and Hannah replied in stereo. Their delight over the situation was maddening. I glared at them both.

"Someone has to make sure your dressings get changed, and take care of you. Someone has to make sure you eat and walk Belle. You're supposed to stay off your legs until the dressings are thinner," Hannah explained. "Dominic is the only one who can take some time off from work and lend a hand. Besides, I think he has a thing for you."

"I am betting that he won't be leaving for a while," Debbie chuckled.

"Nope, I don't expect so," Hannah howled in agreement. "IF he ever leaves!" Both women succumbed to a fit of laughter as I watched in horror. Looking at Dominic for assistance, he laughed. Catching my glare, he snorted in mirth then went back to finding places to put the countless vases of flowers.

"Anyways, about tomorrow," I interjected, trying to change the subject. I did not want to address the implications of Dominic as a nursemaid. The very thought was appalling. From what I'd seen, my thighs were covered with angry red blisters. They were healing nicely, but burns have been never pretty. I tried not to dwell on the horror.

"Yeah, tomorrow," Debbie sobered fairly quickly. "We need to come up with a plan."

"We are all going to the service together. We are going to show a united front. They are going to get the message that if they mess with Hannah, they are messing with us," Dominic stated emphatically. He was now pacing the room in front of the hearth. "The limo will be arriving at ten o'clock in the morning. Take as much time as you need for this. After all the funeral can't start without you."

"We will be ready," Hannah agreed. "We will not hold up the ceremony."

"You are surprisingly upbeat," I suddenly pointed out. It was simply the truth. Hannah was not behaving like a woman about the bury her husband.

"You have no idea how disconnected I feel right now," Hannah admitted, wringing her hands. "This has been a horrible few weeks. On the other hand, Liam and I are now free to live our lives. We never have to look over our shoulder again. I hate that George had to die, but that was his choice. No one can blame me for that. More importantly, I don't blame me for that."

"So, now we bury him and move on," Debbie agreed.

Dominic wondered if it would actually be that uncomplicated. There was still Stephan to contend with. He had yet to tell the women about Chief Alexander's visit earlier that morning. There was a reason why he volunteered to take care of Emma. The women may not be completely out of danger. He would have to remain close, just in case.

"I guess it's time that I get some sleep. My legs are starting to throb again so I need to lay down for a while," I weakly admitted. I felt almost foolish whining about my burns; they were small compared to many patients in the burn ward. However the agony was undeniable, no matter the size of the wound. "I am done."

Debbie and Hannah stood up and followed me to the bedroom. Within a matter of minutes they had me undressed and tucked under the quilt. It was heaven to be in my own bed. Belle jumped up to join me on the mattress. After circling three times, she plopped down in the crook of my arm and emitted a huge sigh of contentment.

"I know how you feel girl," I giggled at the sleepy mutt. One brown eye popped open in annoyance; then slowly closed. "I hope I can fall asleep that easy."

"You will. Take one of these," Debbie said, before handing me a tiny white pill. "It will help you sleep. You'll feel like a new woman in the morning."

"Thank you," I replied gratefully.

"Good night EM," all three companions called as they took leave of my bedroom. Taking Belle's lead, I pulled her close and nuzzled my face into her soft fur. The next time I opened my eyes, the morning sunlight was streaming into the room and the smell of fresh coffee was wafting throughout the cabin.

"Good morning sunshine," Dominic called from the kitchen. "Need some help showering before we leave?"

"Are you serious?" I replied, slightly annoyed. "I just opened my eyes and you were hitting on me already?"

"Not really; you are going to need some help. You can't get the bandages wet. So regardless of how you feel, you need my help. So sit down, enjoy your coffee and let me go to work," he answered.

Sadly, he was right. As soon as I took a seat on the sofa, he went to work immediately. I swallowed my pride and let him unwrap the bandages. He reached for the salve and gently applied the cream. I grit my teeth to keep from screaming out. "There you go; the burns actually look really good. You are healing nicely. Want something for the pain?"

Unable to speak, I nodded. Then gratefully, I swallowed the Demerol tablet he offered. He deftly finished changing my dressing while I waited for the medication to kick in.

"There, you let that settle in. I am going to get your shower ready," Dominic stated when he was done. Before I could respond, he'd gone to the bathroom and started the shower.

"We need to get going," he called.

Two hours later, Debbie and I flanked Hannah protectively as we gathered at George's graveside. Along with Dominic, the two of us formed a united front as Hannah prepared to bury her husband.

Liam slept contentedly in his car seat beside his mother's chair. For the most part, George's parents ignored our ensemble. However, once in while I caught the old man glaring at Hannah. The looks they gave Liam were exactly the opposite. Their longing to possess the infant was evident in every aspect.

Dominic is on high alert. Chief Alexander had called earlier, while they were driving to the service. Apparently Stephan was released on bond yesterday and no one has seen him since leaving the police station.

According to the chief, the police department was preparing for anything.

"We will have plainclothes officers amid the funeral crowd," assured the Chief. "He would be stupid to try something."

"We cannot take that chance," Dominic responded in agreement. "I will be ready for anything."

Standing graveside, I noticed Dominic's vigilant attitude. His eyes were constantly scanning the crowd. Once in a while, he visually scanned the entire cemetery. His nervousness fed my apprehension. Something was still not right.

"Hey - what's going on," I whispered, trying to catch his attention.

"Don't worry about it," he whispered back. "We've got it covered."

"We?" I asked, raising my eyebrow in question. Taking a second glance around at the crowd, I began to recognize faces scattered throughout the group. "Why are there so many police officers here?"

"EM, seriously; everything is fine. Don't worry about it!" Dominic replied, a little louder. Debbie looked over questioningly; I shrugged.

We formed a circle around the casket while the minister offered up final prayers. The service ended with Hannah and George's family laying a single rose on the coffin. Debbie and I stood back, allowing Hannah space to throw a ceremonial shovelful of soil onto the lowered casket, which indicated the end of the official service.

Within moments, mourners lined up and began filing towards the family for the traditional condolence processional. Not wanting to intrude, we hung back a little to allow people to speak to the family. After standing at the grave for nearly an hour, my legs were starting to throb from standing. I looked around for a chair. It was then I discovered the empty car seat.

"LIAM!" I screamed with alarm.

Hannah's head jerked upward. Her eyes flashed with panic as she searched for me in the crowd. Debbie and I were looking in horror at the empty car seat, while Dominic had already sprung into action. At the sound of my scream, he looked up in time to spot a figure dashing awkwardly towards the parking lot. Whoever it was having a hard time running. There appeared to be a bundle clutched tightly to their chest. Liam!

Dominic took off in a flash, followed by several of plain-clothes officers. The horde of suit clad cops jostled their way between grave markers and monuments in an attempt to cut him off.

The culprit was too far away to identify, but Dominic was positive it was Stephan. He caught up with him a few minutes later. He may have been desperate to make his escape, but he didn't want to hurt the baby. Out of breath, the perpetrator slowed to a stop when he reached the parked vehicles. Panting, he leaned against the side of a car panting with exertion. One arm lifted to signal Dominic to stop.

"What are you doing Stephan?" Dominic asked carefully. He took a few agonizingly slow steps towards Stephan, never taking his eyes off him.

"She doesn't deserve him," Stephan gasped in response, trying to catch his breath. "I can teach him so much! She is never going to tell him about his father. George's parents can't have him either; they hated George! They will teach Liam how to hate."

He began to sob, oblivious to the crowd starting to surround the scene. Caught up in the turmoil, the mourners eagerly followed the police, hoping to witness the activity first hand. George's family and Hannah had also joined the curious crowd.

"I have to do this; it's the only way Liam will ever really know about his daddy," Stephan insisted. Liam was no longer sleeping peacefully. Awake and alarmed, he did not know who carried him, he let out a wail.

Hannah burst into helpless tears at the sound of her baby's helpless cries. Liam's wailing picked up in both volume and urgency. Stephan was starting to look panic. His eyes frantically scanned the lot, looking for a hasty escape route.

"Come on Stephan, you can't take the baby. Do you know how to take care of an infant? He needs his mother," Dominic tried to reason with the desperate man. "Look around you; you are not going to get away with this."

Stephan looked around and spotted the wall of officers closing ranks about twenty-feet away. With guns were drawn and aimed in his direction, he was surrounded.

"You're not going to shoot me with the baby in my arms," Stephan cackled. I winced at the sound. There was something demonic and frightening about his laugh. I'd never heard that noise come out of a human before. The man I once loved had gone completely insane with madness and grief.

"Come on Stephan, put the baby down," Chief Alexander called.

"MAKE ME!" he suddenly bellowed. He quickly slung the screaming baby to his left shoulder and reached behind his back. Hannah screamed in agony, having spotted the revolver he'd plucked out of his back pocket. He shoved it roughly against the bawling baby's head.

"NO!" Hannah cried, over and over. Debbie and I moved in quickly and tried to comfort her. I looked frantically around for Dominic but he'd vanished.

"You don't want to do this Stephan; You are going to hurt Liam," the Chief tried to reason. "He's an innocent child. You don't want to hurt him."

"I don't want to hurt anyone. I just want to get out of here. Let me leave and you will never hear from me again," Stephan called back.

"You can't take the baby," the chief yelled back. "Put Liam down and leave."

"What?" Hannah gasped in horror, then looked me and Debbie with shock. "He can't just allow him go!"

"They won't let him go, they are trying to reason with him before he does something rash," I answered, straining desperately to reassure my frantic friend. I could see the terror in her eyes. It was her child. "Graham knows what he's doing. He just wants Stephan to put the baby down. They can't do anything as long as he's got Liam. The risk of hurting him is too high."

"I just want to go home," Stephan sobbed louder.

"Put. The. Gun. Down." Chief Alexander slowly ordered again. Stephan shook his head frantically. He was not ready to cooperate.

"Let me leave!" he shouted back. He drew the pistol away from the baby's head and started brandishing it wildly in the air. The crowd gasped in unison, then collectively took a few steps backwards in surprise.

It was then I spotted Dominic. He was slowly creeping along the line of parked cars, out of Stephan's line of sight. Two more vehicles and he would be hunkering down right behind him. I could almost picture him crouching behind the car, ready to spring on a moment's notice. I held my breath and waited.

"Come on Stephan, it's time to give the baby back to his mother. He's frightened," Chief Alexander continued. Liam's initial complaints had turned into a full blown inconsolable wail. Only his mother would be able to calm him down now.

Stephan glanced down at the purple faced baby, then scanned the crowd looking for Hannah. For a moment we thought he was going to give up. Instead, he brought the gun back up to the child's head. He never got to complete his action.

In a blink of an eye, Dominic launched himself from where he was hiding. Stephan was thrown forward by the impact. As he fell, Liam was launched through the air. Chief Alexander leaped forward and snatched the baby before he hit the ground. Hannah dashed across the cemetery and snatched her terrified son from the officer. Sinking to her knees, she clutched him close and sobbed into his hair while trying to calm down the screaming child. Soon his frantic wails were reduced to a fit of hiccups.

With Liam safe, the crowd's attention returned to Dominic and Stephan, who was still brandishing his pistol. The pair grappled on the ground as Dom tried to disarm the crazed Englishman. Stephan was desperate to maintain the advantage, and he swung the butt of the gun towards his target. Dominic was knocked aside as the gun connected with his temple. He hit the ground hard, but he didn't stay down. Enraged, he rose upward and with a roar of fury landed a well aimed fist, crushing Stephan's nose. Spitting blood, he was knocked backwards onto the ground.

Dominic quickly pinned him down. But the fight was far from over. Dominic grabbed Stephan's wrist and twisted, trying to force him to release the gun. Instead Stephan head butted him in the face, and Dominic was knocked backwards, taking his opponent with him.

Thrashing around on the ground in a tangle of arms and legs, the two men fought to gain control of the revolver.

The struggle suddenly ceased when a single gunshot rang out.

The crowd fell silent as both Stephan and Dominic fell apart to lay still on the grass. The front of both their shirts were covered with blood. It was impossible to who had been shot. To make it worse, neither men moved.

"Dominic!" I shrieked.

CHAPTER TWENTY-SIX

Watching Dominic's body crash to the ground, splattered with blood, I sprang into action. No one tried to stop me. No one dared. Darting forward, I hurled myself onto the ground upon reaching his side.

"Are you all right? Where are you hurt," I gasped, tears streaming uncontrollably down my cheeks. My hands frantically fought with his shirt, lifting it up and looking for the source of the blood. "I don't see where you were shot!"

Dominic reached out and grabbed my hand, forcing me to stop.

"Hey, it's not my blood! I am okay Emmy," he sat up and pulled me into his arms. Wrapped in his arms, I was immediately soothed. Then it hit me, if it wasn't his blood, then who's was it?

I looked up and past Dominic to saw Stephan laying still and lifeless on the grass. He was surrounded by police officers. His once lively blue eyes were staring sightless at the sky. I shuddered, turned away from the chilling sight.

Chief Alexander walked up with a tarp from his cruiser and quickly hid the body from sight.

"Are you okay buddy," the chief asked, turning to Dominic. He smiled knowingly as I extricated myself from his arms. I didn't care.

"I am all right; just some bumps and bruises," Dominic replied, before getting up off the grass. "I will be fine in a few days."

"Good, I am glad!" Graham replied, before turning to direct his officers. "Make certain you get checked out by the medics. They should be arriving shortly with the ambulance."

Word had spread that there was a shooting at the senator's funeral. The media was starting to pull into the street in droves. Camera crews and reporters were dodging gravestones to get to the scene of the shooting.

"On second thought, you need to get the women out of here immediately," ordered Chief Alexander. "Get to the doctor later."

Dominic was already moving forward. Debbie and Hannah were waiting on the edge of the group with Liam, unsure of their next move. Taking my hand, he grabbed me, pulling me in their direction.

"We need to get to the limo and get out of here now. It's about to become a media circus," Dominic insisted earnestly. The women agreed and quickly ran to the waiting limousine. We'd barely jumped into the car and slammed the door when camera crews reached the vehicle. Our driver ignored the horde and pushed through the crowd until we were safely on the street. The police moved in quickly and formed a human barricade, successfully keeping anyone from immediately following.

"What the heck just happened," Debbie finally blurted.

"Stephan is dead!" Dominic replied.

I shook my head in disbelief. At this point of the story, I was having the hardest time digesting what happened. *I was with this man for two years? Wow. Where is my head at?*

"Emmy, don't blame yourself; he really fooled you," Debbie attempted to console me.

"I agree. Both he and George were good liars," Hannah agreed. At the sound of her voice, I looked over at my friends. They were sitting together, with Liam bouncing on their laps. He'd finally recovered from his earlier fright and seemed oblivious to all the drama. Even Hannah looked better than expected.

"Hannah and Debbie are right," Dominic added. "You had no idea. Don't forget - once you suspected things, you were smart enough to start asking questions. If you'd ignored the signals, this may have ended very differently. It may not have been George or Stephan, who is being buried. Sorry for being so blunt, but that's the truth. You need to hear it, so you will take it to heart and believe it."

"So, now what?" Debbie interjected. "Where do we go from here?"

"I suggest that we go back to your place," Hannah replied. "Have a few drinks, celebrate the good times and plan for the future."

"That sounds like a great idea," I agreed. "I am up for a few hours of drinks and friends."

"Then, let's do it," we all laughed.

"Are you okay," Dominic asked, having come up alongside me on the massive seat. His hand felt warm, where he placed it on my thigh. I flinched instinctively. He dropped his hand and pulled away. "I am sorry; your legs."

"No, it's ok, I was only surprised when you touched me," I hurriedly answered. How could I explain that it had been a long time since someone had been so sweet and gentle to me? That I really did not know how to react to basic human kindness.

"Is it okay that I want to put my hand there?" He gently pried.

I could not respond right away. I looked down and tried to ignore the drying bloodstains covering his shirt. I wanted to cry. I don't know what upset me more, the fact that he was covered with Stephan's blood or how close he'd come to being shot. Debbie caught my look and smiled with understanding.

"It's okay, I will give him one of Ron's shirts when we get to my place. You can shower and change into something clean there before we get too involved with our celebration," Debbie offered. "You will be fine Emmy. I promise."

Back in Debbie's back yard, we spent the next few hours sharing stories and getting to know each other further. It wasn't a party but it wasn't a wake either. We were just a group of friends, enjoying a few drinks, trying to come to grips with recent events. It was what we all needed. I was right, Hannah's staying with Debbie's family had brought her into the 'inner circle'. I watched the group interact and it warmed my heart. I may not have a family, but I was blessed with an incredible group of friends. What more could I possibly ask for?

A few hours later, Dominic found me sitting alone on the back porch swing having a cigarette. I was watching the stars when he walked up.

"Are you ready to go home?" Dominic asked.

"I guess so. My legs are starting to burn again, so it is time to go," I admitted. Hannah was in her room tending to Liam and

Debbie was making dinner for her family. As much as I wanted to stay in their tender fold, I needed to get back to my life.

After saying our goodbyes, Dominic and I headed back to my cottage.

I was in the bedroom changing into a night shirt when he finally joined me. I watched as he set down a tray of dressings and ointment onto the nightstand.

"Are you ready?" he asked, when he finally turned his attention to me.

"This time, I took my pill as soon as I got home. I should be fine," I assured. Scooting up on the bed, I sat propped up against the pillows. I watched as he carefully unwrapped the gauze.

"Just so you know, when these burns finally heal you will just have only a tiny puckers left to mar the skin," he softly said. His fingers lightly applied salve to each blister. I gasped.

"Did I hurt you?" He asked, startled.

"No, not at all," I lied. He didn't 'hurt' me; but I did enjoy his touch. The way he gently cleaned my wounds, it was intimate and tender. He could have been a nurse. "You are very good at that."

"That's because I enjoy touching you," he quietly admitted. My leg was twitching involuntarily as I felt myself warm up in a way I didn't anticipate.

"Are you flirting with me?" I giggled, trying to insert levity into the awkward situation.

"Don't laugh. Please, I am serious," he looked up, and our eyes met. I found myself staring into his vivid green eyes, trying to read his thoughts. His eyes darkened, and he started to lean over.

"Dominic!" I moaned. He moved closer. My hand went up to press against his chest, in a feeble attempt to push him away. Instead, I found myself grasping the edge of his shirt and drawing him nearer. Our faces stopped nose to nose. I explored his face, searching for some response or invitation. It came quickly.

He growled and closed the distance. My heart skipped when his lips brushed mine. His mouth was hot and moist, his caresses tender and sweet. Moaning softly, I responded enthusiastically to his kiss. Our tongues battled as he deepened the kiss.

In a moment of sanity, I pulled myself away. We finally broke contact and he pulled back with surprise.

"Are you okay?" his eyes were filled with concern. "Did I hurt you?"

"Oh goodness no," I managed to pant. I was having difficulty talking; and thinking. It must be the pill I took earlier, I reasoned. I was not going to admit that Dominic affected me.

"Then what?" he persisted. His eyes betrayed worry.

"You make me want you," I shamefully admitted. Mortified at my admission, I nearly burst into tears. I was normally not this sensitive, and I hated my reaction.

"You make me want you too," Dominic chuckled. Annoyed, I playfully slapped his shoulder. He pretended to be hurt. "Feel better now?"

"No!" I barked. "Finish my legs."

Chuckling, he returned to the task of wrapping my thighs, taking much longer than needed. It may have been my imagination or wishful thinking, but he was lingering with the bandages. At one point, I opened my eyes to find him tracing fingertips lightly down my leg to my slender ankles.

"You have lovely legs," he admitted, knowing he was caught. He pretended to double check the bandages, then gathered together the supplies.

"I am glad that you like them," I blushed.

"I like all of you," Dominic whispered. I almost thought I'd misheard him, until he repeated more loudly, "I really like you!"

"I like you as well," I giggled. He looked up, startled at my lack of composure. I attempted to look crestfallen. "I am sorry, I think it's the medication. I am not laughing at you."

"Good; I'd hate to think you aren't taking me seriously," he continued. He reached up and brushed a lock of my hair out of my face. I just smiled. The underlying tenderness of the motion wasn't missed.

"Do you remember our conversation at the hotel," he asked. I observed him put the tray on the table by the doorway. He turned back and returned to sit on the edge of the bed. I scooted over and gave him more room. He followed and placed his hands down on either side of me, making further movement impossible.

"Do you remember?" he repeated.

I nodded, but remained perfectly still.

"I asked you to give me a chance, once you were done dealing Stephan," he continued. "Well, he's been dealt with. Maybe not the way you originally planned, but he is out of your life forever."

"That is true," I quietly agreed. For a brief second I felt pity towards Stephan. It was quickly killed by the fact that he got what he deserved. The story played out the way he wanted it. The rest of us were just along for the ride.

"Do I have a chance now?" Dominic implored. Meeting his gaze, I could tell he was serious. This was a man who was laying it on the line.

"I can't make any promises right now," I reluctantly admitted.

"I am not asking for promises; I am asking for a chance. To know you, to love you, to hold you," he pushed. "I want all of you!"

His gasping admission was my undoing. Instead of responding verbally, I reached out and tugged on his shirt. Taking the hint, he leaned over and drew me into his arms. It was all the encouragement I needed. Hungrily, our lips joined with heated desperation. I melted into his arms and felt myself floating away on a cloud of glorious sensation. I allowed him to lay me gently onto the bed, where he soon joined me and pulled me close.

"Mind if I stay and hold you until you fall asleep?" he asked before giving my forehead a tender kiss.

"Is that all you have in mind?" I asked with uncertainty.

"Not really, but under the circumstances, I don't want to push things," he admitted. "You've been through a lot and as much as I would enjoy making love to you, I also understand that now may not be the best time. I am more than willing to wait at least until you are healed up."

His words were endearing and spoke volumes. Instead of taking advantage of my vulnerabilities, Dominic seemed content with offering emotional comfort and not pushing sexual boundaries.

I am not sure how it came about, but I snapped at that moment. It has been said that when someone stares death in the face or has their life threatened they either go into hiding, go insane or look for a way to get rid of that memory. All I knew, was I needed to feel alive; I wanted human comfort and compassion. I needed someone to hold me and say everything would be alright.

At the moment, Dominic was offering what I required - physical and emotional comfort. It was obvious he was sexually attracted to me; and I needed to forget. The decision was simple. Before he could respond, I twisted within his arms and buried my face in his neck. He pulled me in, so I snuggled closer and inhaled deeply. His musky scent both aroused and intoxicated me. He smelt like outdoors and tasted like the sun.

Teasingly, my lips sought his throat, leaving a trail of kisses along his jaw. He moaned quietly with every delicate touch but did nothing to stop my seduction. Encouraged, I carried on. His reaction to my touch was working for both of us. His arousal was triggering mine. It also made me daring. My fingers nimbly progressed across his chest, deftly opening his shirt. As each button released, I pulled his shirt open and began to kiss his upper body. As my tongue playfully teased his torso, his hand came up as if to put a halt to my play. I pushed it aside and chose to ignore him. Before he could obstruct me again, I pulled myself up and straddled his waist., successfully restraining him with my body. Grasping his wrists and forcing them to remain at his sides, I used my lips, tongue, and hair, to tease his face, his neck, and his torso. Not an inch was of his glorious tanned body was spared. By the time I paused for air, he lay in a trembling mess beneath me.

"What are you doing to me woman," he panted. Taking to take advantage of my interruption, he tried to push me off without hurting me. I refused to cooperate.

"You stated you wanted me," I answered sweetly, still straddling his torso. When I straightened, his eyes widened as I tugged my nightshirt over my head and tossed it into the corner. My thick hair spilled carelessly over my bare breasts like a cape. I brushed it aside, exposing the girls to his hungry eyes. His eyes widened with appreciation. Suddenly timid, I blushed and second guessed myself for the briefest of moments.

"Are you certain about this?" He asked, having seen past my false bravado. His eyes betrayed his concern but they also implored me not to change my mind. "I don't want you to do something you will regret."

"I am positive," I replied. For added emphasise, I finished unbuttoning his shirt and tried tugging it off. Laughing at my failed attempts, he sat up and helped me. It was soon joined my discarded clothing in the corner. Once again, he tried to bring me down to lay on his chest, but I stopped him with a well-placed hand. I renewed my earlier attentions and returned to caressing his flesh with my tongue. I lapped at his flesh until he was once again quivering beneath me.

"Hang on," he finally managed to stammer. I paused and let him gently push away and stand up. For a moment, I thought he was going to leave until he started to unzip his pants. I froze. There was a brief moment of panic as the image of George flashed through my mind. I drove the memory from my mind and refocused on Dominic.

I surveyed him hungrily, as his jeans were kicked aside. I had to admit that standing naked and glowing in the glimmering firelight, he was a fine specimen. My eyes devoured his sinewy torso, then followed the treasure trail leading downward. Ogling his manhood, subconsciously I licked my lips in admiration. I could barely contain myself when he finally rejoined me on the bed. I nestled in and let him wrap me up in his arms once more.

"Do you want me to stop?" I quietly asked, trying to hide my disappointment. He seemed content to just snuggle.

"What do you think?" he growled. Instead of explaining, he took my hand and placed it onto his growing heat. He tensed beside me, waiting patiently, until my fingertips accepted the blatant invitation. He groaned loudly when I finally grasped his arousal and began to tease. Soon I was lapping at his tasty flesh in lazy circles. Paying attention to every inch of his body, except the one part of him that could be clearly seen throbbing in the glow of the fireplace.

I was unstoppable, nearly driven to madness by my sudden need to give and receive pleasure. My eager lover started to tremble and pant. Driven to the threshold of self control, Dominic emitted an animalistic growl. Before I could react, he grasped me firmly, and pulled me ups. With hands on my hips, he lifted be slightly, only to lower me onto his torrid heat. I moaned uncontrollably as he slowly filled me. Still clutching me tightly, he lifted me upwards, then drove himself into me deeply. Guiding my hips, he forcing me to ride him hard and fast.

I felt alive and primal.

As I struggled to remain astride, he forced himself into a sitting position without dislodging me from my position, then wrapped his arms around my back. My legs curled behind his back. Reaching up, his fingers laced through my hair. Gently pulling my head back, he exposed my throat.

My soft sighs of pleasure filled the cottage as he nipped the nape of my neck, then worked his way around until he found my waiting lips. His moist mouth pillaged mine, while our bodies rocked together, slowly at first, then harder and faster. The fevered intensity of his kisses, and our frantic dance was pushing me towards the edge.

"That's it, give in," he whispered against my lips. Without breaking our embrace, he urged our bodies to move in unison, as he ground against me. Unable to maintain self control, I surrendered to the intoxicating sensations. I bit back an animalistic scream of pure pleasure when my body finally exploded. Wave after wave of pure ecstasy rippled through me from head to toe.

The ripples of pleasure had barely subsided when I heard him call my name.

"Emma," he cried out huskily.

Dominic's impassioned voice was like a trigger, giving me permission to shoot for the stars. His mouth hungrily devoured mine; his tongue met his thrusts stroke for stroke. His eagerness elicited a delicious response. For a second time, I gave into the sensations and succumbed to my passion as he painted my insides with his heat. I saw stars as my release washed over me. We clung to each other with mutual satisfaction as each wave crashed over us, until they faded away into tiny ripples of sensation.

Still wrapped around each other, Dominic lay backwards, pulling me with him. I collapsed, still convulsing, onto his chest. I sighed with contentment as his arms remained in place, holding me close. Not ready to leave the shelter of his embrace, I did not pull away. Closing my eyes, I listened to his racing heartbeat slowly return to a regular rhythm.

My face still buried within the warm mat on his chest, I beamed with sheer happiness. Within his arms, I felt safe and protected. For the first time in a long time - if ever - I felt whole!

"So, now what?" Dominic asked, interrupting my musings.

"What do you mean, now what?" I quietly asked, unwilling to ruin the moment.

"Well, I didn't exactly imagine that we would fall into bed like this," he continued. "But now that we have, we should to talk about it."

"What is there to talk about? We are two adults, with needs," I offered, not wanting him to think that I was going to become one of those women who expected a commitment after one night of passion. "There is no need to complicate things."

"I don't want to complicate things, but I want this to be a regular thing," he continued. *A regular thing?* I didn't know if I should be flattered or insulted. "What I'm trying to say is that I think that we should continue seeing each other. I want to see where this will go. I don't want this to be a one-time thing."

"Well, you know, I enjoy your company and we are obviously compatible in other areas," I agreed with a giggle. "I have no problem giving this a chance if you want to."

"Oh, I definitely want to," he replied sleepily. "I want to love you, the way you deserve to be loved."

His softly spoken admission made me beam. As I pondered the implications of what just occurred, I heard a soft throaty purr. Lifting my head, I peeked at Dominic. He'd dozed off, with a sweet smile of contentment plastered on his handsome face. I giggled quietly as he emitted another soft snore. Smiling to myself, I slid off to one side, but remained wrapped around him. I nestled closer. There was nothing more satisfying than falling asleep in someone's arms.

As I started to doze off with my head still resting on his shoulder, I couldn't help reflect on wonderful it was to feel genuine love from a man. For the first time in recent memory, instead of scooting to opposite sides of the bed, I didn't want to go.

I felt secure and protected within Dominic's strong arms. He offered more than comfort and security. He also possessed a strong and loving heart. He cared deeply about those who were important to him. More importantly, he'd shown me numerous times that I was one of those important people.

In that moment, I made the biggest decision of my life. It was time to choose to be happy. It was time to let go of the past and to step into the future.

It was time accept that with Dominic, I was not an option - I was a choice!

ABOUT THE AUTHOR

Since the fall of 1997, Marianne Curtis has written for the Dawson Trail Dispatch. She has since published over 7,000 articles in the monthly publication. While she prefers investigative pieces, Ms. Curtis does not limit her expertise. Over the years she has covered hardcore news, political issues, public interest groups, community events, sports and entertainment. She also does her own photography.

In April 2012 she published a memoir called *Finding Gloria* which is based on her life. It has appeared as #1 on several Amazon's Best Sellers list in Canada, United States and United Kingdom. It was also listed on McNally Robinson's Bookstores bestseller list in July 2012. Curtis is also the author of Moondust and Madness: a collection of poetry which is a compliment of Finding Gloria.

When Ms. Curtis is not writing for the newspaper, she enjoys spending time with her family; reading, gardening and spending time with her many friends.

Contact Information
Email: mariannecurtis.author@gmail.com
Website: mariannecurtis.wordpress.com
Blog: Moondustandmadness.wordpress.com
Facebook: Marianne Curtis
Twitter: writerchick68

Made in the USA
Charleston, SC
25 March 2014